Aveoth

I0685679

VLG – Book Seven

Vampires, Lycans, Gargoyles

By Laurann Dohner

Aveoth by Laurann Dohner

Jillian Milzner has lived a life on the run. Her biological sperm donor has made it clear he wishes she'd never been born. Most kids get presents from their dads growing up. He sent thugs to make death threats to ensure she never tries to find him. He needn't have bothered, since she wants nothing to do with Decon Filmore. His father, however, thinks Jill might be useful. Things go from bad to worse when her grandfather's goons snatch her up to deliver her to a man both terrifying…and straight out of her sexiest daydreams.

Lord Aveoth isn't surprised to hear from Decker Filmore. The man is desperate to make the GarLycan lord call off the hunt for his life, and equally determined to reclaim his VampLycan clan. To achieve both goals, he'll offer Aveoth yet another half-human granddaughter from his bloodline.

It's lonely being a lord of a clan, so Aveoth agrees to the meeting—and he's instantly attracted to Jill. He's also angry to learn she's been brought to him against her will, but he still wants to keep her. Even if it exposes his darkest secret…which could tear his clan apart.

VLG Series List

Drantos

Kraven

Lorn

Veso

Lavos

Wen

Aveoth

Aveoth by Laurann Dohner

Copyright © August 2017

Editor: Kelli Collins

Cover Art: Dar Albert

ISBN: 978-1-944526-85-6

Aveoth - VLG – Book Seven

By Laurann Dohner

Chapter One

Jill turned off the flame on the welder and watched the guy, who wore a suit, peer around her large shop. He glanced down at the floor, winced, and stepped lightly across the metal shavings littering his path.

"Can I help you?" Jill didn't like the look of him one bit.

His hands smoothed down the expensive black suit jacket and he frowned at her question. It made him look really sour and only heightened the deep lines near his mouth and cold eyes.

"Are you Mack?"

Her spine instantly stiffened. The protective mask she wore hid her features and made her voice sound strange. The bulky, fire-retardant smock covering her clothes probably didn't help either, disguising her shape. But it was still insulting to be mistaken for a man. "Who wants to know?" She pegged him as a bill collector, and that put her on edge.

"I am looking for Jillian Milzner."

"What do you want with her?"

"I just need to locate her." He stepped closer, stared down at his shoes and grimaced. "What is that?"

"Metal dust and scraps." She decided the guy might dress nice but he wasn't real bright. "You're in a metal shop."

"I'm a lawyer seeking Ms. Milzner."

Her temper flared. "That son of a bitch." She laid the welder down and tore off her gloves. In seconds, she'd removed her helmet to glare at the shark. She wasn't a fan of lawyers. "Patrick is suing me? Are you serious? That prick pinched my ass and totally deserved a broken nose. He's lucky I didn't shove his nuts into his stomach or just do the world a favor by castrating him. He already pressed charges and the idiot judge sided with him. The only reason I didn't appeal was because he only sentenced me to a few hours of that stupid class. It wasn't worth the hassle."

He arched his white eyebrows as he studied her. "You're Jillian."

She untied her bulky smock that protected her clothes, jerked it off over her head, and tossed it on the table. "Hang on." She dug into her back pocket and withdrew the ten-dollar bill she'd shoved there earlier that morning. "Here." She stepped closer to him, holding out the folded money. "That's about all he's going to get. You're an idiot for taking his case. You can keep half and tell him to spend the five bucks on toilet paper, because he's full of shit."

The lawyer didn't attempt to take the money.

"I'm flat busted, broke. You'll never see a dime otherwise, so take it. I don't even own a car anymore since my transmission called it quits. I make ten bucks an hour, part time, and live in a one-room apartment over this building working for Mack. My net worth is about fifty bucks. That's what the tow place offered me to take my car for parts, and I need that for rent. The furniture upstairs isn't even mine. Take the money and tell

Patrick to go straight to hell. You really should be more careful about picking perspective clients. I'm all tapped out."

His green eyes widened. "I don't work for this Patrick you're referring to."

Jill dropped her arm and bit her lip. "Crap. The judge sent you? I went to anger management classes. You can call them and check. That's why I'm short on my rent. They charge for those stupid, um, classes." She shoved the money back into her pocket. "You aren't going to tell the judge I lost my temper, are you? I mean, it was totally justified when I punched that creep. He didn't just grab my ass, he left red marks. You can understand how I'd be angry, thinking he was trying to sue me, right?" She forced a smile. "I'm totally cool. See? No anger here. Those classes really helped," she boldly lied.

He took a deep breath. "No judge sent me, either. I work for Decon Filmore."

The name sent shock through her. It was a familiar one. She had to lock her knees to stay upright.

"He's your father."

"Sperm donor," she amended, her anger returning. "So you came to threaten me? Don't bother. You're wasting your time. I wouldn't try to contact him for anything. Go away and don't ever come back."

"That's not the reason for this visit."

"Is he dead?"

"No."

"Oh." She backed away and nearly bumped into the table. "Is he dying of some painful disease?"

"No."

"Damn."

The lawyer frowned. "This isn't the reaction I'd expected. I've come a long way to find you, Ms. Milzner. It wasn't easy to do. I'm also sorry for your loss."

"My loss?" She clenched her hands into fists. "You have no idea. My mother was a wonderful woman, and her death three years ago devastated me."

He gave a curt nod. "Your father has sent me to—"

"Does he need a kidney?" Hope soared, and she grinned. "Bone marrow?"

The man's mouth hung open. "No."

She crossed her arms over her chest. "This just isn't my month."

"It's very kind that you'd offer, but he—"

"Offer? You're way off. As a kid, I used to daydream about those kinds of situations just so I could stand over his dying body while I told him to burn in hell. As a bonus, I used to hope I'd get to stick around until he bit the big one."

"Ms. Milzner!" He gasped.

"Oh, spare me." She rolled her eyes. "Do you know that asshole?"

"Of course I do."

"Then I shouldn't have to explain my stance to you, but maybe you're dense. He knocked up my mother and threatened her when she refused to get rid of me. Do you really think she didn't tell me the truth? Give me a break! My mother always told me what a douchebag your boss is. He gave her twenty grand and threatened to make me disappear if she ever tried to contact him in any way. He also threatened her with *his* father, swearing Daddy dearest would spend a fortune in court to take me away from her by making her out to be some whore. To add insult to injury, he then promised Daddy douchebag would put me up for adoption just for the sheer joy of ridding the family of an unwanted bastard.

"My mother had to raise me alone, and couldn't even go after that jerk for child support. That twenty grand was mostly eaten up by the hospital bills for my birth and keeping us off the streets right afterward. And every few years, a couple of goons would show up to remind her to never mention his name. Do you *honestly* think I didn't notice her crying after they would darken our doorstep?"

"He felt it was necessary."

Her eyes narrowed, and she remembered how she was supposed to counteract rage. Those stupid anger-management classes and the ten hours she'd endured flashed through her mind, but it didn't help. She threw out her arm toward the welder and hovered her fingers over it while she debated just how long a judge might put her away if she followed through with what she really wanted to do.

"I'm going to count to ten to get a leash on my temper, because I learned that recently, but if you're still here by the time I'm done, I'm going to pick this up and beat you with it. I *feel that's necessary*. Tell your boss to go crawl back under whatever rock he lives beneath and never send someone else to threaten me. I want nothing to do with him."

"Ms. Mil—"

"One." She paused. "Two. And by the way, I'm not screwing with your head. That's an awfully nice suit. I'm totally willing to go to jail, since my life sucks anyway and they feed you three square meals a day in there, from what I hear. Orange isn't my color, but I'm betting black and blue isn't yours, either. Get lost." She took a deep breath. "Three."

"Boon!" The lawyer backed away. "Get in here."

The door to the shop jerked open and a thug stepped inside. The guy was huge, burly, with shaggy brown hair. A scar ran down one cheek and he oozed meanness that he'd probably learned by experience in his estimated thirty-some years.

Jill's heart pounded when she realized she was in trouble. The lawyer had backup. She lifted her chin though as she glared at the scary guy sporting jeans and leather jacket.

"I don't want anything to do with that coward. You can spare me the threats. I'll never contact him or his family. I might be broke, but I have standards. I don't hang out with trash or associate with it. That leaves ol' Decon S.O.L. That stands for shit out of luck."

The thug glanced at the lawyer. "Problems, Cole?"

"She won't willingly come with us."

"Did you explain the situation?" The thug had a deep, grumpy voice. It wasn't pleasant.

"She isn't receptive to hearing my offer. She threatened to beat on me, Boon."

Boon turned his really dark brown gaze on her and smiled. It sent chills down her spine. Jill backed up and bumped the table as her hand bypassed the welder for the needle-nose pliers she kept there to bend metal. The plastic grips weren't easy to grab as she began to sweat. *Oh shit. Where's Mack? Isn't he done with lunch? It would be great if he'd come back right now.*

Her boss didn't magically appear, despite her wish.

The big thug prowled closer, moving in a way that made her feel stalked. He sniffed the air. "It stinks in here."

"I noticed." The lawyer backed up farther.

"What say you?"

"She's Decon's daughter all right. I've seen pictures. You can pick her up and we can go."

"No thanks." Jill inched past the edge of the table. "You're not my type. I don't like being picked up and I'd rather date a homeless dude. They probably have better hygiene than you." She scooted around the table and put it between herself and the advancing scarred man. "Back off, barbarian."

"Your father requests that you visit him." The lawyer smiled coldly, drawing her attention. "You are going with us to Alaska. We have a private jet waiting."

"I don't have a father. I'm a bastard, remember?"

She mentally judged the distance between herself and the door to the alley—then spun on her heels to sprint toward it when the thug drew closer.

She'd almost made it out of the building when he grabbed the back of her shirt. Material tore when he hauled her to a halt.

Jill reacted by crying out and twisting. She swung, the sharp nose of the pliers hitting his arm, but her aim was off and the tool just skidded over the leather instead of stabbing him.

"Stop," he ordered.

"Let me go!" She dropped the useless weapon, gripping his arm to get leverage. Then she brought her knee up hard.

Boon tried to spin away but wasn't fast enough. She nailed him between his thighs.

He roared out loud enough to hurt her ears but his hold on her damaged shirt loosened. She threw a punch at his face as he bent slightly forward from the pain. Her knuckles slammed into his cheek, the unscarred one, and she twisted again to break free.

The creep managed to grab her long braid. Jill screamed in pain as he yanked her back until her body hit his. She shoved her elbow into him as hard as she could, hitting his stomach. He grunted but didn't let her go.

He wrapped his free hand around her throat. "You've got some fight to you. I like that."

Jill couldn't breathe; he had a strong hold on her neck. Terror gripped her, knowing he could snap it if he wanted, or suffocate her. He was big, about six-four and at least two hundred and sixty pounds. Her head didn't reach the top of his shoulder when she was given no choice but to lean against him.

"Don't hurt her." The attorney stepped into her line of sight and frowned. "Don't bruise her up, either. Aveoth won't appreciate that when we deliver her to him."

Who is Aveoth?

"She kneed me in the nuts," the thug growled, doing a great impression of a junkyard dog. It only amplified her fear. He did ease his grip around her throat but didn't let go. "She should at least kiss them better."

Jill sucked in air, filling her lungs when she was able to breathe again. Anger overrode her fear. "Yeah. Do that. Unzip your pants and show me your brains. Not only are you working for a loser, but you're seriously stupid if you think that's ever going to happen without you bleeding a hell of a lot."

The attorney chuckled. He seemed amused by her threat as he stepped closer, holding her gaze. "You take after your grandmother." He looked at the jerk holding her. "Watch her mouth. She's bloodthirsty."

"You have no idea." Jill hated it when the thug holding her released her braid, only to wrap his big arm firmly around her waist. "Get your hands off me!"

The hold on her throat tightened again, as did the one around her middle. She gasped when he yanked her right off her feet. He made her hang there in front of his body, and she couldn't breathe.

The attorney suddenly rushed forward to grab her hands when she tried to claw at the huge one squeezing her neck.

"Easy," he demanded, showing an amazing amount of strength for someone in his sixties at least, as she fought. "You're going to sleep for a little while. We're not going to kill you, Jillian. We're taking you home."

She struggled harder, but black spots appeared before her eyes. Her lungs burned for air and panic gripped her. She couldn't get away, couldn't breathe, her boss hadn't walked in to save her. And they were lying to her. Her father wanted her dead for some reason, and she knew life was over.

God, this so isn't my month. I'm being murdered by a shark and a scarred idiot who growls.

* * * * *

"What do you want?" Aveoth didn't turn when he felt a presence enter the room. He kept his gaze on the open balcony to stare out at the moonlight. A cool breeze wafted across his bare chest as he took a deep breath and knew who watched him. He made a mental reminder to never forget to lock his doors again.

"My brother thought you might desire company."

He turned his head enough to view the woman hiding in the shadows of his darkened bedroom. He would have attacked a man for daring to invade his sanctuary without permission. "When will you stand up to him, Winalin?"

She remained silent and he clenched his teeth, knowing she'd wait there all night if he allowed it. It was the worst thing about his people. A pause in conversation could last for hours. Impatience simmered through him.

"You may go."

She didn't budge.

"I don't want company. Is that clear enough?"

"Elco believes I would be a good replacement for Lane, or possibly a mate, if you chose me."

Aveoth slowly turned his entire body to fully face her. "Your brother only wishes I'd take you as my lover or mate to gain my favor and elevate his status within the clan. You're a bargaining tool to him."

The tall, thin woman stepped out of the shadows enough for the moonlight to catch the tight black gown. Her ebony hair fell to her waist in a thick braid and her pale fingers were locked together over her trim waist. She lowered her chin in an attempt to hide her fear of him. He knew he terrified her.

"You're alone, and someone needs to take Lane's place. You're our lord. It's our duty to see to your happiness."

Bitterness tightened his chest but he refrained from uttering sharp words that would wound her. His plight wasn't her fault. That responsibility rested squarely on his mother's shoulders. He didn't hold it against her, but he resented the consequences of the choices she'd made long ago.

He was the one who had to deal with the fallout if the truth was ever discovered.

"Do you know why I chose Lane to take as a lover?"

She refused to look at him, but she shook her head enough to be seen. "No. She was beautiful..."

"I barely noticed. She had fallen in love with a man who had lost his true mate. He became lonely enough to want another. That meant he had to decide who to spend the rest of his life with, rather than rely on instincts. He picked another woman instead of Lane. I was her solace. She thought it might make him regret his decision, when he'd heard I'd chosen her." His blood seemed to freeze throughout his body. "Being my companion was her version of revenge against him."

A shiver vibrated Winalin's frame slightly. "I don't understand."

"She wanted him to believe he must have misjudged her, if I'd picked her as my lover. Ironic, isn't it? I accepted her because he caused her so much pain. I figured I couldn't hurt her any more than he already had." He shook his head. "You don't wish to be here. Go home."

"Elco wants me to be with you."

"You're no longer a child." His voice deepened with anger. "Tell Elco to earn his *own* way into my good graces. He'd find no favor from me regardless if I took you into my home or not. Tell him to feel grateful for my refusal, or I might decide to cause him harm for using you in this manner. I'm very protective of any woman sharing my bed. I'd feel the need to kill him for such an offense."

"He's honoring you by offering me."

"He's attempting to make you his whore—but I won't stand for it. You shouldn't either."

She lifted her gaze then, her violet eyes showing a spark of emotion.

He smiled. "Ah. You do have some spirit inside you."

"Elco is all I have. Please don't harm him."

His amusement died as quickly as it had risen. "My mistake. I believed you had grown some backbone, but that's fear in your eyes."

"You're cruel," she whispered.

"Yes." He didn't bother to deny it. "Yet here you are, offering to strip out of your gown and allow me to do anything I want to your body. I'm trying to decide if you're very brave or sadly foolish. Which one is it?"

"I obey the head of my household and wish to serve our lord." The purple in her irises darkened. "Did you kill Lane?"

"Is that what they think? That I murdered her in a fit of rage?"

Her silence answered him. He turned, faced the balcony again, and stared out at the partial moon peeking from behind the clouds. Winter approached in a matter of months, and with it would come the oppressive cold.

"Did you?"

"Would you flee for safety if I said yes?"

"No. I've come to serve you."

He chuckled, the bitterness winning out. "That makes it all the more tragic. I didn't kill Lane. She did that to herself. A home is as warm as the person you share it with. Only ice remains here. Go home, Winalin. Do not return. I shall never welcome you into my bed, and that is something the both of us should be grateful for."

"You're lonely."

His shoulders tensed, and he turned once more to stare at her. "I'm dead inside. I no longer feel much of anything. I breathe and exist. Everything I touch seems to die. Run along now, Winalin. This is the last warning I'll give. Never enter my home again." His lips parted and his fangs extended. "Run!"

She gasped and was gone in a dark blur of movement. He listened to her hasty retreat as her shoes struck the rock steps until his door slammed from below.

The silence once more settled around him as he faced the balcony. The moon mocked him as he stared at its beauty. It was so far out of his reach, so unobtainable, like everything else.

He dressed in his outside clothing minutes later, strapped on his weapons and grabbed his cloak. He had hours before the dawn would come, and hopefully with it, he'd find some peace. Sleep seldom came anymore but he knew at some point, his body would weaken.

He strode to the back staircase, toward the spare living space below his home, where he kept an office. His cell phone rang. He paused, dug his hand inside his pocket, and withdrew it. The number wasn't one he recognized.

"What do you want?" He knew his voice came out harsh as he answered but figured it would probably be Elco. The bastard was getting on his last nerve.

"A truce."

The male's voice was familiar—and much hated.

"Decker." He growled low. "Where are you hiding? I'll find you, and when I do, you'll know my wrath. I told you to leave the other clans alone, yet you disobeyed me."

"I have something you need."

"Your death at my hands will be more than enough. I'm leaving now to come for you."

"Her name is Jillian. She's my granddaughter, and she's only hours away. She carries the bloodline. You may have her if you give your word the hunt ends. I need your given oath of honor that I won't be killed, by you or by someone you send after me."

Temptation taunted Aveoth. His resolve to kill Decker weakened slightly at the thought of being given the granddaughter.

He'd never take a Gargoyle as a lover. They were too cold and he needed some warmth in his life. No GarLycan females interested him, and he'd made certain to meet them all. A VampLycan, though, tempted him. They were known for being passionate. She might melt some of the ice that had taken hold of him.

Of course, that would mean Decker would have to kidnap her. That didn't sit well with him. He'd refuse the offer, but at least warn the woman of her grandfather's intentions.

"What clan is she with? I may have met her already and hold no attraction to her, bloodline or not."

Decker hesitated. "My son Decon spent a few years in the human world in college, learning how to manage money for me. He played with a human for a while and got her pregnant. The mother raised her. I only recently became aware of her existence. She's fully grown and healthy. She knows she's to be given to you. I've been told she doesn't resemble your beloved Margola, who you were once promised, but Cole swears she's very attractive. Do we have a deal?"

His heart beat faster at the idea of this human-raised woman. The fact that she had agreed to come to him was almost too tempting to refuse. But price was too high. Decker couldn't be allowed to hold the power he'd once wielded over VampLycans.

It wouldn't hurt, though, to test the bastard regarding what his price would be for the woman.

"I take it the Vampire Council has finally gotten tired of you."

Decker sucked in a sharp breath but said nothing.

"Did you think I wouldn't know who has been helping you?"

Decker growled. "None of that matters. I'm offering you my granddaughter. She's half human. That's her only flaw, but it will make it easier for you to control her if she's headstrong." Decker rushed on, "Some women are at times. I was told she can't shift, so there won't be claws to deal with."

He flashed to the memory of Decker's other two mostly human granddaughters he'd met. Dustina and Batina had both found mates, and were happy with the VampLycans. He envied Drantos and Kraven.

He longed to say yes…but he had others people to consider. "What do you want in exchange?"

The hesitation on the other end of the phone made Aveoth snarl. "I won't give you anything more than your life. I know you wanted to use your own descendants to persuade me to kill your enemies. That will never happen. Peace amongst the clans will remain. I won't allow anything less. You can keep this granddaughter if that's the price. I have to go. I know where you are, and I'm coming," he lied. "It was a mistake to

21

call me, Decker. I have special gifts that help me sense your location every time you speak."

It was a bullshit bluff but his enemy wouldn't know it.

Fear laced the VampLycan's voice when he responded. "Just my life? I've lost *everything*. I also want to be reinstated to my previous position."

"That's never going to happen. I won't hunt you if you stay out of Alaska. That also means you stay far from other VampLycans—and never send others after them again, either. That's the deal. Take it or leave it. Otherwise, I'll find you regardless of where you hide on this planet. Where is she?"

Seconds of silence ticked by.

"I'll see you soon." Aveoth moved his thumb to hover over the screen and end the call.

"The jet carrying her should arrive near dawn, at my private airstrip on the edge of my territory. I just spoke to the pilot."

"You meant to say your previous clan's territory, I'm sure. We have a deal. Don't break the terms we've made or the hunt resumes." Aveoth hung up and shoved the phone deep inside his pocket. *Airstrip*. He snorted. It was really just a long patch of ground that had been paved.

His heart sped up. He was pretty sure that's what it felt like to be alive again. His breathing increased and his fangs elongated inside his mouth at just the thought of a warm, willing female who would share his bed.

He silently swore to protect her. Nothing would happen to this one. He couldn't take the loss of anyone else he grew to care about.

He tapped the screen, found the number he wanted, and connected the call. It was answered on the third ring by a sleepy-voiced clan leader.

"I apologize for the hour, Trayis. This is Lord Aveoth."

"Is something wrong?"

"I just wanted to let you know that Decker has been in contact with me. He seems extremely motivated to find a way to return to Alaska. He's attempting to make deals to earn my help to reclaim his clan. That's not going to happen."

Trayis chuckled. "It sounds as if the Vamp Council isn't his safe harbor anymore. That's great. Wen will be thrilled when I tell him. We'd hoped that crazy Horton would be able to stir up some shit with whatever kind of alliance Decker made with the Vampires before he was taken out."

"Can you contact the other clans and warn them? Decker seems desperate. I wouldn't put anything past him. I also wanted to tell you my scouts will increase their night patrols. Spread the word. "

"I'm on it. I'll call them now and set up a meeting for tomorrow. You're invited too, of course."

"I have obligations already but keep me informed if something happens."

"I will. Thank you, Lord Aveoth."

"You are welcome. We can defeat him if we keep each other in the loop. He's stupid and will come after Lorn's clan again."

He disconnected and guilt surfaced. It would have been best to share all the information with Trayis, but he didn't want them to raise hell about the woman. She was a relation to Batina and Dustina, and therefore they might protest him bringing her to the cliffs.

The landing strip was near the border of his territory but actually on Lorn's clan lands. He knew from the reports of his scouts that Lorn never had guards patrol that section. No enemies would breach from the GarLycans' side. Tonight would be the exception, when that aircraft landed, but he'd be there—waiting and watching.

He'd kill any of Decker's loyal if they did more than drop off the woman and leave in peace.

Chapter Two

Jill plotted murder while she glared at Shark and Scarface. Those were the names she'd dubbed them with. They had her handcuffed and strapped into a comfortable chair inside some small, fancy jet. The turbulence made her feel a little sick but she didn't complain. They might enjoy it if they realized she was suffering.

"We're almost there." Shark gave her a toothy grin. "Would you like some advice?"

"I listen better when I'm not trussed up like a turkey. Let me go and I'll be more than happy to let you totter on about anything you want." A mental picture of punching him in the mouth made her smile. "I'm not mad anymore."

Scarface chuckled. "She's lying. She can't hide the fury in her eyes."

"I see it." The lawyer sipped some dark liquid out of a glass and puffed on a stinky cigar. Both of them had lit up and practically chain-smoked since she'd woken.

"I have to use the restroom."

Scarface shook his head. "We fell for that once already. You ran out with the lid for the trash, threw it at my head, and rushed the cockpit to scream about how you were kidnapped. A wasted effort. Both pilots are more than aware you didn't board conscious. They saw me carry you in over my shoulder. They won't help you."

The plane shook again. It made her stomach queasy, and she prayed she wouldn't throw up her lunch. Not that there could be much left of it.

She wasn't sure how many hours had passed since she'd been kidnapped and when she had woken on the plane. The small windows were dark enough to assure her that the sun had gone down.

The plane swayed, rose up and then dropped.

"She doesn't look well," Shark noticed.

"I'm fine," she lied.

"The turbulence is from the mountains." Shark puffed on his offensive cigar again, the smoke lingering near the arched ceiling. "We'll be past them soon and landing. We have to stay low to avoid radar detection."

Jill didn't want to know that. She imagined crashing into the side of a mountain and turning into a fireball. "You said we're going to Alaska?"

"Yes."

"That's where the douchebag lives?"

"Yes. He did. And do not speak of your father that way. He'd be offended."

"Oh, that would be a shame." She snorted, tugging on the handcuffs. She didn't do it for long since the metal restraints painfully dug into her skin. "He's such a great guy after all, who threatened a pregnant woman and abandoned an unborn baby. To add insult to injury, he then sent thugs every blue moon to terrorize us. Does he kick puppies too? He should put that on his life resume to really impress people."

"She's sexy until she opens her mouth." Scarface licked his lips. "I wish I were the one who gets to tame her. I bet it would be a challenge. She has no respect whatsoever." He spread open his leather jacket and used his fingers to tap the belt looped through the top of his jeans. "I'd take this off and blister her ass with it until she forgot sarcasm."

"Wow, that's so tempting, but I have a better idea, meathead. Why don't you take it off, go into the bathroom, and hang yourself with it? Do the world a favor and make sure you never breed mini idiots. I'm more than happy to lend you these handcuffs to hook your wrists behind your back in case you change your mind at the last second. Be my guest."

He leaned forward in the cushy seat and glared. "What did you say to me?"

"Stop allowing her to bait you," the lawyer sighed. "She won't be our problem much longer."

"She's a bitch, Cole."

"Actually, she's not. You're smelling what I am. She definitely takes after her mother."

"Are you sure she inherited any blood from her father or grandmother? What if she's too tainted?" Scarface snarled. "That would blow our plans to hell if she's rejected by Lord Aveoth."

"Decon said he tested the child once when she was small. He got her alone, away from the mother. She's his child."

"What in the hell are you talking about?" Jill was furious and panicked at the same time. The sperm donor had been near her? It was alarming.

"Your father went to your school once when you were young, to personally inspect you."

27

"I don't remember that." Had the bastard spoken to her? He sure hadn't introduced himself. She'd have punched him in the nuts.

"You wouldn't. He just wanted to get close enough to see and study you. Then he brushed against you and got a blood sample by scratching your arm."

She had no memory of that. "He sounds like a pervert on top of everything else. That's creepy as hell." It also didn't sit well with her one bit. How dare that son of a bitch spy on her. "What a coward."

"Do not speak of your father that way!" The lawyer stubbed out his cigar and finished his drink. "Decon tried to protect you from his father. You have no idea what you're talking about."

"This should be good. Lay it on me. What, pray tell, was he protecting me from? Is Gramps a child molester? I wouldn't be surprised, with that family."

Scarface lunged to his feet, his hand fisted. "How dare you speak so vile of Decker!"

"Sit," Cole demanded.

The ugly thug actually growled at Jill.

"You heard him. Sit, bulldog. That's what you sound like. Need someone to toss you a bone or get you a flea collar to mellow your muzzle out?"

"I'm going to kill her. I'm going to rip her arms off. I'm—"

"Sit, Boon!" The lawyer's face contorted with pure rage and his voice came out deep and scary.

It startled Jill. She gaped at him with her mouth hanging open, then she slammed it closed. Scarface sat, his ass hitting the seat hard, and he grabbed for his seat belt to strap around his waist.

"She should have been drowned at birth," Boon muttered.

Cole lit a new cigar.

"Dear God. Another one? Do you see the smoke haze in here already? I thought you wanted me alive?" She glanced up. "Doesn't this thing have air circulation? Shouldn't it suck that crap out? It's like fog, it's so thick."

"Shut up." Shark puffed on the cigar, blew smoke upward, and relaxed in his seat. "Cities bother us with the stench of so many bodies. This is how we deaden our senses. You reek of them still, and I don't want to smell you."

"I took a shower this morning, and I don't stink. I think it's Fido's dog breath."

Scarface snarled and tried to get up, but forgot his seat belt was on. He was yanked back down before he could move more than a few inches.

"You *do* smell. You're just accustomed to the stench from living with them all your life." Cole smiled. "Have you always been so free with sarcasm?"

"You mean being honest?"

He laughed and turned his head to gaze at his scarred fellow kidnapper. "She has no idea what she is. This is what happens when you resist your true nature. Feel pity for her, Boon. She probably experienced bloodlust in her teens and had no outlet for it. It turned her mean and insane."

"Oh, I'm feeling bloodlust right now. Forget my teens." Jill gripped the armrests her wrists were handcuffed to. "And I'd go find a mirror and a good shrink if you want to talk about who's insane. You abducted me!"

"Your father protected you." Cole ignored her words. "He never meant to have you with that woman. She was a college fling and nothing more. Of course, he knew his father would try to use you in some way. Back then, Decon was naïve. He didn't understand the full scope of what was at stake by hiding your existence or what we could trade you for. Your bloodline makes you valuable. Now he's wiser, and he's learned that what's good for all of us is good for him as well. It was actually quite noble of him to keep you safe."

"Squirrel!"

Scarface sniffed and glanced around, looking for an animal.

Jill laughed and shook her head. "Great. I've been kidnapped by idiots who don't get jokes. You're talking bullshit. Never mind. Blather on."

"I hope Aveoth tears her apart with his bare hands." Scarface glared. "He killed his last lover."

"Great. Another nutjob. Is this your brother? I figure it must run in your family. If not, you should totally hook up with him if he's into killing whoever he's screwing. You need some man-love, Fido."

He reached for his seat belt and growled again.

"Enough," the lawyer demanded. "I won't advise you about what you are, Jillian." He took another puff of his cigar and smiled at his pal. "Whatever you wish to do to her, reality will be so much worse. Aveoth is punishment enough."

Uneasiness pitted the inside of her stomach. "I thought you were taking me to the sperm donor. Can you try to at least keep your crazy stories straight?"

"Your *father*," Cole stressed the word, "needs you. You finally have a purpose, because you carry the bloodline that his enemy wants. You're ensuring our survival by becoming an offering to Aveoth, who currently wishes to track us all down and kill every person associated with our clan leader. That would be your grandfather."

"I like him already." She paused. "I'm talking about this Aveoth, just to be clear. Not the sperm donor or his daddy. Did you say clan?" She glanced down at the stray blonde hairs hanging over her shoulder; Scarface had messed up her braid when he'd grabbed her in the shop. "So, I'm part Irish or something? I wish I'd known that so I could have worn all those cute pins on St. Patrick's Day."

A bell dinged and Cole snubbed out his cigar. "We're landing." He put on his seat belt and secured the whiskey glass by dropping it into the side pocket attached to his chair. "Aveoth should be waiting if Decker was able to make the deal." He stared at Scarface. "Are you prepared, Boon?"

"To die? No. I will fight until I don't have breath left if this goes sideways. You escape, Cole. One of us must survive."

"I usually hate flying, landings especially, but I'm kind of excited all the sudden." Jill tugged on her handcuffs but they refused to break. "You

31

know only cowards run, right? Whoever this guy is, I hope he's some killer freak who hates you. I think one look at me and he'll know I'm not your friend. You don't kidnap them."

"Aveoth is dangerous." Cole glared at her.

"Fantastic. I guess you never heard that saying about the enemy of my enemy is my friend? Want to guess where you stand in my head?"

"She's insane." Boon shot a glare her way.

"That's rich, coming from you, dog boy. At least I'm not barking and growling."

"I don't bark!" he barked.

"Enough!" Cole ordered again, loudly. "We have more important issues to deal with. Aveoth may be out there, and there's no telling what kind of mood he'll be in. But he'll have made the deal with Decker if he is, and he won't be happy about that—and could take it out on *us*."

"Damn." A look of fright crossed the other man's features.

Jill hid her uneasiness. Both men were mental cases but their fear seemed real. Whoever this Aveoth guy was, he must be bad news to inspire that kind of reaction. Her bravado began to waver.

"Who is this badass again?"

"Your keeper, if things go the way we hope." Shark looked nervous.

She didn't like that one bit. "You don't like this guy?"

"He's deadly," Boon warned ominously.

"And you're such a sweetheart. I take it that your lives are in real danger?" She hoped so.

32

The jet landed with a rough bump and the brakes made her jerk sharply in her seat—the pilot hit them hard, slowing their momentum. She wished she could see outside but couldn't. The motion finally stopped and the engines cut out.

"Is this guy really a threat to you?" She peered at Cole.

"Yes."

"Awesome." Inside, she was terrified but she refused to show it. Just because the lawyer wore a suit didn't mean anything. She bet he was far worse than the one who pretended to be all doglike. "Let's stop sitting here, then. Open the doors and let's say hello to this guy."

Boon unfastened his belt and growled at her again. Rage twisted his features. "I hope he's not out there and that he refused the deal. She'll be useless then. I call dibs if that's the case." His fingers tapped his belt. "I'll break you."

"You don't mean that." Cole stood.

"I do. I'll tie her down and whip her until she begs for mercy. I'll make her bleed. And if she's lucky, I'll allow her the privilege of being mounted by me."

"I so hope you're talking about stuffing my dead body and hanging it on your wall next to the deer heads I'm sure you keep in your living room. You totally look the type to kill Bambi." Her gaze lowered to his crotch. "Because *ewww*, if you're talking about sex. I'd rather die."

"You *will* die! That's a given. You'll suffer first, and then I'll fuck you. Hell, I'll let everyone who wants you take a turn."

She hated him...and knew he meant it.

"Well, if you touch me, I'm sure I'll appreciate your friends at that point. Anyone would be a step up from you."

He lunged at her, but Cole moved faster, stepping into his path.

The cockpit door opened and one of the pilots entered the cabin. "We have company." Terror paled the man's features. "There's someone out there."

"Shit!" Cole reached up and ran his fingers through his hair. "Lord Aveoth took the deal." He turned and approached Jill. "Be silent if you have any intelligence at all."

He unfastened the belts holding her down, unlocked the handcuffs chaining her to the chair, and grabbed her shoulders, hauling her to her feet.

Jillian fought, but couldn't get away as the lawyer switched the handcuffs, moving her hands from the front to behind her back. She couldn't do much when both men pushed her forward as the pilot rushed to open the door at the side of the cabin. Built-in stairs lowered as her heart pounded. She hated the company she kept but she had a really bad feeling about whoever they were taking her to.

Things could always get worse. Life had taught her that lesson well.

It was dark and the wind blew, blinding her as loose strands of hair whipped into her face. She couldn't even push it back since the handcuffs prevented it. She tucked her chin down, turned her face into her shoulder, and tried to see the steps. Fear gripped her over the possibility of falling. She wouldn't even be able to grab for the railing with her hands behind her back. She was glad it was summer, at least, and there was no snow to contend with. Still, a nasty spill down onto the runway didn't sound fun or painless.

She reached the bottom and tossed her head, facing into the wind to clear her hair away from her eyes.

This wasn't like any "airport" she'd ever been to.

Thick trees lined both sides of the runway, and the only lights were mounted on poles strategically placed along its length, about every two hundred or so feet. No houses or buildings were within sight.

She didn't see anyone.

Her gaze traveled over what she could make out and there was nothing but blackness behind the lighted airstrip. It sank in that they'd landed on a road.

"Where's the real airport?"

"There isn't one in this area." Cole stood behind her, adjusting his hold from her arms to the chain between the cuffs. "There are some houses a few miles from here but they're abandoned. This was our leader's vacation retreat."

"Why isn't anyone living here?" It wasn't the chilly wind that sent a shiver down her spine.

"Because of him."

Something moved by the tree line to her left, and she watched with trepidation as a large figure stalked forward. He stayed in the shadows for a few steps but then a black-haired man was revealed. He wore some kind of dark cape thing that blew in the wind, and it billowed out as he approached.

Bright, brilliant blue and silver eyes came into view, and she couldn't help but stare into them. They were amazing and kind of scary at the same time. His features stunned her. He was perfection. His bone structure was chiseled to resemble some kind of masculine god. Broad shoulders and an impressive chest wasn't hidden at all by his odd choice in clothing. He wore no shirt and the cape thing hung open in the front. Muscular thighs were encased in tight leather, with some seriously badass biker boots on his big feet.

He paused ten feet away.

"Lord Aveoth." Cole stepped to her side but kept hold of the chain.

Jill glanced his way as the lawyer bowed slightly, his gaze lowered to the pavement in front of his feet. She didn't miss the look of fear on his expression, and seeing him cower was slightly satisfying after everything they'd done to her. She glanced back to find Boon with his head lowered too, looking equally scared.

Her attention fixed once more on the man who frightened them.

He was hot. His good looks and fascinating eyes alone would have drawn any woman's attention, but the size of him was a bonus. His silvery-blue gaze held hers and some of her fear eased. He wasn't glaring at her.

"This is her." Cole gave her a slight push with his hand, releasing the chain linking the cuffs together. "Go to him."

"Fuck you," she muttered so he'd hear, but she walked closer to the stranger.

He held very still until she stopped a few feet in front of him, unsure what to do.

36

He held out his hand as if he wanted to shake hers. "I am Aveoth."

Even his voice was sexy, in a gruff, deeply masculine way.

"I'd shake but I can't." She turned enough to allow him to see her back. "I'd love to if someone would unlock these."

A look of anger crossed his handsome face when she turned again, making his mouth tense into a tight line. He didn't look at *her* with that mean expression, but instead glared over her head. "Where is the key?"

She glanced at Cole and Boon. Shark wriggled a hand into his front pocket and tossed the keys in the air.

Aveoth caught them and he stepped around her, his big, warm hands covering hers. She meekly allowed it, since he seemed to want to let her go. One cuff opened, then the other.

She pulled her arms in front of her, intent on rubbing her wrists, but the big guy moved faster.

He stepped around her and gently cupped her wrists in his larger hands to examine them. She glanced up and saw his anger when he spotted the red marks from her struggles with the metal. He turned his head, and the expression on his face made her instantly like him. He appeared utterly furious at the other two men.

"You bruised her." His voice deepened more.

"She fought." Boon glanced up. "She's a mouthy bitch. It's a miracle those are her only injuries."

"They hurt my throat too." Jill hated her captors, and had no problem screwing them over if this Aveoth didn't like men who abused women. Which seemed to be the case.

The hunk with the incredible eyes released her wrists and stepped closer. "Show me."

She could have stared into his eyes for a while longer, but instead tipped her head back. "Boon choked me while Cole held my arms so I couldn't fight. I thought I was going to die."

He trailed his warm fingers along her throat. His touch was feather-light for the seconds it remained before he withdrew his hand. She met his gaze again, briefly.

He turned his head to glower at her captors. "What do you mean, she fought?"

"She put up a fight," Boon explained. "She wasn't going to come with us. You should be thankful we didn't beat her to a pulp. Wait until you get to know her. She's being nice and meek right now but her mouth is enough to get her killed."

"Decker said she agreed to be mine."

Absolute silence followed Aveoth's words.

Jill stared at Cole and Boon. Both men appeared uneasy, and when she glanced at Aveoth, pure rage showed on his face—all of it still directed at the men.

"Excuse me, Mr. Aveoth?"

Aveoth looked down at her. He was a good foot taller. "You may call me Aveoth. What should I call you?"

"Jill."

"What do you wish to say, Jill?"

He was so polite. "I was kidnapped by them from my work. They strangled me until I passed out to put me on that plane. Can you please help me get home?"

"Are you the granddaughter of Decker Filmore?"

She hesitated. "His son knocked my mother up and abandoned her as soon as she told him that she was pregnant with me. Decon is a sperm donor only. He threatened my mother until the day she died. That family never wanted me, and I don't want anything to do with *them*."

"Why did Decon threaten your mother?"

"He didn't want anyone to know about me. He sent thugs after her every few years to make threats." She shot a nasty look at the men. "Assholes like them. She cried for days every time they found us. After dealing with those two, I understand why. I hate that entire family and anyone who works for them."

"I don't blame you."

"We are gifting you with the bloodline, Lord Aveoth," Cole interrupted. "She's been delivered to you. May we leave now and tell Decker your arrangement is in place?"

"Yes." Aveoth kept his attention on her.

"Wait!" she gasped. "You're just going to let them go?"

His eyebrows arched upward. "What would you like me to do?"

"They kidnapped and strangled me!" She pointed at Boon. "That sick asshole threatened to take off his belt and beat me. You can't just let them get back on the plane. Call the police and have them arrested!"

He hesitated, then spoke. "I am the law here."

"Fine. I demand they pay for the shit they did. Boon threatened to rape me and allow his friends to join in."

All traces of softness left his face. "Halt." His voice came out deep and loud.

She darted a glance at the two men and verified they'd stopped walking. Jill looked back at Aveoth. "Arrest them and put them in jail."

"We don't have a jail here."

"You can't just let them board that plane. They'll fly off and get away with what they've done to me. They could hurt someone else! They're real assholes."

"I don't have much of a choice. I can sternly warn them to change their ways and give you my word of honor they will never grace your presence again."

"We're leaving now." Cole sounded nervous. "We did our part. Can we go?"

"Good luck with that mouthy bitch. Do you want my belt?" Boon glared at her. "Take my advice and whip her into shape."

Her temper snapped. No way was she going to stand there doing absolutely nothing while those pricks just flew off to go back to her sperm donor. Once again, that jackass would win. It wasn't fair. Decon Filmore had terrorized her mother, ruined her childhood, because he'd never stopped sending thugs after them both. They'd had to move every time.

She glanced at the man in front of her. He was bodybuilder-large and looked pretty fit. He also was drop-jaw gorgeous.

"Aveoth?"

He stopped glowering at the two men long enough to peer down at her. "Yes?"

"You said you're the law but you can't lock them up, right?"

"Yes."

"I suppose burying their bodies in a shallow grave is out?"

He nodded. "I swore I'd send them back alive."

She took a good look at the man. He really was a big, muscled bastard. Her gaze slid to the shark in the suit and dog boy. "If you had to, could you take them both in a fight?" She looked back up at him.

"Yes. Easily. Why?"

"I'll do anything you want if you kick the living shit out of them and send them back to my sperm donor bleeding. Can you do that?"

His eyebrows shot up. "Anything?"

Her breath froze in her lungs as his gaze dropped to her breasts. It was obvious where his mind had traveled. She'd had enough men hit on her to recognize the look. Some of her fear cooled instantly while she debated the consequences. He was a stranger, probably the most intimidating hunk of masculinity she'd ever seen in person, but she didn't know anything about him other than thugs feared him.

Boon made that growling noise again, and she turned her head, meeting his glare straight on. Malice shone in his eyes and his hands fisted at his sides. If looks could kill, she'd be in her death throes at that moment.

Decision made. Totally worth it.

She faced the tall badass. "You heard me. You don't have a jail. Murder is illegal, right? So beat the living shit out of them and I'll sleep with you, if that's what you want. Is that clear enough?"

"Yes." He reached up and removed his strange cape. In seconds, he'd wrapped it around her shoulders. "Do you wish to watch them bleed?"

"You bet I do."

"Would you enjoy them having some broken bones?" Amusement gave a sparkle to his eyes and humor laced his voice.

"That would be great." She would probably regret it later, when she regained her sanity, but she'd been through way too much in her life to back down when given an opportunity to get even with someone who'd done her and her mother wrong. Both those assholes were probably men who'd threatened her mom.

"Especially Boon. He loves to threaten women with his belt."

"Your wish is my command."

"Now wait a damn minute!" Boon protested.

"Shit," Cole muttered.

Chapter Three

Rage burned inside Aveoth as he stepped away from Jill. He'd tried to hide his stormy emotions with charm, but he no longer had a need for that. She *wanted* him to unleash his anger on the two clan members who'd brought her to him.

His dick was hard from knowing he'd soon be able to take her to his bed, but he ignored the discomfort it caused as he strode quickly to the strongly Lycan male who'd made threats of sexual torture against the delicate woman now under his protection. The scar on Boon's face would be the least of his issues by morning.

He halted, though, and glanced back, rethinking it. He didn't want to frighten her with a show of too much violence. "Are you certain?"

She nodded. "One hundred percent."

"I'd never do this to *you*. I don't hit women. Remember that."

"No problem." She raised a fist. "Give them hell."

She amused him and he liked her immensely.

He faced the two VampLycans. One was obviously an enforcer of Decker's, but the other was too soft to be a fighter. It didn't matter. He went for the scarred one first.

He moved fast and punched him before he could react. Boon hit the ground with a grunt. Aveoth spun, kicking out. His boot made contact with the one in the suit at chest level, sending him flying a good eight feet.

He bent, grabbing hold of the despicable man who'd threatened to rape Jill. He broke his arm by holding it tight and slamming his knee into his opponent's elbow. Boon roared in pain.

Aveoth spun him before he could recover and dropped him on the ground again. He stomped on his hand next, breaking more bones.

Aveoth glanced at Jill to gauge her reaction. She didn't look horrified or afraid. Her attention was focused on the man now sprawled on the ground, cursing up a storm and rolling in agony.

"Enough or more?"

She tore her focus off Boon to stare into his eyes. "Hit him a few more times. He's really a dickhead."

"Your wish is my command."

He kicked Boon in the ribs and then lifted him, throwing him into the side of the jet stairs. Boon slammed against them and fell to the pavement. The man groaned, still conscious but in serious pain.

The one in the suit had gotten up and tried to run into the woods. Aveoth caught him easily and threw him back toward the plane. He hit the ground rolling. Aveoth stalked after him and grabbed him by the nape of the neck as he attempted to stand.

"You don't mistreat women," Aveoth informed him. "It's bad for your karma." He threw him at the jet stairs and his victim couldn't react fast enough to protect his face from the metal. The scent of blood filled the air. He wasn't an enforcer, so Aveoth figured he'd done enough damage to that one. He'd have broken facial bones.

Boon got up, cradling his injured arm and hand. He snarled and glared at Jill.

Aveoth didn't like the hateful look in the enforcer's eyes. He approached him from behind and dug his clawed hand into the male's scalp. Boon screamed. More blood spilled as Aveoth forced him to turn his head then leaned in until he knew he was all Boon could see.

"*Never* look at her that way again, or even have those thoughts." He reached up and touched some of the blood spilling down the side of the VampLycan's face from the wounds he'd created, as he continued to hold the man's skull still, keeping his claws embedded into his scalp. He sniffed the blood, making a show of it so the jerk understood. "I can track you wherever you go. I know your scent now—and I won't forget it. Kneel down and beg her forgiveness for the mistreatment she suffered at your hands."

Boon didn't do as he was told.

That pissed Aveoth off enough that he stepped to the side of him and used his boot to kick the jerk behind his knees. The enforcer collapsed hard, despite the fact that Aveoth still kept hold of his head. He reached down with his free hand and allowed his claws to lightly scratch the front of Boon's throat.

"Should I offer her your head as an apology, or are you going to give her one yourself?" He whispered the words so Jill wouldn't hear what he said.

"I'm sorry!" Boon yelled. "I'm an asshole. Can you forgive me, Jillian Milzner? I really mean it."

45

Aveoth wasn't impressed with the enforcer's apology. It wasn't a surprise. Decker had no decorum, so his enforcers had probably never learned true respect. He stared at Jill to see her reaction. She took a few steps closer then stopped in her tracks.

"Go to hell, dog breath."

"I can't kill him," Aveoth informed her. "It wouldn't be honorable since I did agree to a deal with Decker, allowing him and his followers to live in exchange for your life."

She had beautiful light blue eyes when she locked gazes with him. "You messed him up. That's enough. I just meant he's *going* to hell. Assholes like that do."

"Would you like me to break a few more of his bones?"

She came closer and studied the enforcer on his knees. Her eyes widened and she paled. Her gaze lifted to him. "What are those things shoved into his scalp?"

"My claws. They aren't fully extended or he'd be dying. They'd be embedded into his brain. I didn't fully pierce the bone but I have a good hold on him."

Jill waivered a little on her feet, but steadied before he felt the need to lunge forward if she appeared she might fall over. She swallowed and inched even closer, staring at Boon's head. Her lips parted, then she sealed them tightly together.

"Do you wish me to break more of his bones?" Aveoth waited for a response.

She shook her head but didn't look at him. She seemed engrossed with his claws. He released the enforcer's head by harshly shoving him away. Boon whimpered and crawled toward the jet.

Aveoth watched Jill as she braved coming closer to him. He held still, allowing it.

She reached out toward his hand. He glanced down at it. His claws weren't fully extended, as he'd said, but they dripped blood. She didn't touch him but inches separated her fingertips from his claws.

"I wouldn't hurt you, Jill. I'm going to retract my claws. Don't be alarmed." He pulled them in until only human fingernails remained.

Jill sucked in a sharp breath. "That's not some kind of weaponized glove. It's your hand."

"Yes."

She lifted her head and opened her mouth yet again, staring at him. "What are you?"

He hesitated. It started to sink in that she must not know the truth about her heritage, or that the others also weren't human. He remembered what she'd told him. Her mother had been human and Decker's son had never been a part of her life. It meant she'd probably been raised totally ignorant about her father.

"I'm a GarLycan."

"What's that?"

"My father was a full-blooded Gargoyle but my mother was half Gargoyle and half Lycan. I believe humans call them Werewolves. I'm

47

predominantly Gargoyle, like all of my people are, regardless of the mixing of our bloodlines."

"Oh." She backed up a step. "So…you have wings?"

"Yes." He reached down and rubbed his fingers on his pants to clean them in case she fainted. He didn't want to taint her with the VampLycan's blood.

"Can I see them? I mean, if you're really a Gargoyle and not just some crazy guy with some kind of fake hand with weapons hidden inside the fingers, like small switchblades."

"Fake hand?"

"You know. Prosthetics. I've seen some that look pretty real."

She was looking for a reasonable explanation to cling to. He felt sympathy. "I'm not lying to you, Jill. I can show you my wings if you wish."

The engine to the jet started, and he glanced back. Boon and Cole had boarded and retracted the stairs. The door was sealed. He could see the pilots through the front windows. They looked terrified as they readied to fly away. He didn't blame them for wanting to flee. Jill was too close to the runway for his comfort, so it made sense to just take her home. He slowly turned, giving her his back.

"Don't be alarmed. You want proof? Here it is." Aveoth concentrated and felt the slight swelling as the skin along his shoulder blades stretched until the usually hidden slits parted. His wings grew outward as the bones shifted. He did it slowly so she could watch, and to avoid the searing pain of a fast transformation.

He extended his wings, showing their full expanse, then tucked them and turned around to see her reaction. Jill's eyes were wide and her mouth hung open. She tried to speak, her lips moved, but no sound came out.

"I'm truly a GarLycan. Don't fear me. I will never hurt you in any way."

"Those bastards drugged me," she whispered. "I'm high as a kite or Boon clocked me in the head so hard I'm hallucinating."

"Would you like to feel my wings?" He carefully extended them forward, brushing her arm with the side of one.

She reached up timidly and he noticed how much her hand shook. Her touch was gentle as she caressed him and it made blood rush to his dick again. She wasn't screaming or trying to run away. He was once again impressed with her bravery.

"And this is why I never did drugs," she whispered. She looked away from his wing to hold his gaze. "I knew you were too hot to be real. They weren't just smoking cigars on that plane. I must have gotten a contact high from hell."

He stepped closer and cupped her waist with both hands. She didn't flinch away. "I'm real. Feel me touching you?"

"Your wings are black. I thought angels had white ones."

"I'm no angel." He looked down at her cleavage. "Trust me. My thoughts aren't pure."

"You want to do me, don't you?"

"I want to take you to my bed. Yes."

49

"Yeah." She placed both her palms on his chest. "This is like the mother of all wet dreams. You're a hot warrior dude who kicks bad-guy ass and then wants to nail me. The wings are a bonus."

He arched an eyebrow.

"But scowling face isn't hot. Smile for me."

It wasn't hard to do. She amused him. "Your mind is trying to come up with a reasonable excuse to explain what you can't comprehend. It's normal, but you aren't drugged and I am very real."

She licked her lips. They were plush, and her mouth looked very enticing to kiss. "Let's just go with the drugs. Otherwise this hallucination is going to transform into some kind of nightmare where you turn into a monster trying to murder me. This is *my* wet dream."

He chuckled. She'd eventually have to accept reality. "Fine. Let's go flying. Have you ever wanted to do that?"

"I just did." She turned her head. "The jet is moving. They're turning it around."

"I'm aware. Flying with me will be much more fun. Put your arms around my neck. I'm going to lift you up and hold you close. Wrap your legs around my waist. It will be more comfortable for you that way while we're in the air."

He bent down enough so she could reach him. She wasn't tall, the way he usually liked his lovers. He'd adjust. She surprised him by doing as he asked. The feel of her arms wrapping around his neck heated his blood. He glanced at her neck and desire shot through him so strong, it astonished him. He wanted to sink his fangs into her and take a taste. It had been so damn long since he'd drank blood from her family line.

50

He clenched his jaw and kept his lips pressed together. He lifted her and she wrapped her legs around his waist. He craved to get her naked so they'd be skin to skin. He adjusted his hold on her, curving one arm under her generous ass he couldn't wait to explore later, and securing his other arm to support her upper back. The cape trapped beneath his arms, still wrapped around her body, should keep her warm.

He flexed his wings and looked at the jet. It had fully turned and the pilots chose that moment to punch the engines.

He glanced upward and leapt.

Jill gasped when they left the ground. "Shit." Her limbs tightened around him.

He soared higher into the sky and away from the runway. They'd reach the cliffs within ten minutes and then he'd have her inside his living quarters. "I won't let you fall."

Jill wasn't sure what kind of drugs she'd been exposed to but they must have been really powerful. Super-hot guy flew with her in his embrace, their bodies horizontal, the night sky and stars above her. She turned her head, staring down. Normally, she'd be terrified. The wind felt chilly but his body was warm. She watched the ominous landscape below. They sped past a lot of dark trees about a hundred feet down.

He banked to one side and she spotted a large mass of what appeared to be a black, glittery substance. "What's that?"

"A river. We're almost home. We're going higher. Don't be afraid."

"Are you kidding? This is a total E ticket ride."

"I don't know what that means."

"You know, like a roller coaster but without the falling. That would totally suck if we crashed."

"We're not going to do that."

He grew quiet, and she turned her attention to his massive wings as they flapped. They were big, probably five feet in length on each side, and black. They hadn't felt like feathers though. They were solid and had a velvety texture. He stopped beating his wings as seemed to glide. It reminded her of a bird. He flapped them again and she looked down. They seemed to soar higher, and when she tipped her head back, looking behind her, she saw the upside-down shape of a huge mountain in the distance.

"That's home."

"You must have an amazing view if you have a home on top of that."

"Inside it. It's the perfect place for my kind to live. It has a sheer cliff face that is near impossible to climb on all sides. It would take a lot of time for someone to reach our homes and that makes it easy for us to defend them."

She let that information sink in. "You live in a mountain? Like a bat cave?"

"There are caves where our homes are built into the cliffs, but you'll find them very comfortable."

"I don't see how."

"You'll see."

"So, you're like a superhero?"

He made a weird growl noise. "Is this helping?"

"What are you talking about?"

"You pretending this isn't real?"

She twisted her head, peering over her shoulder again. They were really high, the dark shapes of trees appearing tiny now. "This has to be drugs. Otherwise I'm going to freak the fuck out. We're flying. You have wings and you dug those white spikes you called claws into Fido's head."

"We're about to land. It's a little jarring. Hold on."

He tightened his hold on her even more, until she almost felt crushed in a bear hug, and did some maneuver that righted them as if they were standing. The feeling of falling had her gasping, but he landed on his feet. She watched him fold his wings back. It was dark but the moonlight was strong enough for her to make him out.

"You can let go now. I don't want to retract my wings into my body while still holding you."

"Right. That sounds dangerous. Could I accidently be sucked in with them or something?"

"No. You'd hear the slight popping noises they make when I fold them back inside, and how it feels, when my skin is pressed against your hands. You'd feel my bones moving around. I doubt you'd find it appealing."

"They just go inside your back?"

"It's complicated. My bones transform into different shapes, you could say. They don't resemble wings while inside my body. Think of a rib cage. My wings contract tight to mimic a second set I guess, while inside me. Does that help explain it?"

He did have a large chest. He'd have to, if he usually walked around with basically two rib cages. She decided she didn't want more answers at that moment. The explanations he gave were only confusing her more. She unwrapped her legs and slid down his body as she eased her hold around his neck. Her feet touched solid ground.

He straightened, breaking their physical connection. "I'll stay close and you'll understand."

His eyes closed and he tilted his head. She watched a look of pain crease his handsome features. Gross little popping, squishy noises she hadn't heard before sounded, but it was otherwise quiet where they were. His wings slowly grew smaller until they disappeared behind him. She glanced down at his chest but it was too dark to make out his skin, so she watched his face again.

He opened his eyes. The color of them appeared a bit startling, since they seemed to glow a little, and now appeared mostly silver instead of blue.

"Welcome to my home. I'll turn on some lights. Don't move. It's a long drop to the bottom if you were to walk off the balcony. There are no rails."

"Does your cave have electricity? I hope so."

"It does. We're not barbaric."

"Of course not."

He walked away and her eyes followed, peering into the utter darkness he'd disappeared into. She turned her head, taking in her surroundings. It appeared as if she was standing on a rock ledge jutting out of the cliff of massive rock.

"Never do acid, kids. It's not for the meek or fearful. This shit is getting weirder and weirder," she muttered aloud.

"I heard that." Aveoth's deep voice came from the darkness. "Hang on—and don't move."

"You told me that. Big fall and screaming involved. Got it."

Lights flickered on, literally. They were dim, then blacked out, but came on again.

She stared into a room. It looked like some kind of library, with couches, a fireplace with a mantel, and tons of wooden bookshelves loaded with books.

"Yeah. This is so realistic," she muttered.

Aveoth stepped into sight and frowned. "What?"

"It looks like a room from an old mansion but in the middle of a cave. Nope. I'm not drugged. This is just so believable."

He walked to her and offered his hand. "I note your wariness. Come inside. I'll close the door."

"Over a cave entrance? I can't wait to see this." She let him lead her forward, stepping onto the hardwood flooring inside, over a metal rail at the entrance running from one side of the wide cave opening to the other.

He released her and waved a hand in the direction they'd just come from. "Watch." He moved to the wall and grabbed the thickest rope she'd ever seen before, a loop that ran from ceiling to floor. He started to pull the front rope downward. A slight squeaking sound, then the wall to the right moved, closing off the opening.

"This consists of four inches of solid metal and rock. The exterior matches the cliff, so our enemies can't spot our homes from the outside when we close these. I don't recommend you attempt to open them yourself. They're on rollers, but it's still a few thousand pounds to shift."

"Right." Jill was reeling inside, trying to take it all in.

The door appeared to be covered in drywall on the inside, like the remaining walls, and painted to match the rest of the library. A painting of the sea even hung there. The seams were noticeable, since there were long strips of dark wood paneling that ran from floor to ceiling on either side of the portion that had moved.

"We do enjoy elegance and comfortable homes."

She turned her head, gawking at him. He seemed so calm and matter of fact, as if he wasn't blowing her mind.

"Are you hungry? Perhaps you'd like a drink?"

She glanced around the room. "I have fallen into the rabbit hole, big time."

He made a soft grumbling noise. "Enough." He walked right over to her and grabbed her arms, giving her a hard shake. The cape he'd lent her fell to the floor. "You're not on drugs and this is real. I'm growing tired of your mind trying to find a way to manage the stress of what you've learned. You aren't high, or going crazy, or dreaming. I'm real, and so is all of this. Stop being as conceited as a typical human can be by believing they are the only ones who share your world."

His grip on her was firm but not hurtful. The tinges of panic started to rise inside her. "I think I'll have that drink. Do you have booze? Something strong?"

"Yes." He backed up and released her. "That might help you deal with the shock. I'm sorry you learned of our existence this way. Your father should have told you what he was and introduced you to the truth."

"The sperm donor is a Gargoyle?"

"He's a VampLycan, and you're half one. You don't carry the scent of a Lycan, so I can only assume you have more Vampire traits. Do you require blood often?"

"I don't drink blood." A horrifying thought struck. "Do you?"

He walked over to a bar in the corner, stepping behind it. His muscles flexed as he lifted a large glass bottle filled with dark liquid and twisted off the lid. He placed two glasses on the counter, pouring a generous amount of booze into each. He set the bottle down and approached her with the glasses. He held one out to her.

She took it and didn't even bother trying to figure out what it was. She just raised the glass and took a gulp.

It was a mistake. Tears filled her eyes, blinding her. It felt as if she'd just swallowed fire that burned from her throat all the way down to her belly. She hissed, almost losing her grasp on the glass.

Aveoth curved his fingers over hers to help her keep hold of it. "Breathe."

"Shit." She rapidly blinked, trying to clear her vision and remember how to fill her lungs. She breathed, all right. It felt as though flames should shoot out of her parted lips as she exhaled.

"What *is* that? Gasoline in a glass?"

He dipped his head, watching her. "Aged Scotch. It's probably a bit strong for you. I could get you wine."

Her insides still burned but it dulled a little. She studied his face. He was really too good looking to be real, but she was starting to believe. She lowered her chin, staring at his tan, long fingers wrapped around hers over the glass. They looked so normal...but he wasn't really a man. Not like any she'd ever met before.

"Remain calm." He had a soothing voice when it came out that low. "You're safe. I wouldn't hurt you, Jill. Your father likely avoided being part of your life because your mother was human. Decker Filmore hates that race. His son was probably ashamed of having a daughter with one. Decker wouldn't have approved of him taking a human as a lover, much less breeding a child. It's still no excuse for you never having learned the truth of what your father is."

She tried to pull out of his hold and he opened his fingers, letting go. She lifted the glass and took a smaller sip, expecting the backlash that time as she swallowed. It still burned but it didn't make her eyes water.

Panic and fear fought for dominance inside her. She couldn't look at Aveoth's face. He had freakin' wings and claws. It wasn't some drug-induced fantasy—it had really happened. Reality was sinking in fast. She backed up and bumped into a couch. She twisted her head, staring at the leather monstrosity. It was a big, heavy piece. *Did he fly that here? Up a cliff? Oh shit!*

"I can smell your fear, Jill. There's no need for that. Talk to me. What are you thinking?"

She finally found the nerve to meet his gaze. Those amazing eyes, blue with silver in them. *No one should have eyes like those, though. They're too beautiful.* "You're telling me the sperm donor is some kind of half Vampire, half Werewolf?"

"Yes. We call them Lycans, though."

"My mother just said he was a selfish asshole." She took another drink.

"He wouldn't have revealed the truth of what he was to her unless they were bonded for life. It's forbidden."

"Right." She wanted out of there. She glanced around and spotted an open doorway. "So you're telling me Scarface was growling because he's *really* a dog?"

"He smelled strongly of his Lycan heritage. He's also part Vampire."

"And the lawyer *really is* a bloodsucker then?" She took another sip. It helped.

"He smelled mostly Lycan too. It's rare for them to actually crave human blood."

"I'm not in Kansas anymore." She bit her lip, the reality of her situation bitch-slapping her hard. She downed the rest of the drink. "Fuck me."

59

She hurled the glass at Aveoth's broad chest and spun, rushing toward the only exit, an open doorway.

She had to get out of there.

It was pitch-black once she left the room. But she needed to escape. She bumped into a wall and put out both hands, blindly trying to feel her way around for another light switch.

Aveoth cursed loudly from nearby. He was coming after her.

She shoved away from the wall and just ran blind. Her foot caught on something and she pitched forward. Pain exploded into her ribs where she impacted with a solid and unforgiving object. It moved, and she cried out as it seemed to collapse under her, then her head struck something, hard.

Aveoth's strong, warm hands gripped her. "Damn it. You're bleeding."

She couldn't see a thing. Her fingers touched what seemed like hard wood, whatever she'd landed on. He adjusted her, rolling her gently. She ended up lying on the floor, on her back.

"I'm going to carry you to bed and tend to you," he rasped.

"Get away from me!" She tried to wiggle out of his reach but her head hurt. It felt as if she'd been nailed with a hammer on her forehead.

"Be still, my little rabbit. I'm going to take care of you. You're safe with me."

"Rabbit?"

"You're the one who said you fell into a rabbit hole. I understood the reference. You saw the books in my library. It's one in my collection."

"Great. Gargoyles read."

"We do a lot of things." He released her, sliding his arms under her back and behind her knees. "Don't fight me. There's no need."

He lifted her and nausea made her stomach roll. She reached up and touched her throbbing head. It was wet and warm. "I *am* bleeding."

"I'm aware. You ran right into one of the guards."

"We're not alone?"

"It's a large carved wooden statue of a guard. I own a few of them. You knocked him over. I think you hit your head on the shield he holds."

"I don't even want to know." She was afraid enough. She closed her eyes and didn't fight when blackness stole in to take her. She'd never fainted in her life, but it seemed like a good time for it to be a first.

Chapter Four

Aveoth carried Jill into the bedroom next to his. He didn't bother with the lights. His night vision was excellent. He gently deposited her on the bed and walked into the adjoining bathroom they'd share. He grabbed a hand towel and turned on the water. It would be cold but she couldn't object. She'd passed out. He just hoped it was from fear and not a severe injury.

He returned to her quickly and cleaned away the worst of the blood. Only then did he reach out to the lamp and turn it on. The slight cut near her hairline was small but it bled a lot. He held his breath, focusing on her. He listened to her slow and steady heartbeat. It was normal for someone sleeping. The scent of her blood instantly tormented him.

That wasn't all that did. He glanced at her cleavage.

So much for him taking her to his bed and stripping her naked. Jill was injured and afraid.

He'd never liked Decker's youngest son. He'd met him on a few occasions, when Decker had sent him with messages into GarLycan territory. The VampLycan had seemed spineless. His dislike increased for Jill's sake. He wanted to kill Decker, and now his son as well. Decon had a child with a human and had abandoned her to be raised in the human world.

It was a miracle a pack of Lycans or a nest of Vampires hadn't killed Jill. She smelled mostly human but he picked up the faint trace of other on her. They would have too. Then again, he hadn't smelled it until she'd bled. Decon had to know his daughter would possibly be hunted without a clan to protect her. She also could have been born with traits that revealed she wasn't fully human. He assumed she didn't have any special talents, or she wouldn't be so shocked by what she'd learned.

He calmed a little when he realized she wasn't severely injured. The cut wasn't deep. The Scotch might have been too strong for her. She did seem totally human, and she wasn't a big one. He leaned in and watched her expression in sleep. Her features were attractive. She had a straight, near perfect nose and full, kissable lips. The urge to brush his mouth over hers became strong, but he resisted.

The blood on her forehead drew his attention.

Vamps had the ability to heal small wounds on humans. He wondered if he could do the same. He'd never had the opportunity to test it. He licked his lips and then drew even closer to her, bracing his hands on each side of her shoulders. He opened his mouth and gently ran his tongue over the small cut.

He closed his eyes and suffered a massive, instant hard-on as the taste of her sweet blood hit him. His fangs shot out of their own accord and it caused him to jerk back. A raw hunger clawed at him to bite that inviting neck of hers. He even glanced at it, looking for the perfect spot. He could almost sense the pulsing vein.

No!

He turned his head and fought his instincts. No one had *ever* affected him that way. He'd had to take some blood from Lane, but it had seemed more of a chore than real pleasure when he'd bitten her. The urge hadn't risen much in the years she'd been his lover. They'd been strangers, for the most part, who shared intimate moments when she went into heat. He avoided her unless she needed him.

Thinking of the tall VampLycan who'd shared his home helped him cool his lust. Lane would always be a grim reminder that he seemed fated to lose any woman he allowed to get too close to him. Lane had been unhappy but she'd refused to leave when he'd offered her freedom.

Then one day he'd gone hunting...and returned to find her gone.

At first, he believed she'd just decided to visit her family living with one of the clans. He'd asked the sentry when she planned to return. The confused look on the man's face had alarmed him. There had been no way for Lane to leave without one of his men flying her from the cliffs, and none of them had seen her.

It had taken him five minutes to locate her body where she'd plunged to her death.

It might have been an accident, but Aveoth didn't believe it. And Lane's scent had been the only one inside his home. It meant that she'd ventured out onto the ledge by herself. She never did that since she feared heights. The only reasonable assumption was that she'd taken her own life. She'd chosen death over remaining with him or returning to her family.

"I'm not going to let that happen to you," he softly rasped. "That's a promise, Jill." He picked up the cloth and tenderly dabbed her forehead to clean away the rest of the blood. More surfaced. The wound wasn't healing.

He frowned, wondering what he'd done wrong or if he hadn't obtained that gift with his minimal Vampire traits.

He leaned forward, his fangs still out. He licked at the wound again. The taste of Vampire was weak but there. The Lycan in her was so faint it was just a slight aftertaste. She was mostly human. He paused and leaned back. The wound bled still.

He remembered something then, and used a fang to pierce his tongue to draw his own blood. He leaned in and licked the wound once more before easing back again.

It no longer bled. He watched, amazed, as the cut began to heal. Aveoth smiled and bit the same spot on his tongue, running it across the slight cut a few more times. He stopped and watched as it completely sealed. Her skin mended so much that within a minute, he couldn't even see where she'd been injured. He tended to her injured wrists the same way. The tiny scratches disappeared.

He rose up and removed her shoes. He studied her clothing, wanted to take those off too but didn't. Jill might believe he'd done something nefarious to her if she awoke naked in a strange bed. He did cover her with part of the blanket by folding it from the other side. He left the lamp on so she wouldn't waken in the dark. That might frighten her too.

He entered the bathroom and closed the door. He had blood on his pants from his earlier fight. He turned on the shower and tried to ignore the state of his body. Arousal wasn't something he suffered often but Jill was in the next room. He wanted her.

A list of precautions formed in his head as he quickly stripped. Jill would try to escape again. He would too, in her place. All the exterior entrances needed to be sealed. She wasn't strong enough to open them on her own. He could barricade the stairwell to the lower floor with a large, heavy piece of furniture. A guard placed at the front door would not only keep her in, but protect her from anyone trying to reach her.

Some of his clan wouldn't be thrilled to have Jill at the cliffs. The full-blooded Gargoyles would attempt to turn his people against him. That was a given. They'd question his leadership, his mental stability, and even his loyalty to the clan for taking a human with VampLycan blood as a mate. Vampires had been the enemy of Gargoyles for millennia. That old hatred remained strong in the ancient ones. GarLycans, for the most part, were more tolerant since they'd aligned with the VampLycans. They just didn't breed with them.

Aveoth finished his shower and dried quickly, entering his room from the bathroom. He put on black sleeping pants and located the secondary cell phone he kept charging on his bedside table. He picked it up and placed a call. Kelzeb answered on the second ring.

"What's wrong?"

That amused him. "Who said anything was?"

"This isn't your official line. It's your private one."

"I need to speak to you. Come to my living quarter—and be silent. I have company."

"I'm on my way."

He hung up and checked on Jill. She still slept. He used the door out of her room to gain access to the rest of his home, and crept down the hall until he reached the living room and open kitchen area. It didn't take long for his best friend to step out of the darkness. Aveoth grinned at the sight of Kelzeb gripping a sword, a dagger strapped to his bare thigh in a holster while he sported a pair of loose boxer shorts.

Kelzeb sniffed and instantly frowned.

"You can lower your blade. There's no threat here. Decker called me with a deal. You're scenting a granddaughter we never knew about. Decon had a human lover, got her pregnant, and abandoned them both in the human world. Decker had a few of his enforcers grab the now-adult daughter and bring her to me."

"Let me guess. He wants you to give him his clan back *and* your promise to help him wipe out the other clans?"

"He would have tried if I hadn't cut him off. I gave him nothing except the promise he could live as long as he doesn't return to Alaska or start more shit with the clans. I won't actively hunt for him until he gives me cause." Aveoth curled his lip. "He will."

"She agreed to be given to you?"

"No. Her name is Jill, and she didn't even know anything but humans existed until Decker had her snatched."

"Fuck." Kelzeb placed his sword on the table, then ran his fingers through his sleep-tousled hair.

"I apologize if I woke you."

"You should have woken me before you went to get the woman. It could have been a trap."

"That's why I didn't take you with me. One of us needs to survive to keep the peace."

"You took backup with you?"

"No."

"Damn it, Aveoth! You know Decker would love to kill you."

"He could try, but I doubt he's smart enough to do it. I was careful."

"Why didn't you take a few enforcers?"

"I'm not certain how the clan will react when they learn I've brought Jill here."

"Right. VampLycan. I have to say, she smells mostly human."

"But?"

"I'm scenting blood. Is she well?"

"She'll be fine. It was a slight cut."

"It's acceptable for you to keep a lover. No one can say anything as long as you don't breed with her. What's the problem? They didn't bat an eye when Lane lived here."

Aveoth studied his friend. "Lane had no human blood. You're forgetting biology."

"Shit. I'm not fully awake yet but I'm getting there. You could have her sterilized. That way there's no accidental pregnancy."

"No."

"It will cause major problems if you get her with child."

"I'm aware. But I'd like to have children." He paused. "I don't plan to just have her as my lover. I want to create a family."

Kelzeb softly cursed.

"Exactly. There is going to be a lot of fallout."

"Probably not with the younger generations, but some of the pure Gargoyles are going to rise up against you if you mate a woman with VampLycan bloodlines."

"I'm aware."

"A few will side with you."

"Name one."

"Fray and Chaz's father, Hawk. He's pretty mellow about that shit. He might get Gorzak on his side. They've both lost mates and are lonely. They'd understand your need to take one, despite her bloodlines. They also don't want a full-blooded Gargoyle lord again. You know they didn't get along with Abotorus."

"Vampires killed both of their mates."

"But they are friendly to VampLycans and humans. I'd say you were shit out of luck if that woman was a full Vamp, but then again, having children wouldn't be an option if she were."

"Agreed. I sometimes wonder why I bother to stay."

"You do it for the good of all. The other Gargoyle clans would attack us if they heard you were no longer our lord."

"No. They fear us."

Kelzeb snorted. "The other clans fear *you*. They'd challenge *me*."

Aveoth scowled.

"You are the one who killed Lord Abotorus. No one ever beat him until you."

"I get it. I need to stay."

"How is this Jill handling being here and meeting you? You said she was unaware of anything not human."

"She's brave. I got the impression she gave Decker's men a difficult time when they kidnapped her."

69

"I like her already."

"So do I. She asked me to beat the shit out of both of them."

Kelzeb chuckled. "You didn't."

"I did."

"How did she react to seeing violence? Most humans abhor it."

He grinned over the memory. "She has spunk. That's why I'm considering taking her as my mate."

"Don't rush into anything."

"She's going to need time to adjust to me and this life first. I won't force the issue until she's ready."

"That might never happen. Her mind could shatter. Humans are pretty frail with their beliefs."

"She's no weakling."

Kelzeb sighed. "You hope."

"I have faith."

"That's new."

"I'm attracted to her, Kelzeb, and lonely. It's motivation. But I wanted your assessment skills right now. How do you think the clan will react when they learn I've brought what they will believe is a human here?"

"They'll be shocked, since Elco has spread word that Winalin is yours. It's expected that you'll take a full-blooded Gargoyle female as your mate, since there is one here."

"Elco needs to be beaten, and I'd *never* touch his sister. Life with Winalin would be pure misery. That's never going to happen. And I can handle shock. What do you think will be their second reaction?"

"Some will assume you're going to use her to breed children. And no lord uses a breeding vessel unless there are no other mate options or our clan numbers are decreasing. It's been that way from the beginning. That will likely cause outrage, since we stick to tradition, and this doesn't fall under either of those situations. Once they realize you plan to mate this Jill..." Kelzeb sighed. "I can't even guess."

"I want change."

"I do as well, but this is pretty bold, mating with a woman with Vampire bloodlines, especially if your children show any signs of a need for blood passed down to them."

"There's a way we could avoid that entirely if I do mate her and she gets pregnant. I'd need your assistance with that."

Kelzeb lowered his gaze. "Damn."

"I won't kill you. You're family to me. To let her drink your blood would ensure any offspring are strongly Gargoyle. Is that asking too much?"

His friend lifted his gaze and peered at him. "If your bond will allow it, I'll offer my blood in a cup for her to drink. It would be an honor."

"Thank you."

"You're welcome."

"I also need to continue to protect my secret."

Kelzeb stepped closer. "It would be hell if they realized."

"That's why I'm asking you to share your blood at some point."

"Done."

Aveoth relaxed. "Thank you again."

71

"Look on the bright side. We won't have to take any secret trips in the future."

Aveoth nodded. "True."

"You've got your own blood supply when you need it."

"She's more than that to me, or she will be. Thankfully, I don't get the urge often."

"You could have always taken my blood. I've offered."

Aveoth grinned. "I knew you'd be uncomfortable with that. It's intimate to share blood."

Kelzeb chuckled. "True." A teasing spark flared in his gaze. "Although it's been so long since *anyone* has been intimate with me in any way that I might have appreciated it."

"I keep telling you to take a few days for yourself." Aveoth reached out and gripped his friend's shoulder. "When things settle, go find a woman to warm you."

Kelzeb shook his head. "I'm not looking for a mate yet, and my ravage is years away still. I'm good. It's a complication I don't need. Humans are so drawn to us that I feel guilt over their attraction, and Lycans always seek to mate."

That piqued Aveoth's curiosity. "What do you mean, humans are so drawn to us?"

"You're never around them. I forget. Remember when I had to spend four days in Anchorage?"

Aveoth nodded.

"I hated being cooped up in the hotel, waiting to see if any of Decker's men showed up there. They had a gym for humans to alleviate some of their energy. I decided to try it. I lifted some weights, ran on a treadmill, and then did some pull-ups. Before I realized it, about twenty human women had surrounded me. They were drawn to me in an unnatural way."

Aveoth frowned. "How?"

"I'm not certain if it was the sight of my body or maybe the scent of my sweat, but we seem to attract them. I could smell arousal on all of them. A few of the more aggressive ones approached me for sex, and two of them almost came to blows fighting for my attention. It might be a pheromone thing. I wasn't sure. I broke it up and got the hell out of there. A few tried to follow me back to my room. It felt wrong to take advantage of them, considering I wasn't certain why they were so sexually interested."

"You never told me."

"It wasn't necessary. We usually avoid humans and it's extremely rare for our men to stay in hotels. When they do, they aren't exactly social. They check in, sleep, and leave after they're rested. I didn't think it was a big enough deal to bring up."

"It's not, but perhaps I can use that information to help Jill accept me."

Kelzeb arched an eyebrow. "I'd call that an unfair advantage."

"I need one. She's going to be very resistant to becoming my mate. I want to keep her."

"We don't have a gym."

"No, but we train. You could spar with me. That usually causes me to sweat."

Kelzeb grinned. "I don't take it easy on you."

"I appreciate that. Everyone else fears being too aggressive."

"You know I have no reason to take your head, so I don't have to worry about you mistaking my actions for veiled attempts on your life."

"True."

"In the morning?"

"Afternoon."

"I'll arrange for the training area to be empty except for the two of us and your Jill."

"Thank you, Kelzeb."

"I'm going back to bed."

"Sorry for waking you."

"I just wish you'd done it sooner, and had me go with you when you retrieved the woman. Don't do that again."

"I make no promises. Lock the lower doors, please."

Aveoth watched his friend lift his sword and leave down the back staircase. He waited moments, sealed the door by putting a large piece of furniture in front of it that Jill wouldn't be able to move on her own. He did the same to the front entrance. He just wanted to keep her upstairs in his private area and away from the mirrored space on the floor below that guests visited him at times.

He returned to the bedroom and found her peacefully sleeping. He lifted a chair and placed it next to her bed, took a seat, and watched her.

A good hour passed before he stood, finally going to his own room. He planned to sleep for an hour, then return to her side so she'd wake to find him close.

His phone buzzed before he could lie down. He answered it. "Yes?"

"You hurt my men."

"So?" He gritted his teeth. The bastard had nerve.

"I want retribution."

"Fuck you, Decker. You gave me the impression your granddaughter willingly agreed to become my lover. Your men traumatized her by stealing her from the world she knew. Your enforcer roughed her up and made disturbing threats. They *deserved* the abuse they received. Feel lucky I didn't send them to you in pieces."

"I want to return to my clan."

"You should have been happy when you led them previously, but instead your greed cost you everything. I told you to leave the other clans alone and to keep the peace."

"I don't have to listen to you. It's a VampLycan matter."

"You made it my business when you tried to blackmail me into doing your bidding. You can't take them on your own. We both know it, and so do they. My men will never attack a VampLycan clan just so you can rule them all."

"Lorn murdered the men I left behind! That bastard needs to die."

"He challenged for leadership, and won fair, Decker. I like Lorn much better than I ever did you. He has my blessing."

"It's not up to you!" Decker snarled the words, clearly outraged.

It amused Aveoth. "You're right—but Lorn has my support and that of my clan. We will help defend *his* clan if you send anyone after them again."

"I don't know what you're talking about," Decker yelled. "And it's *not* Lorn's clan. It's mine!"

The ease in which Decker lied killed Aveoth's good humor. The asshole had no honor whatsoever. "You're full of shit. You've been working with the Vamps for a while. You put a hunt order out for your own granddaughter with their council and every Lycan pack, in the hopes they'd capture Batina for you. Then you sent Vampires into VampLycan territory as revenge because Lorn took over your clan. You probably thought it would make him appear weak to the clan, having a VampLycan kidnapped by a Vamp during his reign."

"That's not true!"

Aveoth snorted. "Spare me your lies. Were you worried your clansmen didn't miss you? Did you think being attacked would encourage them to believe they were better off with you there? Wrong. Lord Abotorus taught me the art of manipulation. Your plan failed. The VampLycans aren't stupid, and every clan is aware of who is *really* responsible for that Vampire attack. You are."

"They're setting me up and trying to blame me," Decker spat.

"Give it up. You have your life, but it's forfeit if you don't leave everyone alone, including me. I beat the shit out of your men. So what? I left them alive. Feel gratitude. I'm going to hold you responsible if there are any more attacks on the clans. That includes from suckheads, Lycans, or even humans. Don't call again, Decker, and stay the fuck out of Alaska if you want to remain alive." He disconnected the phone.

"Fucking idiot," he muttered.

Chapter Five

Jill woke to the sight of a rock ceiling. It took her a few seconds for memory to slam home. She'd been kidnapped and flown to some Gargoyle cave.

She sat up, peering around the bedroom.

She had to admit, it was extremely elegant for a cave. The furnishings appeared antique and high end. She shoved off the covers and her bare feet touched thick carpeting. It turned out to be a large area rug. She stood, taking in the entire room. The tops of the walls weren't exactly even, seemingly built to fit the rock ceilings. The floors were smooth though. Flat.

Where's the hot dude with wings?

She listened but the silence didn't clue her in. She rounded the bed, stepped off the large area rug and onto cool stone flooring. She stopped, staring down at the polished stone. *Impressive.* She had to give them credit for craftsmanship. They took cave dwelling to an unthinkable level of class. She found her shoes and put them on.

Jill left the bedroom and entered a bathroom. It seemed to be surprisingly modern, with a toilet, shower, and tub. She quickly peed and washed her hands. One toothbrush was in a glass cup on the counter. She figured that belonged to Aveoth. She used his toothpaste and her finger to deal with her morning breath. Her hair was a mess but most of it remained trapped in the braid. She left it alone.

There was another door out of the bathroom, and she carefully opened it, trying to be very quiet. The sight of another, larger bedroom surprised her. Sunlight filled the room from a large opening in the wall. A warm breeze fanned across her skin. She crept inside and her gaze landed on the massive bed.

The sight there made her freeze, lips parting.

Aveoth lay sprawled in the center of the mattress and black bedding, face up. His eyes were closed.

His chest rose and fell but he didn't snore. He wore a pair of black, silky pajama pants without a shirt. She took in the sight of his flat stomach and beefy arms, one of them stretched out across the bed. He took up a lot of space because he was a big man. She crept closer, wondering if he really slept or if it was some kind of ruse. He didn't stir.

She hugged her waist and swallowed hard, unsure what to do.

He shifted his leg, bending a knee and arching his hips a little. Her gaze lowered down his body. His stomach tightened, revealing a lot of muscles. His wings were gone. She wasn't about to forget he could grow them, though.

She spotted something on his nightstand—and hope flared when she realized he had a cell phone. She could call for help.

She tiptoed forward—but froze when he suddenly rolled onto his stomach. He spread out his limbs and she was left staring at his broad back.

There was no sign of where his wings had been the night before. Smooth, unmarred skin stretched across his shoulder blades. She lifted a foot to inch closer to the nightstand, and that phone, but he made a low grunt.

Jill backed away. It might be possible that he could sense her as she got near him. There was no telling what kind of other freaky things he could do. Though he didn't move or make another sound.

Her gaze remained fixed on the phone but she didn't dare go for it. He'd probably wake and catch her red-handed. She turned toward the opening in the wall instead, quietly crossed the room and stepped out onto a flat ledge. The sight that met her as she stared out at the world left her breathless.

The view from that height revealed what appeared to be endless wilderness. She didn't spot any signs of a city, buildings, or even homes. Just trees, and a jagged line through them revealing a river in the distance.

She turned her head, spotting another ledge some distance away. She also saw cuts in the rock, perhaps handholds, that led to a third ledge much farther below, probably twenty or thirty feet.

She backed up and returned to the bedroom she'd woken in, exiting to enter the room Aveoth had brought her in through the night before. The wall remained sealed. She walked down a hallway and found another door. A large piece of furniture blocked it. More exploration took her to another large room, with a living space and kitchen.

Son of a bitch. There seemed to be no escape with that doorway blocked. She returned to that spot and studied it. Aveoth had done blocked it. She felt certain of that. She tried to lift the heavy armoire but it had to weigh hundreds of pounds. She tried to tug and pull but the wood scraped the floor a mere inch, the sound loud. She stopped and listened, fearing it might have woken him.

Damn it!

She needed to escape. The only way out had been that open ledge inside his bedroom. She chewed on her bottom lip, debating it. She turned, retracing her steps, searching for another phone. She found none. Finally, she returned to Aveoth's bedroom. He still lay on his stomach, in the same position she'd left him. She tiptoed toward the phone but when she got close to it, he rolled onto his side.

Her heart pounded as she backed up, glancing over her shoulder to make certain she didn't bump into anything or trip. Aveoth grunted in his sleep, and as she watched him, he reached up and rubbed his cheek. He appeared to be dreaming, possibly having a nightmare.

Fear struck that he was about to wake. She turned and rushed as quietly as possible to the ledge. Heights had never been her thing but she feared them less than the man on the bed. She needed to get away from him. He was a Gargoyle or a GarLycan or whatever. He had wings and an association with her sperm donor's fucked-up family. That was more than enough to tell her he was bad news. She couldn't forget his clawed fingers either, or the sight of them buried in Boon's head.

It was a beautiful, sunny day. The breeze felt good on her skin as she eased onto the side of the ledge. She faced the rock wall and put the view at her back. It helped not looking down or seeing how far she'd fall to her death that way. She scanned the rock and found places to grip with her fingers and where she could put her feet.

"Damn." She turned her head, seeing the cuts in the rock to the ledge below. It seemed like a really long way to climb down, but she didn't have a choice. It was possible there might be a way out if she entered through another ledge. Aveoth had mentioned caves the night before. If there were a lot of them, maybe he'd only used some of them as his living space.

"I want the hell out of here," she muttered and shoved back her fear. "I can do this, even if I have to climb all the way to the bottom of this damn cliff. I'm going home. Fuck this messed-up shit."

* * * * *

Galihia gripped Aveoth's arm, preventing him from stepping into the moonlit courtyard. He paused, turning his head to stare into her cobalt-blue eyes. They were the same ones he saw every time he looked at his reflection. Her silky black hair was piled in an elegant braided bun.

She'd given birth to him but he never called her mother. It wasn't allowed.

"Do not show emotion regardless of what he says. He'll test you. Don't fail. I realize the sixteen years you've lived are too few to learn control, but your life is at stake."

The warning stiffened his spine. She took a risk even speaking those words. He resisted the urge to ask questions. They didn't have time. Lord Abotorus waited.

Galihia released him and stepped back, waiting for him to exit. He inhaled slowly and held the air in his lungs as he faced the event he dreaded.

82

The full moon mocked him. Aveoth kept his attention on the silent forms waiting to witness the moment when two clans sealed an agreement for continued peace. He wasn't happy with the way it had come about, but he hadn't been asked. His father never took his wishes into consideration.

Three tall figures stood unhooded near Abotorus, but it was the smallest one, still completely shrouded, who deflated his lungs. He didn't know her name, nor anything about her personal life. To ask questions would have been an offense. It was his duty to heed his lord's demands. Any show of hesitation would be viewed as defiance.

He couldn't even look directly at her, instead staring at the altar. He did use his peripheral vision to gather every detail he could about the young woman. The hood hid a lot but not all of her. She kept her chin down and her black hair hung to her waist down the front of her cloak. Delicate shoulders, and her slight height deeply disturbed him. She was either a very dainty teenager or hadn't even hit puberty yet.

His hatred for his father, Abotorus, grew stronger.

"We gather here today to deepen the links to our clans." Abotorus paused. "Let us hope we are more successful than the last time we attempted this."

Aveoth allowed the insult to roll off him. He knew he'd been a disappointment since birth. He'd never been allowed to forget it. Memories of being punished flashed through his mind but he kept his emotions masked. He could feel his father watching him for a reaction, so he gave none.

"Let us begin, Lord Abotorus. This shall permanently cement our clan bonds." The VampLycan allowed his impatience to sound in his voice.

"Doubtful, Decker. I don't see any of my kind living with *your* clan, yet I keep being expected to take yours into mine."

The VampLycan clan leader softly growled. "We've offered, but your clan members have refused to leave the cliffs."

"That's because we're not heathens."

Aveoth focused on his heartbeat, keeping it steady. Lord Abotorus seemed determined to insult their guests. It was one time he didn't feel embarrassed by the rudeness. The VampLycans might take the girl away and cancel the agreement.

His luck wasn't that good, because no one moved.

"Do you concede to our agreement, Decker? I grow bored. What is her name?"

"Margola. She is the younger sister of my own mate." The leader of the VampLycan clan reached out an arm and steered her closer to the altar.

"Wait." Abotorus grumbled. "Didn't your mate come from another clan? Does this girl belong to your clan or another?"

"Mine," Decker stated clearly. "She wanted to live with her sister and I accepted her. Let's get on with this." Decker motioned to the girl. "Give your agreement to accept Lord Abotorus's son as your lover to unite our clans."

Aveoth silently urged her to decline. It would be best for both of them if she did. She raised her chin, not that it helped make out her features without looking directly at her. He didn't dare.

"I do," she whispered.

"Aveoth agrees as well," Abotorus muttered.

"That's not how it should be," Decker protested. "He must speak the words."

"I accept her as my lover," Aveoth stated loud and clear.

The small female shivered. He didn't blame her if she felt fear. It was an indication of intelligence. He also pondered why she'd agreed to allow him to house her inside his new home. It had been his gift months before on his sixteenth year. He'd been kicked out of father's dwelling. He figured his father didn't want him underfoot any longer. That had been fine with him.

Aveoth had been assured the VampLycan he was to take as a lover was mostly Lycan, but even a drop of Vampire blood made it impossible for him to ever accept her as a mate or allow her to birth his children. Did the VampLycan clans fear a war between their people so deeply that they'd encourage one of their women to agree to this madness?

His hatred for his father notched a little higher. The bastard had probably enjoyed concocting the hellish deal. Lord Abotorus felt the VampLycans were beneath them, and asking for one of their women to offer her body for sex with his son until Aveoth found a mate was insulting to all concerned. He didn't have fond thoughts toward the VampLycan Decker, either, for basically whoring out one of the women under his protection.

Pity surfaced next. He might have no choice but to agree to take her as a lover. But he silently swore to never visit her bed. What happened behind the closed doors of his home would be no one's concern. He only wished he could tell her of his decision. She wouldn't be afraid of the future.

Aveoth steeled himself for what would come next. He couldn't show any compassion. That would come much later, when they weren't under the steady watch of his father.

"I hereby decree that the alliance has been reset, and grant the date five years from this night when Aveoth fully claims her," Abotorus announced.

Decker hissed his displeasure. "I believed you'd take her now and our alliance would be immediate."

"She'll be of legal age at that time. My son doesn't want a child in his bed."

Aveoth did the math and hid a cringe. The girl was only thirteen. He was surprised his father had enough compassion to not force her to his home at her current age. His fingers stiffened but he forced them to relax. He wanted to hit Abotorus for forcing a mere child into that kind of promise in the first place. He wasn't much older than her, but he'd had a harsh life. He'd aged beyond his years.

"I'll give you an older woman," Decker offered. "You're the one who chose this one."

"I did it for a reason. You're too eager, and I don't trust you. This will give me time to watch you."

Aveoth glanced up at the VampLycan leader to see the effect of his father's words, not liking him much, either. What kind of man would offer up a young girl from his own clan and try to trade away her childhood innocence for an alliance? Not much of one. Decker Filmore had made himself an enemy today.

"It's time to seal this bargain with a blood oath." Abotorus motioned with his finger for Aveoth to approach the altar. "Take her wrist and bleed her. The heathens insisted."

Aveoth's stomach heaved but he moved into place and finally lifted his gaze to stare into her delicate features. Pure fear showed in her pale blue eyes. It proved she knew of the danger he represented. Her pending beauty couldn't be denied, even at that tender age. He felt monstrous as he held out a steady hand with his palm open. It would infuriate his father, but he refused to brutalize her further by making her put her skin against cold stone.

She trembled when she placed her wrist over his hand. He reminded himself that Abotorus would be studying him carefully, and parted his lips, forcing his fangs to slide down. He bent without pause, sealing his lips to her skin. He didn't sink his fangs into her, but instead licked over a vein with his tongue to give her warning. Her gasp of surprise could be taken for pain. He hoped that's what his father believed. He waited a second to allow her to prepare before he pierced her flesh. He did so gently.

Warm blood flowed and he drank slowly. He didn't want to take too much and leave her weakened. She wasn't fully grown. He took his time to give the impression he held no regard to her health by being greedy.

When he finally pulled away, he released her and spun around, holding Abotorus's cold gaze.

"It's done." He made sure not to lick his lips to clean them. That way there could be no doubt he'd actually taken some of her blood.

A muscle in his father's jaw twitched and his mouth compressed into a tight line. "You didn't make her thank you."

Aveoth didn't want to do that to her. It would humiliate her in front of everyone present in the courtyard. He spared her that by uttering harsh words instead. "I will when she's of age and I get to fuck her. *That's* when she'll kneel before me."

The girl whimpered behind him. Aveoth knew she'd fear their future, but it was best to save her from being forced to her knees to grovel in public.

Approval curved Abotorus's lips into a hideous smile. "We are of the same bloodline."

Aveoth inclined his head, saying nothing. He really hated the man who'd fathered him.

"You're dismissed." Lord Abotorus directed his attention to the VampLycan clan leader. "In five years, the girl will belong to my son."

"You can have her now," Decker offered again.

"No. My men will fly you home. Leave my cliffs," his father thundered.

Aveoth never glanced back but he could hear their words. He entered the doorway and met Galihia's tearful eyes. He hated to see the moisture there. He kept walking until he reached the lower corridors, her soft footsteps behind him. He paused, allowing her to stop at his side. She glanced around before stepping closer to him, making sure they were out of hearing of anyone else.

"Please tell me you didn't mean that."

"She's a child. Would you have preferred I say obscene words or actually hurt her? My lord would have expected me to grab her by the neck, lower her to her knees, and make her praise me for being a bastard. He made his wishes clear before the allegiance ceremony. He wanted it blatantly shown that they are not our equals."

Galihia paled and raised her hand, gently resting it on his forearm. "Don't become anything like him."

"Did he humiliate you when you mated to him? Did he make it clear he thought your Lycan blood made you lesser than him?"

Her gaze lowered. "Never ask. You'd kill him."

His gums throbbed, his fangs trying to extend. It happened when he was really angry. He placed his hand over hers. They didn't show affection often anymore but there were stolen moments when they did. Abotorus would punish them both if he ever found out.

"I'm nothing like my father. The day will come when I challenge him. I already plan to take him out."

"Good," she encouraged. "Practice your sword skills often and grow stronger. He's an excellent fighter. But you will be able to beat him within a few years."

Footsteps sounded and she sprang away, taking off quickly in the opposite direction. He turned, waiting. Abotorus appeared. He came to a halt.

"What are you doing standing there?"

"Waiting for you," Aveoth lied. He wanted to stall him to make certain Galihia got away without being caught. "Couldn't you have given me a woman I could take to my bed now?"

Abotorus smirked. "You're not of age yet."

"Years mean nothing."

"You *are* of my bloodline. I felt the same urge to have a woman trapped under me. I know why you refused to make her grovel. It's already sickening enough to have to deal with those lower breeds, but they do serve their purpose. Decker is too eager to form an alliance. I don't trust the bastard. It's why I chose the girl."

Aveoth really detested his father but he masked his features, hiding his feelings.

"The biggest flaw with them is they're emotional." His father appeared disgusted. "That's why they insist you drink her blood every month. They think it will help you develop some kind of attachment to her."

It was the first Aveoth had heard of it. "What do you mean?"

"She is to be returned here the night after the first full moon every month, weather permitting, until the five years pass. Those imbeciles think it will make you learn to care for her and form an attachment. I only agreed because she was the best of what they offered in that age range.

She has very minimal Vampire blood, but those idiots actually think you might mate her one day." Lord Abotorus snorted. "As if I would allow that kind of abomination at the cliffs. We'll have her sterilized once she's brought to us for good. It's best not to take any risks, and you shouldn't be limited as to what you can do to her once she belongs to you."

Aveoth hid his horror. The girl would never be able to give birth to a child, even after she was freed from living in his home and able to search for her true mate.

It was too cruel. He wouldn't allow it to happen.

"I hope for your sake that she's not a whiner." His father sneered. "I made that mistake with Galihia. Tears are a disgusting thing to see."

Rage boiled deep inside Aveoth. He hid it from the man regarding him coldly. He'd never treat any woman with the cruelty that his father did his mother.

Abotorus dismissed him, walking away.

Aveoth watched him go and allowed his fists to curl. One day he'd kill him. Rage built just thinking about how much he wished to spill his father's blood.

* * * * *

Aveoth jerked awake and opened his eyes, relieved the memory from his past had ended. He was out of bed in a heartbeat, striding to the wardrobe and donning a shirt. It was tempting to go check on Jill. He'd slept longer than he thought but he wasn't ready to face her yet after dreaming of the past. He moved to the ledge instead, staring out over his territory. He breathed in the fresh scent of the woods from far below.

Memories rarely haunted his sleep, but Jill linked him to that moment in time. Her relative had escaped her fate by dying before reaching the age when she'd have been sent to live with him. Aveoth had taken control of the clan by then, but he would have been forced to honor the deal his father had made by accepting Margola into his home. He just wouldn't have sterilized her or forced her to suffer his touch. After a short amount of time, he'd planned to announce they weren't a good match and have her returned to her clan.

Margola's face had faded from his mind but he could remember how timid she'd been when she was brought to him every month. Not once had she held his gaze or stood before him without trembling.

Jill was drastically different. Amusement struck him. He liked her spirit. She didn't back down from him or cower. The feisty woman had even pitched a glass at his chest.

That amusement quickly faded when a slight, odd noise sounded from below. He stepped to the edge of the ledge, peering down. "Son of a bitch."

The object of his thoughts stood on a thin line of rock twenty-some feet below. She faced the cliffs as she inched sideways, clinging to the uneven rock.

He judged the distance between them. Rocks crumbled under her right foot as he watched, and she froze.

He reached up and ripped off his shirt. The material tore easily in his hands.

Is Jill trying to get herself killed? It pissed him off. The fall to the ravine below would definitely kill her. She'd hit trees before a mass of jagged boulders at the base of the cliffs. There would be no soft cushion. Her bones would shatter on impact.

He studied the face of the cliff. He could climb down to her but debris might strike her off her precarious perch. He couldn't risk it.

More tiny rocks tumbled away below, bouncing off the cliff. She would fall if he didn't do something fast. Pain ripped through his back from the force of the quick change. He dove forward into the air and let himself fall a good hundred feet below her.

A rush of adrenaline always hit when he spread his wings. He didn't want to startle her, but she must have heard his wings flap even from that distance when he turned, circling back, and began to gain height to reach her. He was usually silent for a predator but speed had become his priority.

Jill turned her head, and he saw her features pale. Her eyes widened and she wavered, about to fall back. One of her feet slipped and she gasped. He flapped his wings hard, closing the distance.

Aveoth wasn't gentle when he grabbed her around the waist. He was too angry over her recklessness. He got a good hold on her and glanced up. He hadn't sealed the wall to his lower living space, since he'd blocked the door to it. He adjusted her in his arms and backed away from the cliff sharply, turning toward the ledge to his right. His legs absorbed the impact to prevent her from being hurt when he landed on the ledge.

His anger exploded once he had her safe. "What the hell did you think you were going to do?"

He eased her down until she stood and lessened his tight hold. She trembled against him. He paused and drew in his wings. His shoulder

93

blades throbbed a little as the skin started to mend around the damaged flesh.

She tried to wiggle away, and he allowed it. He stayed between her and the edge. She spun, her eyes still wide and her lips parted.

"You could have fallen to your death. You don't have wings!"

"I know that." She took a step backward, then another.

"Watch it. There's a planter behind you. Don't trip."

"I want to leave here." Her voice sounded stronger but she still looked unsteady on her feet.

"That was your great escape plan? To plunge to your death? Do you know how easy it is to fall? You don't even have climbing equipment. You're damn lucky I happened to wake and see you. Otherwise I might have heard your death scream on the way down."

Jill glanced back, spotted the tall round planter, and surprised him by taking a seat on the edge of it. Her knuckles whitened from the grip she kept on the rim. "You can't keep me here forever."

Some of his temper cooled. He didn't blame Jill for attempting escape. "I can. You're not safe anywhere else, Jill."

"You're wrong."

He strode forward but she jerked back, landing on her butt in the dirt-filled planter. He crouched down in front of her. "Take a deep breath."

She blinked a few times and sucked in air to her lungs. It would have amused him at any other time, seeing her in that position, sitting on a large pot resembling some ancient toilet. He reached out to touch her but she flinched away. He withdrew.

"I'm not going to hurt you. I just saved your life." He didn't want to lose another woman to death. "Let's go inside and get you fed."

She shook her head. "I'm good where I am."

"I didn't mean to frighten you but those holes you were using to cling to aren't stable. Do you understand that? Never do that again. It's safe for us since falling isn't an issue. You can't fly, Jill."

"I just wanted to leave."

"By killing yourself?" His anger returned. "How far do you think you'd have gotten?"

"There were other ledges but they were all blocked by rock. I couldn't see that until I got lower. This one didn't have any holds to reach it."

"Those are homes of other members of my clan. Be happy they were sealed. Otherwise you'd have invaded their space and they would have attacked you, believing you were an enemy."

She paled.

"Let's assume you managed to climb all the way down. You wouldn't have stood a chance, but what then? Do you know where you are? How far you are from one of your cities? Would you like to talk about the kind of wildlife you may have run into if you'd managed to sneak out of my home undetected or get past my clan members? There's nowhere for you to run."

"I don't belong here."

95

Regret surfaced. He didn't blame her for desiring her old life. "You know about us now, and I can't protect you if you go home. Don't you think those two men I beat the living shit out of might want to seek revenge if they're ever given the chance?"

"They won't come after me again. They'll think I'm here with you."

"Are you certain they won't keep checking?"

She bit her bottom lip. "I'll be prepared for them."

"They are VampLycans. Do you know what that means?"

"I can't forget. Half Vampire, half Werewolf."

"How will you prepare? You shoot one and they get up. You're lucky they wanted you alive and unharmed. They are stronger and faster than anything you've ever faced before."

"I'll buy silver bullets. Those kill Werewolves, right? I could soak them in holy water and have a priest bless them. That way I'm covering both my bases for those half-breed freaks."

He grinned. She did amuse him.

She suddenly appeared annoyed. "What is so funny?"

"That's in movies and books. It's not reality. Crosses and holy water don't work on Vampires, and silver bullets don't hold any special qualities besides being harder to come by. You'll only injure a Lycan with bullets but they won't stop coming."

"What *does* kill them?"

He considered it. "I could."

"I mean stuff that I could get where *I'm* from."

"Do you have grenades? Blowing one up would work. Of course, they're fast. They'd just see it coming and jump out of the blast range. At best, you'd end up with a slightly injured one who's super pissed off."

She seemed to be considering it, and he bit back a laugh. He loved her spunk. He moved closer to her again and extended his hand. "Come inside. You're shaken up." He could see her trembling.

"I'm fine here."

"Do you really want to learn how to kill other races?"

"Yes."

"Then come inside."

She seemed to debate it for a few seconds but refused his hand. She got up on her own and brushed off the back of her pants. "Just stay back."

He retreated a few steps but kept between her and the edge of his balcony, not willing to risk her doing something else that could endanger her life. He made a mental note to seal every opening inside his home immediately. He wouldn't give her the opportunity to climb outside again.

"How do you kill them?"

"Inside," he reminded her. "I'll make you breakfast."

"I'm not hungry."

He didn't believe that. He could hear her stomach grumbling. Her tactics made no sense. He'd fill up on food, making him as strong as possible, and plot his escape if he were in her place. She seemed to be on a hunger strike. *Women. I'll never understand them no matter how long I live.*

She entered his lower secondary living room and glanced around. She didn't like it, from her frown. He studied the room for the first time, trying to imagine what she might be thinking. It was masculine and dark. The fireplace probably needed to be cleaned. He had stacks of books on a few tables from his library. The smaller kitchen he'd had put in for Lane's use was across the open space. Down the hall were two bathrooms and bedrooms.

Jill walked to the table and fingered the cover of a book.

"You like to read?"

"Yes." She turned and faced him. "Some of these look really old."

"They probably are. You won't find a bookstore out here."

"You have internet, don't you?"

"No."

She glanced around. "No TV, either?"

"Not in my home. Some of the others have satellite dishes."

"Oh my God." She strode over to his couch and sat down hard. Both of her hands rose and she covered her face. "It's like hell."

"It's not that bad."

She lowered her hands to her lap and glared at him. "What do you do all day?"

"I rule my people and keep them safe."

"I mean in your off time?"

"I read. I take walks in the woods or go for a fly. Train for battle."

"Stop." She glanced away, staring at the fireplace.

98

He didn't like to see her unhappy. "I could get a television for you."

"How nice."

He identified her sarcasm. "I want you to be happy here."

"That's never going to happen."

He strode over to the fireplace and leaned his arm against the mantel. "Do you understand that you can't go back?"

"Why?"

"You're being stubborn. I already told you of the danger you'd be in."

"I wouldn't be if you killed those two men who kidnapped me. Situation handled." She stood up. "What would that cost me?"

"I'm not…" He paused, unable to tell her he wasn't a killer. He'd done a lot of that in his lifetime and would again. "Your grandfather would just send more of his enforcers after you if I let you go…or worse."

"What does that mean?"

"He could have Vampires, Lycans, and everything in between hunting for you. He's done that before to another like you."

"What other kind of supernatural beings are out there?"

"You want a list?"

She nodded.

He really liked her. "Lycans aren't the only kind of shifters. There's bear shifters, large cats, and a few other breeds. Full-blooded Gargoyles. Vampires. Ghouls. Halflings—think humans with unnatural abilities like you see in movies. Humans used to mistake them for witches and warlocks. Heard enough?"

She chewed on her bottom lip.

"They'd all go after you if your grandfather put a bounty on your head."

"So kill *him*. Problem solved. Also, don't call him my grandfather. He's an asshole."

"I concur, but I gave him my word that I wouldn't hunt him down if he obeyed my demands. I have honor."

"*He* doesn't have any."

"I'm aware, but I do."

"So you're a nice kidnapper?"

"I didn't take you from your world. I just accepted you into mine." He tried to calm his temper.

"I don't want to stay here!"

"You made that clear. But I wouldn't ever hurt you."

"Gee, thanks."

Sarcasm. He began to detest that tone in her voice. "We can make the best of this situation. You're safe here under my protection."

"Great. I'm a princess in a tower now. I'll let my hair grow and hope my prince comes to rescue me one day."

He laughed.

Her eyes narrowed as they gazed at each other. "You can't keep me here. I'm not like you. I don't have wings." She glanced at his bare chest, then back up at his face. "We're not even the same species, are we?"

"You're part VampLycan. Your father—"

"Sperm donor," she corrected.

"He was VampLycan. That makes us compatible, and humans *have* bred with my kind."

"Bred? Oh, hell no!" She backed up and her knees hit the couch, sending her to her ass to sit again. She remained there. "Stay back, Wings."

"My name is Aveoth."

"I'm not having your bat babies. *Ever.*"

He grinned, not insulted. She was refreshing, even if she didn't mean to be. "They wouldn't have wings at birth."

"They won't have anything because it's never going to happen. I'm not going to bed with you!"

He was disappointed by her words, but an idea came to him. "I'll make a deal with you."

"You already did. I came inside. Tell me how to kill those jerks who came after me."

"I'll teach you how to fight with a sword. Beheading them always works."

"You know it's not like seventeen hundred and something, right?" She waved a hand around the lower living space of his home. "Even if it looks like your decorator came from that era." She suddenly paled. "How old are you?"

"I don't keep track. Time has no meaning here."

"Shit. Give me a ballpark figure. Just toss out a rounded number."

"I don't think you're prepared for that yet."

"Hit me with it anyway. I'm sitting down. I want to know."

He took a breath, slowly blowing it out. "I haven't bypassed one of your human life cycles yet, but close."

"What do you consider a cycle?"

"Don't humans live to be about a hundred years old? I'm younger than that, and considered very youthful for someone ruling a clan. Lord Abotorus ruled before I did. Now *he* was ancient."

"Give me a number on *him*."

"A few thousand years."

"You live that long?" Her eyebrows shot up.

"Gargoyles do, and he was a full-blood."

"But you're not?"

"No. My mother is a GarLycan."

"How long do they live?"

He shrugged. "No one has any idea."

"How does someone not know something like that?"

"They were only created about two hundred years ago. Some of the firstborn are still alive and going strong. None have died of old age that I'm aware of."

"Fuck me."

His dick stirred, more than willing to do that. He knew she didn't mean it but decided to tease her a little into hopefully getting into a better mood. "My bedroom is upstairs. Would you prefer my bed or on the couch?"

"You wish."

"I do."

Her lips parted but she closed them. She shook her head, giving him an angry look again. The silence stretched between them. She refused to speak.

He stepped away from the fireplace. "I'm going to make you breakfast." He strode across the room.

Her gasp stopped him and he swung around. She'd risen to her feet. "What's wrong?"

"You're bleeding."

He'd forgotten about his back. "It will heal. It happens when I don't prepare myself for the change. Reaching you before you plunged to your death was more important than taking the time to allow my body to shift slowly. I'll go take care of it if you swear on your honor that you won't leave this room while I do."

Chapter Six

Jill felt horrified after seeing all the blood on his back. She wasn't about to admit it to him, but climbing off that ledge hadn't been her smartest idea. She'd thought she was a goner until Aveoth had literally swooped in to save her.

His wings looked even more intimidating during the day than they had the night before. They were big and scary looking as he'd flown at her. There had been no sign of them when he'd started to walk out of the room, but she'd seen the jagged tears in his skin from where they must have sprouted from.

Guilt came next. He had gotten hurt because of her.

"Will you remain here while I wash off my back? I need to climb up to the higher floor. I'd blocked the doorway leading down here to keep you safe upstairs."

Those amazing blue and silver eyes regarded her, waiting for an answer. It was the second time he'd asked. She licked her dry lips and cleared her throat. "Yes."

He arched one of his eyebrows, as if he didn't believe her.

"I promise that I won't try to escape for at least half an hour. I nearly fell."

"Forgive me if I'm leery of your word."

"What does that mean?"

"Last night you offered me sex to beat up your grandfather's men."

She felt heat rush to her cheeks, having forgotten about that. "That was before I knew all the facts. I thought you were a man."

"I *am* a man."

Her gaze ran over him. He sure looked like one when he wasn't sporting wings or claws. A really attractive one. "I swear I won't go cliff climbing again. Lesson learned. I'm also freaked out about what you said about your neighbors, so I won't be searching for exit doors. I don't want to meet any of them."

"I believe you. I'll go deal with my back."

"Can I do anything to help?" She did have a few first-aid classes in her past.

"Do you want to join me while I shower? You could wash away the blood for me."

"I'll pass."

"You're welcome to join me at any time. Just say the word." He turned away, striding out onto the balcony. "I'll hurry."

He didn't make any bones about wanting to nail her. She had to give him credit for honesty. She waited a few minutes and followed him out the gaping hole in the room that led outside. It was easy to spot him above her. He used rocks as handholds, and he moved faster than anyone she'd ever seen climbing, disappearing over the ledge of his room.

She reentered the living space, studying it. It felt like stepping back in time. His decorator probably *had* lived in the seventeen-hundreds.

This was so crazy. *Gargoyles, Lycans, and Vampires are real. Bear shifters? Large cats? Halflings? Half of what? I don't even want to know.*

105

Shit. She took a seat on the couch and covered her face with her hands, using her elbows to prop her arms as she leaned forward. Deep breaths helped. Last night, she'd hoped she'd been drugged, but she'd given up on that. Life sucked—and she was smack-dab in the middle of a monster's lair, or whatever he wanted to call it.

She thought of the sperm donor, hating him even more. This was all Decon Filmore's fault. It wasn't bad enough, what he'd done to her mother, but now his family had pulled her into weird world. They'd never wanted anything to do with her until they'd suddenly felt the need to give her to Aveoth. It pissed her off.

Jill stood, pacing.

"Fucking asshats," she spat. "Like I'm furniture. 'Oh here, give her to wing guy and let them have bat babies'." She halted, staring around the room. "Who doesn't own a television? He reads and leads his people. What the hell does that even mean?" She began to pace again. "I don't care. I'm going to get his phone and get out of here."

She walked over to the wall opening and peered out at the expanse of woods far below the ledge. "Great. I can just see how that 9-1-1 call is going to go. 'Hello, I'm trapped in a cave on the top of a huge-ass mountain, and could you please trace the call, then send a damn helicopter to save me from people who can fly? Yes, I said fly. They can grow wings out of their backs.' Fuck! They'll hang up on my ass and think I'm just another crazy person bugging them."

She turned away and entered the room again. "So screwed. That's what I am. I'm going to murder Decon Filmore with my bare hands! It

106

wasn't bad enough he knocked up my mother and treated us like shit. Nope! Now he drags *me* into this mess."

"Who are you speaking to?"

The voice startled her so much that she screeched and jumped, spinning to face the man who had spoken. Her mouth fell open. He was tall, muscular, and wore all black leather, with some kind of body armor over his arms.

"I'm Kelzeb. My apologies for startling you, Jill."

She recovered. "How do you know my name?"

"Lord Aveoth told it to me last evening. I called him a few minutes ago but he didn't answer. I hope you didn't attack him." His voice deepened, growing a little cold. So did the look in his eyes. "I smell his blood."

"I didn't hurt him. He's taking a shower." She pointed at the rock ceiling. "Somewhere up there."

The man's expression softened. "You're safe. I'm a friend."

"Not one of mine, unless you want to fly me home."

He smiled. "I can't do that."

"Do you have wings?"

"Yes."

"Then you could but you won't. That's what I figured, but it was worth a shot to at least ask."

"You'll adjust to life at the cliffs. I understand you were unaware of our kind until last evening. Aveoth is a good man who will treat you extremely well. There's no reason for you to fear any form of abuse."

"That's comforting, as opposed to you warning me that I'm in for some hurt."

His eyebrows arched.

She decided to change the subject. He wasn't human and probably didn't have a sense of humor. "Do you own a television?"

"Of course."

"Your buddy doesn't."

"I'm certain he'll order you one if you just ask. Aveoth will want you to be happy."

Kelzeb studied her. "I feel badly for you, Jill. I do. This must be difficult."

"Badly enough to take me home?" She'd take pity if it worked.

"Aveoth needs you."

"Right. To have bat babies. No thanks."

Shock showed on his face.

"Sorry." She glanced at his sword. It wasn't a good idea to piss off the muscular, weapon-carrying stranger. He probably wanted some woman to have *his* bat babies too and wouldn't appreciate her calling them that. "I'm out of my element big time."

"You'll adjust to life here."

She highly doubted that. "So, what do you do? Besides being Aveoth's friend?"

"I'm his advisor and lead enforcer."

"And that means what?"

"He looks out for me and helps me stay alive." Aveoth walked into the room. His hair was wet and he'd changed clothes. He wore leather pants and a black short-sleeved shirt that showed off his biceps. His feet were bare. "You've met Jill."

"I have." Kelzeb turned to face his friend. "An issue has arisen. I apologize. I attempted to call you but you weren't answering your phone. You're needed immediately in the judging chambers."

"What's wrong?"

"Delbius and Paltos are having a dispute and are demanding to see you. It can't wait. They need you to settle the matter for them."

"Fuck. What's the problem?"

"Delbius is starting a new training group this afternoon, and Paltos insists his son join. Delbius refused, stating the boy is too young. The father disagrees. They couldn't come to terms so they want you to assess the boy yourself."

"What skill is being taught?" Aveoth glanced at Jill but then regarded Kelzeb. "Do you know the boy?"

"No. The group will focus on daggers and small-blade fighting." Kelzeb sighed. "Nothing too dangerous."

"How old is the boy?"

"Six."

Jill listened quietly but that got a response. "Wait. What?"

Aveoth inched closer, his gaze fixing on her. "What's wrong?"

"If I'm following this right, some six-year-old's dad wants this kid to learn how to use sharp weapons and the instructor is saying no, right?"

"That sums it up." Aveoth turned away. "I'll be right back. I need to put on my boots and change shirts."

Jill stared at Kelzeb after he left. "This is actually an issue?"

"Aveoth will listen to both father and instructor, hear their concerns and opinions, and then make a decision."

"It sounds like a no-brainer. The kid is six. That's a baby. Who in their right mind would want their little boy to play with anything dangerous?"

"It's not that simple, Jill. These are not human children and they need to learn how to fight. The point of conflict is the child's age. That's two years younger than normal for that training skill."

"You people are nuts."

Kelzeb grinned. "We're not people. We're GarLycans."

He probably had a point. "Why do you need daggers and small blades anyway? Can't this kid grow claws like Aveoth showed me last night?"

"He can, but they would only be effective on other races."

"And in layman's terms that means what?"

Kelzeb explained, "Claws hurt in a fight against, say, a human, Vampire, or Lycan. They don't when we fight our own kind. Have you seen Aveoth shell his body?"

She shook her head. "He's got more extras? Great. What does that mean?"

"We're mostly Gargoyle-blooded. Watch, but don't be frightened. I'll slightly shell my skin. Are you prepared?"

She braced herself to see whatever freaky trick he planned to perform. It couldn't be more shocking than growing wings. "I'm ready."

Kelzeb's skin began to darken. The texture of it changed, seeming to harden. He started out tan and normal looking but ended up a light gray.

She managed to keep her mouth from falling open and the curse words that sprang to mind from spilling out. She hesitantly approached him. He looked like a rock mannequin someone had dressed in badass clothes and strapped a sword to the waist. She reached out, her hand trembling a little, and pressed a finger to his exposed arm. What should have felt like flesh now had transformed to a hard, almost smooth, cool marble feel.

"Wow," she whispered.

She lifted her chin, staring at his face. His eyes were alive but the rest of his face seemed frozen, gray, and it gave her the chills. He really looked like a stony mannequin or a life-size garden statue, but with a real person trapped inside that body staring back at her. She pulled her finger away and pressed her entire hand around the curve of his arm, giving it a squeeze. He felt solid and real.

The color of him started to lighten, and she felt heat against her skin. She let him go and backed up fast. It took him only seconds to appear normal again. He shrugged.

"That's what we call mild shelling. Claws couldn't break my skin if I were to fight in that form. It's why weapons training is so important."

"How can you fight when you're frozen in place? Do you just stand there while someone tries to hurt you until they wear themselves out and give up?"

He laughed. "That was just partial shelling. I could have moved if I'd wanted to but you already looked spooked. I didn't want you to scream or try to flee from me."

"I probably would have," she admitted. "It's like something right out of a horror movie. Do you guys impersonate statues and then scare the shit out of people just for the fun of it by moving?"

"No. It's forbidden to allow humans to know what we are."

"So why am I so special?"

"You now belong to Aveoth, and you're not completely human."

"I would point out that it's illegal to own someone these days, but I highly doubt that would matter to people who still live in caves. I don't have fangs, and I can't even grow my fingernails to a decent length, so that makes me a shitty non-human, doesn't it? I'm usually sporting acrylic ones, but it's been a while since I could afford to have them done."

"Acrylic?"

"Fake nails. My real ones are thin and break. In other words, I don't have claws. Not even close."

He glanced at her hand, then held her gaze. "What is the point of fake nails?"

"They're pretty and makes me feel girly. Don't judge, Stone Garden."

One of his eyebrows arched. "Stone Garden?"

"I like to stick people with nicknames. That's how I'm going to think of you from now on. You looked like you belonged in someone's backyard with the other garden statues when you were gray."

"Statues are harmless. I'm not. Do you know how youngling GarLycans learn how to hunt?"

"Tell me."

"We teach them a game called 'snatch the prey'. We let an animal see us and give it a chance to run away. Then we fly high, circle around it, and swoop out of the sky to grab it off the ground. I was excellent at it as a boy, but now *nothing* gets away from me when I'm on the hunt."

He was scary alright. She wasn't going to be intimidated though. "I usually don't tell people *what* name I tag them with, but I don't give a shit right now if that upsets you. Maybe you'll want to be rid of me, and take me home to save your friend from being subjected to me."

"I see. What do you call Aveoth?"

"Wings."

He chuckled. "You are entertaining, Jill."

"I don't mean to be."

Aveoth returned. He'd put on a long-sleeved white shirt that looked as if he'd raided the costume wardrobe on the set of a pirate movie. It was loose fitting, the top of it split to reveal some of his chest. The boots appeared to be military, black, and he'd added a sword to his waist too. She'd have laughed at anyone else in that getup, made jokes, but Aveoth pulled it off. He would probably look sexy in anything. She resented that, too.

Kelzeb withdrew a cell phone from his back pocket. "I'll see if Fray or Chaz are available to keep Jill company. They are human friendly and loyal to us."

"No." Aveoth walked over and snagged Jill's hand. "I'm taking her with us."

"I don't think that's a good idea."

"I don't either." She agreed with Kelzeb, and tried to pull free of Aveoth's larger hand.

He tightened his hold. "I'm not letting you out of my sight. Do you want to survive?"

She stopped jerking on her arm. "Yes."

"Then stick close." He placed her hand on his arm. "You belong at my side. Stay there."

"Shit," Kelzeb grunted. "You know word will spread fast. They'll only smell the human scent on her and assume you've chosen her to be your breeding vessel. Then they'll wonder why you're allowing her out of your chambers. Some will be offended she's not chained."

"Breeding vessel? Did you just call me that?" Outraged, she glared at Aveoth. "Is that what I think it is? And I heard 'chained'. Don't even think about it, Wings."

"It's a term some of the older generation uses for women we choose to have our children. It was customary to chain the woman if she was human. They feared us, believing we were demons. Some women jumped to their deaths to escape giving birth to what they called our 'spawn'. We'll discuss this later. I must play judge."

"That's so insulting! And your people aren't demons. You're actually all outdated-thinking caveman. How would *you* feel being called a sperm-giver or a baby-making machine?"

114

"Or Stone Garden," Kelzeb mused.

Aveoth scowled. "What does that mean?"

"I shelled a bit to show your Jill how we look. She compared me to a statue and has dubbed me with that nickname."

Aveoth had the nerve to smile.

"Don't do that." It irritated Jill that Kelzeb had a point. She *had* called him a nickname that might have been a bit insulting, despite that not being her intention.

"You do amuse me, Jill. I don't think of you as a breeding vessel. Some of my people are what you'd call old fashioned." Aveoth made a small bow. "I apologize for the offensive term."

"I can think of worse names to call your people who think that way," she admitted.

"I'm sure you can." Aveoth rubbed her hand resting on his arm. "We can discuss this later. You're highly intelligent, so I'll tell you exactly what kind of danger you'll face." His expression sobered and his eyes did some weird thing where the color began to change, silver and blue sparking like some electricity ball. "I'm about to expose you to my clan. They will attack us if you don't do exactly what I say."

She watched his eyes do that crazy thing they did, had to admit it was mesmerizing, if not freaky, and carefully considered his words. "I'm listening."

"Act submissive to me in front of my kind. I won't ask that of you when we're alone, but in front of others, it would be a harshly punishable offense if you do not. I'm their lord, and we aren't forgiving. It wouldn't sit

115

well with anyone if I allowed you to get away with things that I'd beat *them* for doing. Do you understand? It would make me appear weak if I didn't punish you swiftly and without mercy."

"They could turn on us," Kelzeb warned. "We'd all die. Damn it, Aveoth. Just leave her here. We can expose her to the others once she has more of an understanding of our culture."

"Someone might have seen her when she tried to climb from my ledge to another one." Aveoth kept his gaze locked with Jill's. "Rumors may already be circulating. I spotted a few flyers when I went after her."

"She *what*? What the he—"

Aveoth cut Kelzeb off with a shake of his head. "She ventured outside while I slept. It's best to take a preemptive measure by showing them I'm not trying to hide that I have a woman in my chambers. They'd wonder why I'm so secretive and possibly make dangerous assumptions."

Kelzeb grumbled, a deep, unpleasant sound. "She isn't dressed appropriately to make acquaintances."

"We'll move up our sparring session to begin right after I judge. It is a large enough space there. Our women wear pants when they train, and I'll make it clear that I intend to teach her self-defense. It will excuse her appearance, since this was a priority matter and wasn't scheduled."

"I'm hearing English coming out of your mouths but I don't understand what either of you are saying." Jill glanced between them.

Aveoth leaned forward a little, drawing her full attention. "Just be silent and stay by my side as if our lives depend on it."

She swallowed. "You said you're their lord. What kind of place do you run?"

Kelzeb answered before Aveoth could. "You asked about television. Did you ever see a show or movie about a leader of a state or country being betrayed and assassinated by his own people?"

She peered at him and got a sinking feeling in the pit of her stomach. "I hate those."

"Welcome to the cliffs."

"What's their issue?" She stared at Aveoth.

"We must go." Aveoth stepped forward, tugging on her. "I'm not a full-blooded Gargoyle. Some would be happier if my father still ruled. He was pure."

"Where's he?" She walked with him, not really happy about it, but he had her hand trapped between his side and his arm.

"Dead."

"Did they kill him?"

Aveoth gave a negative shake of his head. "We'll speak of history later. Just be silent and pretend to be submissive. I apologize but I'd rather live out the day. Wouldn't you?"

"Yes."

* * * * *

Jill remained very quiet, but Aveoth's repeated quick glances at her told him she was having a difficult time taking in her surroundings as they strode down stairs and through inner tunnels to where they needed to go.

He tried to imagine what her thoughts might be. She probably hadn't spent much time inside a mountain. He doubted many humans had.

Delbius waited outside the double doors leading to the judging chambers. A small boy and Paltos stood a few feet away. He spotted their surprised expressions before each man masked them. The boy was another matter. He gasped. Paltos reached over and slapped his hand on his son's shoulder to silence him.

Kelzeb unlocked the doors and threw them open. Aveoth paused, had Jill halt next to him, and indicated the other men enter first with a motion of his hand. He wasn't about to expose his back to either GarLycan. They weren't ones he explicitly trusted. He noted how Paltos used his body to shield his son from the trainer and Kelzeb. It meant he cared about the boy's safety.

Jill looked up at him and he met her gaze, shaking his head. Her mouth tensed but she said nothing. He hoped her compliance lasted until business concluded.

He entered and led Jill to his throne. He positioned her to stand at his side and took a seat, keeping hold of her by reaching out to wrap his fingers around her leg just above the back of her knee. She shot him a slightly irritated look but didn't try to shake off his touch. Kelzeb sealed the doors and blocked them with his back, nodding at him to proceed, now that they had privacy.

"Lord Aveoth." Paltos bowed, adjusted his sword more to his back and then clasped his hands together at his waist, locking his fingers together in a show of non-aggression.

"My Lord." Delbius bowed as well, but kept his hands at his side and the sword hilt strapped to his waist within easy grasp.

Aveoth wasn't alarmed. Delbius was a weapons trainer. His sword had become a part of him. It wasn't meant as a threat or an offense. He took a deep breath and blew it out. "I was about to spar with Kelzeb and show this one some defensive movements. Let's skip the formalities, shall we?"

Both men glanced at Jill and inclined their heads. He could see their curiosity but neither were rude enough to ask about her. Aveoth relaxed.

"I've been given the highlights of the issue. Paltos, why do you feel your son should start training with weapons? He should still be focusing on flight drills at his age."

"He excels, my lord." Paltos's tone exposed his pride. "Hawk raved that Jobi is the best he's taught. His dives and rolls are superb. Even the scouts were impressed. They take my son out some nights. Yesnor said he'd vouch for Jobi if you want references."

"That's true," Delbius conceded. "I conferred with Hawk. It's the boy's size I object to. None of my students are close to his weight and height. They would have an unfair advantage over him."

"I see." Aveoth could understand the problem. Children two-plus years ahead of the boy would be taller and stronger. "Jobi? Let me see you better."

The kid hesitated, glanced at his father, but Paltos nodded. Aveoth felt a bit sorry for the boy. He knew his reputation made the younglings terrified of him. Jobi jutted his chin out and stepped away from his father to come forward. Aveoth hid a smile and used his free hand to motion him to get within five feet of him.

Jobi seemed average in size for his age. It would have helped his case if he'd sprouted earlier. It happened. Some kids grew faster than others, packing on height and muscle. Aveoth had been like that. He released Jill and stood. He moved slowly, so as not to frighten the child, and crouched down before him. The boy revealed his fear in his eyes but his body remained steady.

"I don't hurt children." Aveoth softened his tone. "Your father would try to attack me for getting this close to you if he wasn't aware of that. You're safe. Have flight drills become boring?"

"Yes, my lord."

Aveoth cocked his head. "Why?"

"I don't need Hawk to ever assist me. I can pull out of a straight dive without trouble and I mostly help the others. I'm stronger than I look, and fast."

That was impressive it if was true. He glanced at Delbius for confirmation, trusting that he would have spoken to Hawk at length about Jobi's proficiency. The instructor nodded.

"I saved Kob," Jobi whispered.

Aveoth stared at the boy. "How?"

"He was playing and didn't see how close he'd got to the cliffs. He slammed one wing into a jagged edge of rock and didn't have time to shell since he didn't see it. His wing crumpled. I dove after him and snatched him before he hit the ground. I got him to a ledge safe. He's a year older."

"It's true, Lord Aveoth."

He ignored the father, remembering hearing that one of the youths had broken a wing a few weeks before and had almost been killed. Hawk had assured him it would never happen again but hadn't given him further details. "You understand that the other boys in training will be larger?"

"My father spars with me. He said I'm really fast on my feet."

"It's true, Lord Aveoth. He's a quick learner and—"

Aveoth leveled a glare at the boy's father and growled. Paltos instantly shut up and ducked his head. Aveoth peered back at the boy, hiding his anger at his father. It wasn't the kid's fault his parent didn't know when to stay silent.

"Remove your shirt and show me your wings. I'd also like to take a look at your fighting shell."

The kid leaned to the side a little, staring at Jill. Fear showed in his eyes again. Aveoth shifted his body in the same direction and blocked the boy's view of her.

"It's okay. She belongs to me and is aware of what we are. I need to know your wing strength and how fast you can react if you wish to train with weapons. It's difficult to motion shell enough to avoid real harm from steel."

"She smells and dresses funny. What is she?"

"Jobi!" Paltos thundered.

Aveoth glared at the father again. "Silence! Not another word." He looked at Jobi and lowered his voice. "That was rude...but you're young.

She's human, and she just arrived here. Those are the only garments she has until some can be made for her. Now remove your shirt and show me."

Jobi had paled and trembled when his father had harshly reprimanded him but he seemed to recover fast. He took off his shirt and dropped it on the floor. His eyes closed and he eased his wings out, fully extending them. Aveoth smiled. He could see why the kid might excel at flying. He had a remarkable span for one so young. Aveoth rose up and walked behind the boy, studying his wings from the back.

"Motion shell for me," he urged. "Now!"

The kid's coloring changed fast, the softness of his wings disappearing and the grooves sharpening. Aveoth ran his fingers along the top edge of one wing, then pinched it hard. The boy didn't flinch. He rounded the kid, sparing a glance to see how Jill reacted. Her eyes were wide but she hadn't made a sound. He crouched in front of Jobi again and touched the boy's chest. His shell was solid, no soft spots. Aveoth extended one claw and tapped at it. Jobi held still, not trying to retreat.

"I'm going to throw my right and left straight punches at you. Avoid them. On the count of three. One. Two. Three."

He threw some easy punches at the boy but Jobi dodged each one, his little body moving swiftly from side to side. Aveoth stopped and lowered his hands.

He studied the boy again, looking for any softening around his rib cage and throat, but there were no signs of weakness. Those were the two places VampLycan children were the most vulnerable during training. "Revert."

122

The boy closed his eyes, and Aveoth was impressed by how fast the six-year-old could skin and completely retract his wings. Jobi peered at him when he was done. Aveoth smiled.

"Your father has reason to be proud." He winked and stood, returned to his throne and took a seat. "Put on your shirt, Jobi. Thank you. Go stand with your father."

Aveoth reached out and curled his fingers around the back of Jill's leg again, his gaze locking with Delbius's. "Assign Jobi to someone for private instruction, see how he does, and we'll reassess if you still feel reluctant to add him to your classes after a reasonable time frame. Let's say one month. It would give him an advantage over the others if he has one-on-one weapons lessons from a scout. They are adults, so children a little larger than him shouldn't be an issue at that point."

Delbius grimaced. "Yes, my lord."

"I'll volunteer to work with Jobi," Kelzeb offered. "I have some free time in the mornings. Will that work, Delbius? I know you hate to ask for assistance from any of the scouts. I'll spend an hour with him, then drop him off with you. He can at least watch what you're teaching your students. That way, he doesn't come in blind."

Surprise crossed the instructor's face but he nodded. "That would work."

"Good. It's settled." Aveoth released Jill, rose and took a few steps forward. "Let's all get on with our day. We're adjourned."

He waited for the room to clear and Kelzeb to close the doors. Their gazes met.

"That's one happy kid. He's going to brag to his friends that the lead enforcer is his personal trainer. Why did you do that, Kelzeb?"

His friend shrugged. "I remember being that young, and the father isn't a dick. He's just very supportive of his son, which I find endearing. Jobi has promise, and one day he might become one of our best scouts."

Aveoth turned, still smiling—until he saw that Jill had collapsed into his throne. "Are you okay?"

"I thought you said kids don't have wings."

"I said they aren't birthed with them. Do human children walk, talk, and run right from the womb?"

She regarded him with narrowed eyes but didn't speak.

"What is it, Jill?"

"Nothing."

She was lying, but he decided to wait until they were alone to prompt her more to share her thoughts.

Chapter Seven

Jill stayed seated as Aveoth and Kelzeb removed their shirts. Her eyebrows arched when both of the men withdrew their swords. "What are you guys doing?"

"Training." Aveoth didn't spare her a glance. "We do this often. Just remain where you are."

They faced each other, backed away, and then lunged forward, swinging their swords. The shocking sound of metal clashing made her wince the first few times until she adjusted to it. They fought, striking at each other, doing a dangerous dance. It was like seeing something out of some medieval movie. She adjusted in the big fancy chair and tried to get more comfortable.

With the men shirtless, it didn't suck, noticing how their many muscles bunched and flexed as they battled. A fine sheen of sweat coated both of them after a while and it amazed her that they kept going at it for so long. She would have fallen to the floor from exhaustion after a few minutes.

She caught her breath when Kelzeb almost took a blow to his arm and shelled his body at the last instant, spinning away. The blade missed by a hair. Aveoth leaped back and both men stared at each other. Kelzeb unshelled, his skin turning tan again instead of light gray.

Aveoth chuckled. "Sorry."

"My fault." Kelzeb grinned. "I was too slow that time to recover. Perhaps I should spar with you more often. I'd be a shitty lead enforcer if I couldn't hold my own with you."

"It's *my* fault. I've sent you on a few missions lately and we've missed sessions." He sheathed his sword.

Kelzeb did the same. "My wings are stronger though. Want to fly with me tonight?"

Aveoth turned his head, peering at Jill. "No."

"I don't blame you." Kelzeb strode across the room and lifted two bottled waters from a table. He spun back around fast.

Jill was amazed when he chucked it hard about twenty feet at Aveoth, but he just caught it as if it hadn't been hurled at his head. They both drank them down and Kelzeb returned to his friend, bent, and picked up his shirt, putting it back on.

"I'll go guard the door so you can teach her some defensive moves. She may need them." Kelzeb strode across the room to the closed door, opened it, and stepped out. He shut the door behind him.

Aveoth faced her and tossed the now-empty plastic bottle toward a corner. He used one hand to motion for her to come closer. "You need to learn how to defend yourself."

"I've taken self-defense classes."

"Show me."

She didn't budge from her seat. "I'm not going to sword fight with you."

He unbuckled his weapon and laid it down. "No swords. Not yet. I need to see how you move and react first before we advance your training that far."

"No thanks." She glanced at the stone floor. It would hurt if he put her on her ass, and she knew he could. She'd just seen him fight with Kelzeb.

Aveoth advanced with a smile on his face. "I won't hurt you, Jill."

She leaned back in the chair and gripped the arms. "No."

He reached her and bent, gripping her wrists. He pulled, easily yanking her out of the chair despite her bracing to keep him from doing so. She found herself being led by him to where he'd originally stood. He released her and his smile faded.

"I plan to keep you close and protected but there might be times where it's paramount that you can get away from someone like me. Do you understand?"

"That's just another reason you should return me to where I came from."

"It's not going to happen. Are you aware that when you bleed, you scent faintly of VampLycan? You get that from your father's side. It would put a target on you from anything not human. It's amazing you reached your age without being attacked."

"Don't call him that! He was just a sperm donor."

"I apologize. I understand. I hated my father too."

"At least you said yours is dead. I still dream about that day."

She regretted saying that instantly when she swore she glimpsed pain in his eyes. She'd had a hard life, and tended not to understand when someone complained about things she couldn't relate to.

"Sorry. It was tough growing up without a dad, and it made it worse knowing mine was such an asshole. I have some issues. It's foreign for me to think of fathers as good things."

"You were lucky he wasn't a part of your life. Mine raised me. Lord Abotorus was cold and cruel." Aveoth stepped closer, lowering his voice. "He limited the time I got to spend with my mother and ordered me to call her by her first name. I was a year old when he took me from her."

Jill tried to understand what he was saying. His life seemed so strange to her. "They got divorced?"

"No. She lived here at the cliffs, and still does. They were mated but he kept her in separate quarters. He never would have allowed her to venture outside and leave him. He put me in his quarters. She wasn't permitted to visit me there. I only saw her during social events." He licked his lips and glanced away, then back at her. "I'd sneak away as I got older and visit her when I knew he was busy. She'd leave her bedroom balcony open and I'd fly in to see her."

That was so sad. "Why would he do that?"

"She loved me. He considered that a weakness."

It made her feel bad for Aveoth, trying to imagine such a childhood.

Aveoth cleared his throat. "Those are some of my best memories. I was four the first time I went to see her. I had so much curiosity. I always caught her watching me when my father assembled the clan. I feared she'd turn me in to her guards and want me punished for breaking the rules. That wasn't the case. She welcomed me with a hug and tears when I figured out which room was hers and landed on her ledge. It was the first time I could remember when someone had embraced me with gentleness, instead of for battle training, to prove I wasn't fast enough to avoid capture."

Jill studied his handsome face and tried to imaging him that young. The boy she'd just met had been six. Aveoth had been flying at four. He'd have been smaller, and had only wanted to talk to his mom.

"Of course, she made me promise not to return. She was terrified someone would discover me there and I'd be severely punished. I realized she didn't fear for herself, but for me. How could I not take the risk to see her again? Spending time with my mother was the only happy times I had as a child. She wanted to know everything about my life, and she always told me she loved me, how important I was to her."

Aveoth was breaking Jill's heart. "Why would your father keep you from her?"

His smile faded. "Gargoyles regard emotions as a weakness. Not all, but most. Lord Abotorus was very old." He shrugged. "He had no empathy for anyone, especially for his own family. He felt forced to mate a GarLycan, and resented my mother, especially for birthing me. I was a disappointment."

"Why?"

He hesitated. "I wasn't able to hide my emotions from him at first. I learned to at a young age, but it was too late. He'd seen weakness in me as a baby. As I grew older, I also didn't make him proud with acts of brutal rebellion like some of the other younglings did. It angered him."

129

She hesitated. "I'm afraid to ask but...like what?"

"Bressor was my age, and my sparring partner for years. In our fifteenth year, he snuck out one night and went for a flight. The scouts caught him returning before dawn with blood on his clothing." Anger harshened Aveoth's expression and his tone. "He was taken before my father and forced to confess what he'd done. He had flown to a human town, grabbed a woman, and murdered her."

The idea horrified Jill. "Why would he do that?"

Aveoth's jaw clenched. "Women at the cliffs are off limits and protected. He was fifteen and wanted to have sex with one. So he kidnapped a human, abused her, and killed her when he was done to hide his crime. The scouts had to go out to find her body and dispose of it so it was never discovered. My father punished him for leaving the cliffs without permission...but not for the murder or abuse of that poor woman. She was just human, he said. As if they didn't matter."

Aveoth's voice deepened even more, almost into a snarl. "Then my father pulled me aside and asked if I'd ever done anything similar before. Of course I hadn't. I'm not a sick fuck who would rape and murder someone. He said I was a great disappointment, and actually encouraged me to do the same one night, because it would prove I was more like *him*. He just ordered me to be smarter about not getting caught the way Bressor had."

Jill needed to sit down. She hesitated for a moment and then just took a seat on the floor. She had no words. "So this Bressor is here somewhere?" She was human, or at least mostly, according to Aveoth.

Aveoth crouched in front of her and sat on the floor. "I challenged my father a few years after that happened."

"You fought him?"

"It was a fight to the death to see who would lead the clan. I won. Bressor was one of the clansmen who challenged me for leadership afterward. I killed him…and had no regret over doing so."

She stared into his eyes, seeing the truth there. It didn't break her up that Bressor was dead. He sounded like someone who more than deserved it.

It also sank in that Aveoth was saying he'd killed his own father.

"Sometimes people need to die. They are too cruel and selfish to be allowed to live, Jill. There's no telling how many other times Bressor snuck away and harmed women. Are you afraid of me because I've admitted to killing him and Lord Abotorus? The more I learned of my father, the deeper my sense of rage and hatred burned toward him. He encouraged some of the clan to do atrocious crimes, and to look down on other races. I took over the clan, and some of my people aren't happy about it to this day because I won't stand for that shit. Most of the full-blooded Gargoyles still here are as cruel as he was, and resent the laws I've written. It's punishable by death if they murder for sick entertainment. But I still have to hide most of my emotions when I'm dealing with the clan. They see them as a weakness."

Everything he said made sense, and she agreed. The world was a better place with some people not in it. "I understand. I'd kill my sperm donor if I could after everything he did to my mother. She died because she got sick and refused to go to a hospital because it would have cost money. By the time I realized how sick she really was, and called an ambulance, it was too late. The pneumonia had damaged her lungs and she was too weak to respond to treatment. We had a little savings at the time, but she knew he'd be sending assholes after us soon, and that money would help us go on the run again. I hate that son of a bitch."

"I'm so sorry, Jill."

"Me too."

He slowly lifted his hand, holding it out to her. "You do need to learn how to fight. Aren't you tired of running? I can teach you how to kill assholes like the two who kidnapped you."

She hesitated then gave him her hand. He rose up and gently pulled her to her feet. "I'm not so sure this is a good idea."

"I'm nothing like Lord Abotorus but sometimes I have to act that way. I never want you to fear me. I'll never hurt you, Jill. Can you trust that?" He released her hand.

"Do I have a choice? I'm kind of trapped here for now."

"I didn't take you from your life," he reminded her. "I just accepted you into mine. Decker might have either killed you if I hadn't brought you here, or used you in some other horrible way to gain something he wanted. He and Lord Abotorus were very similar. A bloodline means nothing and if you aren't useful to them, they seem to think you don't deserve to live."

She took a deep breath and blew it out. "I took some self-defense classes because I was raised in some bad neighborhoods." She studied him from head to foot. Aveoth was a big man with a seriously buff body. Then she glanced at the hard floor. "Don't you guys use mats when you

132

tussle?" She met his gaze. "I can't harden my body to protect myself from breaking bones if I slam into something solid. I'm assuming that's what you plan to do with me?"

"I'm going to come at you but I won't let you fall. Try to avoid me grabbing you."

It was the only warning she got as he lunged forward and tried to snag her around her waist as he bent a little. She threw out an arm and knocked one of his hands away, twisting to the side and kicking out the way she'd learned. Her shoe made contact with his pants just above his knee.

The hit to his thigh actually made him take a step back and he straightened. He arched one eyebrow.

"What? I wasn't going for your nuts."

"Thank you."

He lunged again but faster.

She gasped as his arms wrapped around her and she was lifted right off her feet. He had her in a bear hug with her side pressed up against his chest. It put their faces very close together. His skin was hot and a little damp. Whatever cologne he wore smelled amazing. She actually had to fight the urge to lick him to see if he tasted as good as he smelled.

He smiled. "I have you. You need to do better."

She was grateful he spoke; it forced her to stop thinking about running her tongue over his skin. "I didn't even see you move."

"You aren't completely human. Stop acting as if you are." He lowered her to her feet and let her go, taking steps back to put a little space between them. "You've got some Vampire blood. We need to discover what advantages it gives you. I'm going to come at you again and this time, avoid me. Ready?"

"No." She put more space between them, glanced at the hard surface of the floor again, then back at him. "Put down mats and then we'll do this. I know if one of us ends up on their ass, it's going to be me. I don't want to break my tailbone or something."

"We don't use them here at the cliffs."

The door to the hallway opened and Kelzeb stepped inside. "I couldn't help but overhear your conversation. May I make a suggestion?"

Aveoth appeared irritated. "What?"

"You have guest bedrooms in the lower section of your quarters. I'd remove the mattresses from the beds and use them to cushion the floor. I think your lower hosting room would be big enough to place them down if we moved the furniture against the walls." Kelzeb grinned. "I'll help you prepare the space, and then leave you two alone."

Aveoth suddenly smiled. "That would work."

Jill glanced between the two men and noticed that both of them looked amused. The idea of her and Aveoth on what amounted to one large bed in some room made her leery. "Maybe we could just not do this."

Aveoth held her gaze. "You wanted mats. It's the best we can do." He strode over to his shirt and put it on. He strapped on his sword next, then approached her. "Let's go, Jill."

134

"Shit," she muttered. She had walked right into that and it was her own fault.

Aveoth just grinned and took her hand, pinning it between his arm and chest. He led her out of the room and back to his home.

Once they got there, she excused herself to use the restroom upstairs. Mostly, she just wanted to hide as both men went to put mattresses down on the floor.

* * * * *

"Your Jill watched you closely," Kelzeb whispered, leaning the mattress against a wall. He pushed the couches and tables to the side of the room, out of the way.

Aveoth frowned. "She didn't scent of arousal. So much for pheromones and sweating for her."

"This is a much smaller space, and she may have felt uncomfortable in the judging chambers. It's cozy here."

"It is," he agreed.

Kelzeb put his mattress down first and shoved it into place. "You should just carry her to your bed, tie her down, and seduce her."

Aveoth dumped the other mattress on the floor and held his friend's gaze. "Did you get that advice from a Gargoyle?"

Kelzeb cringed. "True enough. I can't imagine how difficult it's going to be to persuade a distrustful human to let you get between her thighs."

Aveoth checked the mattresses, making sure that they lay close together with no gaps between the side seams. "I want Jill, but I'm not willing to push her too fast. She might resent that, and she's already angry that I'm keeping her here."

"She asked me to fly her home."

"What did you tell her?"

"No."

Aveoth sighed and stared at the stairwell. "She's probably barricading herself inside her room. Go. I'll secure the doors so no one can get in. I'll call you later."

"I'll take the meeting with the scouts and go over the lists for winter supplies with our stores this afternoon. That will leave your day free. Just keep your phone within hearing range. I'll call if an emergency arises."

"Damn. I'd forgotten both were scheduled for later."

"You have a lot on your mind." Kelzeb walked over to him and reached out, gripping his shoulder. "I have you covered. It's my honor as your friend to take whatever burdens I can from you." He smirked. "Just focus on getting laid. You really need that."

Aveoth snorted and shook his head. "That's the Lycan side of you. Sex doesn't fix every problem."

"It would be nice if it could though. I know it would improve *my* mood most days."

"You need to look for a mate."

"The timing isn't right yet. Women need a lot of attention, which I don't have to give. The price would be her unhappiness." Kelzeb released him and waved. "I'll call if I need you. I won't interrupt unless it's very important. Good luck."

Aveoth followed him to the exit and secured the door. He ran upstairs and went to his bedroom first, closing off the balcony. The reminder of how close Jill had come to falling to her death had already made him secure all the lower-floor cliff openings. They were now safely sealed. He heard sounds in her bedroom and walked through the connecting bathroom to knock on the closed door.

"Are you ready, Jill?" He tried the handle and found the door unlocked.

She stood by the bed and turned when he stepped inside. "These aren't really the right clothes for workouts."

That reminded him that she needed outfits. "They will do for now. After we see what you can do, I'll have Renna come measure you. You're welcome to wear anything in my wardrobe until she's made you gowns."

"Gowns?"

"We aren't in your world anymore," he gently reminded her. "We dress a certain way here at the cliffs."

"Are we talking a ton of material that goes from the shoulders to my feet?"

"Yes."

"I'm not leaving your fancy cave again if that's true. No way am I going to put on some getup from the eighteen-hundreds."

He didn't blame her. She was a modern woman, used to wearing the clothing of one. "Luckily for you, we're just going downstairs into another part of my home right now. Let's go."

"Why are you so determined to kick my ass?"

"I'm not. I just want to see how you can defend yourself and if you have any traits you weren't aware of before. We need to test your skills."

"You mean like if I have any super-secret kickass things I can do? I don't."

"You didn't know what your bloodlines were before."

"I've gotten into plenty of fights in my lifetime, Aveoth. Nothing weird ever happened."

"You were around humans. Now you're not. Let's go, Jill."

Her gaze flashed down his body, then she stared into his eyes again. He watched her swallow hard but she walked toward him. "Fine. Let's get this over with. After you."

He crossed her bedroom and opened the door to the hallway, more than aware that she kept close behind him as he took the stairs to the lower level and entered the living room. The two large king-size mattresses were squared together in the center of the room. He paused, then took a seat on the floor to remove his boots.

"Why are you doing that?"

"Take off your shoes."

She sat far from him and removed them. It surprised him when she didn't argue. He stood, unbuckled his sword belt, and then stripped out of his shirt. Jill kept glancing at him, but she said nothing. She got up and hesitated near the edge of the mattresses. He didn't. He walked to the center of them and pointed at the space in front of him.

She came over and stopped two feet away, a frown firmly on her attractive face. He thought she was incredibly cute. He rolled his shoulders, relaxing.

"Show me something you've learned with this self-defense you spoke of."

Her eyes narrowed. "Okay." She turned and pressed against him, her back fusing to his front. It stunned him. She turned her head, looked up at him, and smiled. "No bear hugs, but wrap your arms around my shoulders like you've just come up behind me to mug me or something."

He gently wrapped his arms around her...but then remembered what she'd said earlier. "Don't hit me in the nuts, Jill. I won't be amused by that."

"I won't."

She looked away from him to peer straight ahead—and suddenly reached up.

One of her hands gripped his forearm and the other clasped the curve of his shoulder. She bent suddenly, kind of twisted her upper body to one side, yanking on him.

He hadn't expected that, and it knocked him off balance. Surprise held him still while he stared at her from his back on the mattress.

She'd flipped him.

Jill straightened up. "It worked! I thought you might be too heavy."

He stayed down, staring up at her. Part of him was amused, another impressed. She looked pleased with herself. It turned him on more. He sat up and got to his knees, twisting around to face her.

He tackled her a heartbeat later, taking her down flat on the other mattress.

He was careful to do it gently and not crush her under him when he pinned her flat to her back. He crawled up a little so they were face to face. She felt fragile under him, so he braced his arms more and took some of his weight off her.

Her eyes widened and her breathing increased as she gazed up at him.

He grinned. "Get free."

Her hands pressed against his chest and she pushed. It tickled a little. She stopped. "I'd have to hit you, and then you'd hit me back. No thanks."

"I doubt you could hurt me unless you went for my groin. Don't."

She licked her lips and his focus lowered to her pink tongue. Desire shot through him and his dick reacted. Blood surged south. He wanted to kiss her.

"Your eyes are doing that weird thing where they're reminding me of a lightning ball."

He stared into hers. "A what?"

"Never mind. Your eyes are amazing and scary at the same time. What causes that? Silver bolts are flashing inside them right now, and the blue is moving around as though it's liquid being poured around your irises, then disappearing behind all the silver."

"I'm part Gargoyle. The colors can swirl with my emotions. I'm not hiding mine from you. Vampire eyes brighten to an almost neon color when they want to control a human's mind or when they're sexually aroused."

"Good thing you're not a Vampire because I'm still not having your bat babies. You can't mess with my head and change my mind."

He was tempted to confess his real heritage to her, but it was too dangerous. It would probably make her fear him more. He imagined her pregnant with his youngling and longed for it. He'd been alone all of his life. With Jill, he'd create a family, and they'd form tight bonds together. "Would it be such a bad thing?"

Her lips parted, then closed. She pushed against his chest again. "Get off. I thought you wanted to fight with me."

He'd rather fuck her. He lifted up though and got to his feet. He bent, offering her a hand. She ignored it, rolled over, and got up on her own. They faced off against each other.

"What kind of cologne are you wearing?"

"I'm not."

She inhaled. "That's just you I'm smelling?"

"I apologize for sweating earlier. Is it offensive? We do use deodorant." He tried to contain his excitement. Kelzeb might have been right about them excreting pheromones that would attack sexual interest. He got closer, making it easier for her to inhale his scent. "Do I smell horrible to you?"

"You don't stink. It's actually the opposite."

He needed to keep her close. "You're stalling."

"I am," she admitted.

He lunged at her again and wrapped his arms around her. "Get free from me. Show me what you've got, Jill."

She put her hands on his shoulders, staring into his eyes. "You're really strong. You're holding me off my feet like it's easy as pie."

"You are very light."

"Could you tell that to my doctor? He recommended I lose twenty pounds the last time I went in for my annual checkup."

That pissed him off. Humans were idiots. "You're perfect. This doctor was incompetent."

Her lips parted again but she didn't say a word. That was rare for her.

Her hands slid over his skin, and the sensation felt so good. He liked her touching him...a hell of a lot. So did his dick as it stiffened inside his pants. He'd have adjusted it but he held her in his arms, her body against his.

Her eyes widened. "Put me down, Wings."

"You're supposed to break free from me."

Panic showed in her eyes. "Please?"

He lowered her to the mattress so she stood on her feet and released her. "There's no reason to be afraid."

She lowered her gaze, staring at the front of his pants. She backed away from him, then lifted her chin, staring into his eyes. "We aren't going to do this."

"We need to discover if you have any defensive traits you weren't aware of."

"The only thing I've learned is you have a huge bulge in your pants and touching me seems to be the cause. I'm not having your bat babies. Wrestling around with you isn't going to change my mind. You never fed me. I'm hungry." She cleared her throat. "For food, to be clear. I'd like a shower, too."

Regret surfaced. He'd forgotten to feed her. His desire to get her into bed had been foremost on his mind. She'd seen through his plot, too. That's what he got for listening to Kelzeb. His friend spent way too much time with full-blooded Gargoyles. "I'll fix you something now. You can shower after that. Let's go upstairs." He led the way.

She followed him to the upper level of his home. "Thank you."

He turned away from her and crossed the room to his kitchen. "Eggs, bacon, and toast okay?"

"Sounds perfect. I would have been happy with a bowl of cereal."

He smiled. She wasn't like any other woman he'd ever known. The possibilities intrigued him.

Chapter Eight

Jill felt a lot better after a shower. The cave had hot water. Aveoth had told her a bit about the cliffs as she'd eaten. It amazed her that a small city had been built inside a mountain. She dried off her skin and used another towel to scrub at her dripping hair.

Aveoth had laid essentials out on the counter that included shampoo, conditioner, plastic razors, body wash, and a new toothbrush. They were all brands she normally couldn't afford. He'd even thought of deodorant. She put some on and hesitated. Would Aveoth be waiting outside the door? He'd promised to leave her something clean to wear on the bed she'd slept in the night before.

"I can't stay in here forever," she muttered and opened the door. The bedroom was empty but there was a robe laying on the bed. It was a silky black material and looked skimpy. It was a reminder that Aveoth expected her to have sex with him. "Shit."

"Is there a problem?"

Aveoth's deep voice startled her, and she spun as the door to the hallway opened. He strode in as if he owned the place, which he did. She clutched at the towel. "I was hoping for a real outfit. You know. Pants. A shirt. Underwear. Maybe a bra."

He kept about four feet of space between them. "I apologize. I didn't have time to prepare for your arrival. Decker called minutes before I flew to that landing strip to pick you up. It was the first I was told of your existence. I've asked my mother to send Renna here. She'll measure you and have garments made."

144

She eyed his outfit. He'd put on a black pirate shirt and matching loose pants that could be described as breaches. His feet were bare. "I'm almost afraid to see what those will be. Do I get to look like a pirate too?"

He glanced down and frowned. "This is casual wear."

"Sure. If the year were seventeen-fifty, maybe."

"I see your point. You're going to dislike the dresses our women wear. They are formal gowns."

"How formal?"

"Long gowns that cover women's legs to the ankles."

"That's a joke, right?"

"No."

"I refuse." She held his gaze as she clutched at her towel, making sure she didn't flash him. "I'd prefer to dress like a wench. Those at least look comfy. You're not getting me into a some gown. No way, no how. I wore one once for a Halloween party. Can you say miserable? I did, about a million times in the course of four hours. It was bulky and I kept tripping on the skirt."

"I'm sorry. You'll only have to dress that way when we leave my home."

"How often will that be?"

"I'm not leaving you alone, so you'll go to work with me."

"More judging?"

"Sometimes. I have a lot of meetings, too, in the main hosting room with various clansman about our general welfare and needs."

"That's what Kelzeb called your living room downstairs."

"That's the formal living room. We host friends there. It's an old term. We have a clan hosting room where I keep a desk and hold meetings. It isn't inside my home."

"Oh." She gave her attention to the robe and lifted it, studying it. "Nice. It belongs to a woman. Who donated it?"

He said nothing, so she stared at him. He looked uncomfortable.

She dropped the robe as if it were hot. Jealousy was the emotion that hit her. She resented *that*, too. It shouldn't matter if Aveoth had tried to give her something that had probably belonged to one of his ex-girlfriends. She sure didn't plan on becoming his new one.

"I'll just put my dirty clothes on."

"Use the robe."

"No thanks."

The frown lines around his mouth deepened.

"I'll guess that belonged to someone you used to sleep with." She figured that wasn't a far stretch to make. "Tacky, Wings. Very tacky."

"She never wore it. It was something I bought as a gift. She died before her birthday."

A flash of pain showed on his face. It made her inwardly wince at her harsh words. "I'm sorry."

"I wasn't in love with her. The robe is new. You should wear it. It's the only feminine thing I had. I sent her belongings back to her family but forgot about the robe until I was searching through my closet to find something for you to wear."

"I'm good in my own clothes."

"I never slept with her." He stepped closer. "We were occasional lovers but she slumbered in a guestroom below. This room and my bedroom were off limits to Lane."

Jill found that kind of sad and cold at the same time. "That doesn't help any."

Aveoth lifted his hand and ran it through his hair. He strode over to the bed and sat down hard. "Damn. I'm making a mess of this." He locked gazes with her. "You're as foreign to me as I am to you. Everything I say seems to make you dislike me. I want things to work between us."

To see him looking and sounding so vulnerable tugged at her heart. It reminded her of what a crappy childhood he'd had, the stories he'd told her. An image flashed of a small boy with wings breaking the rules to spend time with his mother. There was so much she didn't know about him. "Tell me about this ex of yours."

"I'm the lord of this clan, Jill. Certain things have been expected of me. Lane was one of them. She was a VampLycan."

Jill moved closer and actually sat on the bed a few feet from him. "I don't understand. What did your girlfriend have to do with your clan?"

"Unmated lords tend to keep a lover. It's a status thing." He sighed, rubbing his legs with both hands and staring at the rug on the floor. "I didn't have one for years. It wasn't a secret, so sometimes women in the clan would offer to become my lover. I turned them all down. They didn't want *me*. To be the lover of a lord puts them in a position to expect certain favors and advantages. I only accepted Lane because she wasn't from my clan, and she didn't want anything from me except to escape her own. I understood that."

147

"Why did she want to escape her clan?"

"She had fallen in love with a man she'd become a lover to. They were together for seven years. He was an enforcer who was sent on missions sometimes. He went to help a Lycan pack that was being attacked by Vampires and met a woman there." Aveoth turned his head to stare at her. "This VampLycan had lost his own mate to death years before Lane came into his life. He swore he wouldn't take another mate, but Lane had hoped he would fall in love with her. Sometimes a deep bond grows between lovers. They aren't true mates, but they make a lifelong commitment to be together. Instead, he fell in lust with a Lycan on that mission, and she agreed to come home with him if he'd make her his mate. He made that commitment to her. It deeply hurt Lane."

"Oh man. That's so messed up." Jill felt bad for the woman.

"Lane couldn't stand to see them together, and told me as much when she pleaded her case to become my lover. I accepted her. I thought I was doing a good thing. It would give her time to heal and part of me hoped she'd meet someone here who would pull at her heart."

That stunned her. "You wanted her to fall for someone else while she was with you?"

"We weren't what you'd consider in a relationship. I allowed her to live in my home. Lycans go into heat, and Gargoyles experience the same thing, only we call it the ravage. Do you know what that is?"

"I can figure it out. I fed a stray cat for a while. She wasn't fixed and I couldn't catch her to take her to a vet. She'd go into heat and disappear for days to go meet up with boy cats."

Aveoth nodded. "It's the only time I went to Lane's bed. And she needed me when *she* was in heat. It was just sex. I didn't even sleep next to her. I'd leave her bed to go to my own. It worked for us both. Then one day I came home and couldn't find her. She'd jumped to her death. I didn't know she had grown despondent here. She could have returned home at any time. I made sure she knew she was free to leave."

Unlike me. Jill didn't say it aloud. "I'm sorry. I've heard most people who are really set to commit suicide don't give warning signs that are easy to pick up, or it's often a sudden decision. They just do it so no one can stop them."

He stared at the rug again. "I was angry that she died. Some of my clan believe I might have thrown her off my ledge. I didn't. I'd never harm a woman." He looked at her again, his expression pained. "Please believe me."

She didn't have to think about it. He hadn't hurt her and she wasn't afraid of him. "I do."

"Good. I liked Lane here. I had my selfish reasons."

"Sex?"

He shook his head. "She kept other women from approaching me."

"How long did she live with you?"

"Four years."

She did the math. "What happened to the lover you had before her?"

"There wasn't one."

That surprised her. "She was the only woman you've ever had sex with?"

He smiled. "No. I'm older than I look, remember? I flew to human areas and had one-time sex encounters with women, but it was rare." His humor faded fast. "The woman who was supposed to be my first lover was arranged by my father. He couldn't resist using me to form an alliance with Decker. I was sixteen at the time and had no say in the matter. Neither did the girl. She was a blood relation to you. I discovered later that she was the younger sister of Decker's mate. Your grandmother's sister. I—"

Shit. "You did my great-aunt?" That was creepy and a big ewww factor.

He shook his head. "We never became lovers. She was only thirteen at the time the alliance was made, and it was luckily decided to wait until she reached eighteen to be sent to live with me. I wouldn't have touched her if she'd come to me that young. I'm not sick enough to steal someone's childhood away from them, unlike Decker and my father. It wasn't long after that when I had to challenge my father."

He paused. "Decker offered her to me as soon as word spread that I'd won. I refused, demanding we keep the original timeline in place. I should have taken her from her clan, but I didn't know she was in danger. She would visit once a month but never told me what she was being ordered to do."

"What was that?"

He clenched his hands into fists. "Decker had a tendency to use some of his unmated clanswomen as assassins. I believe he trained Margola to be one so he could one day order her to kill me. That bastard said she died from drowning in the river, and that's why he couldn't show me her

150

body. He claimed it was never recovered. But I dug deeper. He'd sent her after a VampLycan who'd fled the clan. She lost when she tried to take out her target."

"How did you find out she was an assassin?"

"Not everyone in Decker's clan liked him. I got my information from someone who despised Decker, and tracked down the VampLycan who'd fled to find out if he'd been the one to take her out. He was."

"Did you kill him?"

Aveoth shook his head. "He was only trying to protect himself and his human mate. She was pregnant with his child. That's why he'd fled. Decker had sent him on a mission. He'd fallen in love and they were expecting a child. He felt terrible, but Margola forced him to kill her. He'd begged her to just let them escape. She attacked and wouldn't yield."

Jill nodded. "Makes sense. She was probably afraid she'd be killed anyway if she returned without getting the job done."

Aveoth frowned, staring at her with narrowed eyes.

"I've watched hitmen movies and read books about them. You flub a job and it's a death sentence."

His features relaxed. "She only had to tell me what Decker was making her do and I would have protected her from him. You're of her bloodline, but the two of you are drastically different. She wasn't headstrong, from what I knew of her. You'd have refused to do his bidding."

It reminded Jill of what she'd heard Boon and Cole discuss. "What's the deal with the bloodline thing? Those jerks who kidnapped me said it made me valuable. At the time, I chalked it up to them being crazy, but now I know so much more… They implied you wanted me for my bloodline."

"Margola visited me once a month specifically for me to drink a little of her blood. It wasn't sexual," he added quickly. "I'd bite her wrist. It was because her clan felt if I drank her blood, I'd form some kind of attachment to her. They believe Gargoyles have no ability to feel. Not that I blame them. Some don't seem to, or hide it so damn well, even I can't detect their emotions. Decker is convinced I grew addicted to her blood. That's why he thought I'd make any deal he wanted in exchange for you. Because you're her descendant, with the same bloodline."

"*Did* you become addicted to my great-aunt's blood?"

He smiled. "I can't tell you all of my secrets, beautiful. Give it time." He stood. "I'll get you something of mine to wear."

She watched him use the connecting bathroom to leave and couldn't help but feel confused. It had been a simple question, but the answer must be complicated since he'd fled to another room. She was pretty sure his answer would be a yes. It also meant he wasn't going to give her up easily or without a fight, if what ran through her veins was something he craved.

She'd met plenty of addicts growing up in the neighborhoods she'd lived in. They'd committed terrible crimes to get their next fix.

Was her blood Aveoth's high? What was he willing to do to gain access to it?

He returned soon, holding a folded shirt and soft pants. "Here. I don't have underclothing that would fit you. Come into the living room when

152

you're dressed. You said you enjoy reading. We'll see if I have any books that you like." He left through the hallway door, closing it behind him.

"You're not getting off the hook that easily, Wings," she whispered.

* * * * *

Aveoth lowered the glass he sipped from when Jill walked down the hallway, and swallowed hard. He'd given her one of his shirts and a pair of cotton stretch shorts that should have fallen just under her knees. All of his pants would be too long on her much shorter frame.

It appeared she had chosen to only wear the shirt. The view of her bare thighs teased him as she walked.

"It's a good thing your home is warm."

He tore his gaze off her lower half to stare into her eyes. "I gave you more to wear."

"The waist on the shorts was too big."

"They have drawstrings inside them."

"Oh." She shrugged. "What smells so good?"

"Don't get too excited. I just warmed some leftovers. I was hungry. You're more than welcome to join me for a snack. I hope you enjoy elk stew."

She wrinkled her nose. "I've never had it, to be honest." She walked up to the island that separated them, hiding her legs from his view. Her expression smoothed out. "I'm adventurous though. I've tried some weird foods while on dates."

He didn't like to think about her with other men and forced his attention back to the pan in front of him. "Like what?"

"Sushi. Know what that is?"

"Of course. I might live here but I'm not that cut off from the world. Did you like it?"

"Some of it was decent but I prefer my food cooked. I was taken to a seafood place that served shark and eel. It wasn't for me."

"It's a good thing we're not too close to the ocean then." He turned off the heat to the pan and spooned stew into two bowls. He lifted them and walked around the island, placing them in front of the pair of barstools. He went to the fridge. "What would you like to drink? I have soda, water, beer, and milk."

She didn't answer.

He turned, lifting one eyebrow at her in question. "What?"

"Milk? Is there a grocery store around here somewhere?"

"We have cows."

She looked momentarily surprised, then sighed.

"We're civilized, Jill."

"Do you have chickens, too?"

"I'll tell you if you let me know what you want to drink. I'm hungry."

"Soda, please."

He grabbed two cans and sat next to her, the silverware and napkins already something he'd set out. "We do have chickens. We let the younglings tend to the animals near the base of the cliff. It teaches them responsibility."

"Younglings. You mean kids."

"Yes."

"Why at the base of the cliffs?"

"In the warm months, we allow the animals to go outside. Do you know how difficult it would be to fly a cow thousands of feet down to the base of the cliff? They need to be kept inside during the winter months or they'd die from the cold."

"Okay. I guess that makes sense." She took a bite of the stew.

He watched her, gauging her reaction. Part of making her happy would be serving her foods she enjoyed. She took another bite, so he relaxed, digging into his own bowl. He figured Jill would complain if she hated it.

He ate fast, used to not sharing his meals. He got a second bowl and polished that off as well.

"What other kinds of animals do you have?"

It seemed a good thing that she showed interest in anything at the cliffs. "Goats, lambs, sheep, cows, chickens, and a few bulls for breeding."

"I can see the cows for milk and the chickens for eggs. Even the bulls, but why the others?"

"To produce wool, meat, milk, and they're good animals capable of surviving at the cliffs. We don't like to be completely dependent on hunting for meat or fish that are plentiful in the nearby areas. I happen to love scrambled eggs once in a while. Horses didn't fare well. They hated being contained inside for month after month."

"Do you have a garden?"

"The conditions are too harsh with the dense growth of the trees, so it's not feasible. Not enough sunlight to sustain a large enough area to grow for the whole clan. We order some supplies from large companies. They are delivered to a warehouse the clan owns near a larger city, and we transport them in over the summer months to store up for the winter."

"It would be so much easier to live in cities."

He smiled, guessing where her mind went. "It probably would be but we couldn't fly in populated areas. It would be a risk that someone would catch us on camera and post the footage to the internet. Out here, we're free to be ourselves. My territory is clear of humans."

"*I'm* in it."

"You aren't fully human."

She stopped eating and put down her spoon. "I don't have fangs or a hair issue. I don't belong here."

He looked at her, spotting the sheen of tears in her eyes. "I'm sorry you were dragged into this, Jill. You seem to be a very reasonable woman. I wouldn't lie to you. It's not safe for me to return you to the life you had. I'll be completely frank. Are you ready to hear it?"

She nodded. "I'm waiting with baited breath."

He admired her spunk. "When you ran into that guard statue, you bled. Do you remember?"

"Yes."

"You don't smell completely human when you're injured. It's a miracle that you were never attacked by Lycans or Vampires. The scent of your blood would have told them you weren't completely human. It would have put a target on your back. They hate VampLycans and probably would have killed you or, like your grandfather, tried to use you to gain something they wanted. The best outcome would have been if they'd bargained with the VampLycans for your life. The worst would have been them turning you over to some crazy-ass Vampire master who wanted to torture you. Your bloodline makes you unique. To be blunt, you're a sick fuck's wet dream."

"Why?"

"Why would they want you? You don't have the strength of a VampLycan so you aren't a threat to them. You may even be immune to mind control from a Vampire. When they get excited, their eyes begin to glow. Typical humans are entranced by the sight, hypnotized. See the problem if a Vamp wants to induce terror and screams? It kills their fun. You'd be perfect. They can be vicious bastards. Plus, they really despise VampLycans."

"Why do they hate them so much?"

"You should know your history." He sighed. "A nest of Vampires and a pack of Lycans paired up a few hundred years ago, after both of them were tired of being hunted by humans. Vampires can erase and mess with human memories, but sunlight kills them. They had to hide during the day. That often meant being trapped in small, confined spaces with no escape if they were found. Meanwhile, Lycans had to live nomad lives to avoid detection. Humans caught on that Lycans were different when they were around them long enough. Plus, they tend to shift out of extreme fear or anger. So the Lycans protected the Vamps while they slept, and the Vampires made sure humans never remembered if they saw something off with a Lycan."

"A perfect pairing," Jill murmured.

"It was at first, until a few Lycans and Vampires became lovers. I should say they were more than that. Lycans take mates, and Vampires have companions. It's basically the same thing. They commit to each other for life and deep emotions are involved." He shrugged. "It was considered a good thing to strengthen their alliance. The problem arose when the Lycan women mated to Vampires became pregnant. Vamps are sterile—but they'd finally found a loophole. The nest turned on the Lycans. The strongest Vamps tore into the minds of Lycan women and convinced them they were mated to get them to ovulate."

Jill had to close her mouth. It had fallen open. "They can hypnotize Lycans too?"

Aveoth nodded. "It's complicated. A master or someone equally strong can. The Lycans realized what was going on quickly, and they fought to be free. You see, mind control over Lycans doesn't last long term the way it does with humans. Once the Vamp releases a Lycan mind, they're immediately aware of what was done to them. They remember every single moment of when they were being controlled. It was paramount that the Lycans escaped before the Vamps could weaken them and imprison their entire pack. Then all the Vampires, regardless of their age or strength, could control their minds."

"How do you weaken a Lycan?" Jill had a feeling she wasn't going to like the answer but she was curious.

"Torture, beatings, blood loss, and starvation."

"Shit." She felt sick.

"The Lycans ran away. They came to Alaska, where there weren't enough humans at the time to feed a Vampire nest. VampLycan children were born, and they police Vampires now. VampLycans never want the past to be repeated. They'll send hunting parties after any nest that preys on Lycan women. It's a death sentence to force the women to birth their children. Vampires like to think they're at the top of the food chain, but they created something far stronger than they are. It's caused a lot of resentment and rage on their part."

"Is anything stronger than a VampLycan in this food chain?"

Aveoth nodded. "We are—but I will never go to war with VampLycans. We're allies. They have honor and don't abuse their powers. We share values and want to keep the peace between all races. Bad guys need killing and good guys should win."

She peered at him with interest. "Decker is a VampLycan. You don't seem to like him. I know *I* sure don't."

"He and his enforcers are a rarity. They need to die because they have no honor and don't value *any* life. Decker wanted to enslave his own people and others. There's evil in every race."

"True enough."

"You aren't safe around Vampires or Lycans, Jill. Both live in your human cities." He stared at her with sincerity. "A cut of your finger near one, and they'd know you're not fully human. Lycans live in packs. Ones that don't are considered a threat to their existence because it's unnatural to them to be solitary. Most rogues are rule breakers, killers, and packs actively hunt them. They could see you as one."

159

"Nobody ever bothered me."

"You've been lucky. They try to blend with humans. It helps them fit in and gain a footing in your world. You could get into a car accident and the police officer or the paramedic might be non-human." He paused. "They take jobs that give them access to blood, to cover up incidents that might reveal what they are, and some even work with the government."

She let that sink in.

"You're safe here, Jill."

She frowned. "It doesn't seem that way. You're worried about your own people turning on you. I was paying attention this morning."

"True, but I'd fly you to safety if that ever happens. I'd take you to the VampLycans. They'd protect you while I dealt with the mess here."

"They might turn me over to Decker or Decon."

"Never. I'd leave you with Velder's clan. They have honor, and you have family there."

"I think I'd like to avoid any Filmores."

"You have two cousins who are half human. Both women mated to VampLycans in that clan."

That news surprised Jill. "I do?"

"Decker's daughter fled to live with humans, and mated to one. She had two daughters. Decker tricked them into coming to Alaska and their mates saved them from ending up being used by him."

She opened her mouth, a hundred questions filling her head.

A loud pounding sounded before she could voice any of them.

Aveoth stood fast. "Go to your room. Wait for me there and don't come out." He strode away, down a hallway that led to the stairs.

His abrupt and curt tone implied danger. She got up, but instead of doing as she'd been ordered, quietly followed him. If they were going to be attacked by his people, she wanted a heads up. She crept down the stairs and tiptoed toward where the beds had been put on the floor.

"I asked you want you wanted. Get to the point." Aveoth's tone wasn't friendly.

"You had a human brought to you?" The voice was female, and ice cold.

"What I do is none of your concern, Winalin. Leave."

"Would you like to have this discussion here in the hall where anyone could happen upon us or would you prefer to let me pass to allow for privacy?"

"I have nothing to say to you. I made that clear." Aveoth's voice deepened.

"I have things to say to *you*." Winalin's tone rose. "Let me pass, or gossip-spreaders will be busy today."

"Fuck," Aveoth rumbled. A door slammed.

Jill hesitated, not sure if she should keep eavesdropping or rush upstairs. He must have slammed the door in that woman's face. The real question that bothered her was, who was Winalin to him?

"Say what you have to and then get out," Aveoth snapped.

Jill tensed, realizing he must have let the woman inside.

Silence stretched and no one spoke. It made Jill want to sneak closer to the opening and peer into the other room to see what was going on.

"Goddamn it," Aveoth thundered, making Jill jump. "You wanted to talk, so do it. Stop staring at me. I'm in no mood to waste a day waiting for you to form words. Spit it out, Winalin."

"What have you done to the hosting area?"

"It's none of your business, but I'm using the mattresses for training. Just say what you must and then get out."

"There was no need for you to send for a human breeder, my Lord. I am right here. My brother and I have discussed this many times. Your younglings should be born of strong bloodlines for the sake of the clan's future."

"I see you're still eager to become a whore for Elco. Get out, Winalin. I've told you, I'll never visit your bed, nor you mine. I'd rather fly through a wildfire than touch you. It would be a more pleasurable experience for me."

"You insult me?" The woman's voice remained calm and cool.

"As if I could. You do that to yourself every time you come to offer your body for my use."

"I'm a pure-blood Gargoyle willing to mate or breed with you. That's a high honor."

"One I have no interest in. Have I not made myself clear?"

"You would choose a human breeding vessel to birth your youngling over a pure-blood?"

162

Aveoth snarled. "Why do you and your brother assume the human is here for me to breed?"

"There's no other reason, my lord. You'd have chosen another VampLycan if you sought a lover. I offer to become your mate. It would settle you as our lord."

"*Settle* me?" Aveoth laughed. It sounded harsh. "I *am* your lord. Elco may challenge me if he believes otherwise. I'd happily take his head in a fight."

"You're twisting the meaning of my words! A mated lord with strong sons is best for the clan's future."

"Did Elco tell you this? I would never have been born if bloodlines weren't mixed. One of my first executive orders was changing the title of our clan to GarLycans after I challenged my father. I beat *him*, and he was a full-blood. Do you know why? That Lycan blood of mine gives me some advantages. Do yourself a favor and find a GarLycan who makes you feel something, anything, Winalin. Step out of your brother's shadow and take control of your future. Elco is archaic in his ways and thinking. It's not a crime to seek happiness in your life. You don't want to be with me any more than I wish to be with you."

"You need to choose me. I'm better than a human. "

"No." Aveoth paused. "You're not. I've made my choice. Get out."

Jill strained to hear the door open and close but only silence could be heard.

"Goddamn it!" Aveoth yelled. "Don't undress! I don't want you, Winalin."

"I'm offering you my body, my life, and all that I am. You can take me as your mate or as your breeding vessel. I will not return to Elco without your child inside my womb."

"I'll toss your ass out into the hallway naked if you keep removing that dress. Do you understand me?" Aveoth sounded pissed. "I feel *nothing* for you."

"Your Lycan side will rise. Bare skin will incite your lust."

"Another bit of bad advice you got from your brother?" Aveoth's tone sounded bored now. "Your breasts are doing nothing for me."

Jill's mouth dropped open. It sounded as if the woman was really stripping in the other room.

Emotions hit—and none of them were good. Jealousy took the lead. She didn't like it one bit that someone was trying to seduce Aveoth. Part of her wanted to storm out there and tell the bitch to stop acting like a ho. He'd made it abundantly clear the woman's advances weren't welcome.

The silence bothered her more, making her wonder what in the hell was going on.

"I still don't want you." Aveoth actually yawned. "Get out, Winalin."

"I'll touch *you* if you won't touch me."

"Don't do it. I'd hate to hit a woman, but I will if you get any closer."

Jill had had enough. Aveoth had spent the morning flirting with her. She'd be damned if he had sex with some Gargoyle bitch, since he wouldn't let her go home. It wasn't going to happen.

She pushed off the wall and stormed the few steps to the opening, stepping into the room.

The sight that greeted her was Aveoth's back as he stood with his legs braced apart and his arms crossed over his chest. Winalin was stark naked and crossing the room slowly toward him. She had a tall, pale body that was on the thin side, but otherwise she had a killer figure, with small, firm breasts that jiggled with every step and a patch of black pubic hair.

She halted when her unusual gaze landed on Jill.

The fact that the Gargoyle was drop-dead gorgeous and looked like something out of a high-end porn movie pissed Jill off more. "Am I interrupting something, my lord?" She managed to not grit the words out.

Aveoth didn't turn his head to glance at her, or even tense. "Not at all. This is one of those unpleasant things I have to deal with. I'm glad you're here, Jill. Our guest needs to redress and leave."

Jill glanced up and down Winalin. That was the last thing she'd have said if she were a man. Most of them would have loved to let someone who looked like the Gargoyle get naked for them. They'd be all over her. The woman made Jill feel a little self-conscious, too. She sure didn't have that kind of body or those model-worthy looks. It made her wonder why in the hell Aveoth wasn't tossing *her* out instead and keeping the naked woman. Winalin wanted to have his bat babies pretty badly, and made no bones about it.

"That's her?" Winalin curled her lip. "She's puny." Her glacial gaze raked up and down Jill. "She's also not very attractive."

"Beauty is in the eye of the beholder," Aveoth replied. "Jill is stunning to me. You're blind to the important things in life, Winalin. Get out of my

165

private chambers. I strongly suggest you put something on before you do or I doubt you'd make it home without inciting *someone's* lust. It just won't be mine."

The Gargoyle dismissed Jill with a wave of her hand. "She's nothing, my lord. I stand before you offering you the best. Don't settle to breed with that pathetic creature."

Pathetic creature? Jill wanted to punch the bitch but she wasn't that stupid. She had seen what these people were capable of, between Aveoth's ability to fly and Kelzeb shelling his body. She'd get her ass handed to her in a fight. Instead, she walked up to Aveoth, keeping slightly behind him instead of at his side, in case the Gargoyle attacked. She had faith he'd protect her, since he'd made it clear she was safe with him.

Jill hesitated for a heartbeat—and then pressed up against his body. There were other ways to win a fight.

She smiled at the bitch and raised her hand, running her fingers lightly down Aveoth's arm in a caress, and then placing her hand on his hip. "Will she do that soon? We had plans to go to your bedroom."

That got a reaction from Winalin. She hissed, and her unique-colored eyes brightened, turning into moving orbs of violet. Her white skin began to darken a bit, becoming gray. It shocked Jill a little, and she realized she clutched Aveoth tight with her hand. That was one scary bitch.

He reacted by chuckling and uncrossing his arms. He turned, putting them around Jill and jerking her against his tall frame.

"Don't even think about it, Winalin. Jill is under my protection. You strike out at her and I'll not only knock you out, but you'll wake imprisoned for the next four months. I'll put your brother with you so you're not alone."

"She's *human*. It's an insult!" Real anger showed on Winalin's face but with her graying, shelled skin, cracks appeared on her otherwise flawless features. "You dare choose *that* over me?"

Aveoth glanced down at Jill. "This is an example of how to never behave. Conceit is an ugly trait, isn't it?"

Jill almost smiled. "Yes, my lord."

"Perhaps Winalin needs a lesson on why I prefer *you* in my bed over her."

Amusement sparked in his eyes, and she narrowed hers. She realized he planned to take advantage of the situation. She glanced at the Gargoyle, the sight of her naked and glaring at Jill enough to make her play along.

"What do you have in mind, my lord?" She shot him a warning look. It better not be something humiliating. She had her limits on what she'd do or say to get even with someone who'd insulted her. There was no way she'd go to her knees to fondle him or act like some slutty sex slave.

He slid one hand up her back and cupped her head. He lowered his face toward her and she closed her eyes, guessing he planned to kiss her. Her heart hammered and she tensed a little, but tried not to outwardly show it since they were being watched.

He brushed his mouth very softly over hers and licked the seam of her lips. She opened up to him to deepen the kiss. Aveoth didn't hesitate.

Jill was glad his arm was hooked around her waist and he was strong enough to hold her against him when a wave of sexual need exploded inside her.

Her body heated from the inside, as if she were being lit aflame under her skin. His taste, scent, and the aggressive way he kissed had her body responding with a near terrifying intensity. Her breasts ached and her clit throbbed. She clutched at him, the desire to tear at his clothes overwhelming.

He broke the kiss and she stared up at him in shock, panting. His eyes were silver and blue liquid orbs of moving, flashing colors. A deep growl rumbled from his chest, and then he broke contact with her gaze. His features hardened, his eyes turning bright blue as he glared to her right.

"Get the fuck out, Winalin. Never come to my home again. You're not welcome." He eased his hold on Jill, then bent and grabbed her around her hips. His shoulder hit her lower stomach gently before he rose up, with her body draped over his shoulder. He hooked her behind her knees with one arm, his other hand resting on the curve of her ass. "I have much more pleasurable things to do with my time than spend it with you."

Jill hung upside down reeling from the way she'd reacted to Aveoth. That wasn't normal. She wasn't some blushing virgin. Admittedly, she hadn't had all that many sexual partners but none of them had turned her on that fast or hard by just kissing her.

He's not human, she remembered. Not only did Aveoth have wings, the ability to shell and fly, but he must have some freaky hormone thing going on that accounted for the way she'd gone from zero interest on a sex scale to fuck-me-now.

Oh shit. I'm in trouble.

"Get out," Aveoth thundered.

Jill winced at the loudness of his voice but she didn't struggle to break free. Confusion and jumbled emotions kept her still. She focused on his ass. He had a beefy one, and she longed to grope it to see if it was as firm as it looked. She fisted her hands instead of touching him. That empty feeling inside was making itself known, and she knew exactly what would cure it.

She mentally went there, imagining the big, muscled guy naked, nailing her. Panic came next over how much she wanted Aveoth. One kiss had turned her into a raging sex fiend.

Aveoth moved and the door opened, then it slammed. She heard metal scraping, probably as he locked the door. "She's gone." He turned, walking toward the mattresses that lay on the floor. He bent.

Jill's feet touched the soft thickness of the mattress and his hold on her loosened. She straightened and he totally let her go, standing before her. She jerked back suddenly, trying to put more space between them, and fell over, landing on her ass.

Aveoth frowned and crouched down, staring into her eyes with a frown. "Are you okay?"

Her mouth opened. "What the hell was that?"

"Winalin is a pain in my ass. I'm sorry about that." He reached out a hand, probably to help her back up.

She rolled, scrambling to get away. She was afraid if he touched her, she'd lunge at him. The need to touch him and get naked was nearly

169

overbearing. It wasn't the most graceful of moves, but she got to her feet to bolt away. Jill ran as if the hounds of hell were on her ass to put space between them, and didn't stop until she reached the bedroom he'd given her.

She got inside and turned, only to find him coming at her with a concerned look in his eyes. She slammed the door.

"Stay away from me!"

"Jill? What is wrong?"

She saw the lock and twisted it. A second later, he tried to open the door. She backed away, breathing hard from her wild sprint up the stairs and down the hallway.

"Jill?" He softened his tone. "I apologize if kissing you upset you, but I needed to show Winalin that I wasn't interested in her."

She hugged her body, flinching over how oversensitive her breasts felt under the shirt. Her nipples were hard, her skin too hot. She backed up more and spun, heading toward the bathroom. A cold shower might dilute whatever weird thing he'd done to her.

"Jill?" He knocked on the door. "Talk to me."

"Fuck off, Wings. Keep your freaky mouth and whatever the hell kind of drug you secrete away from me," she yelled over her shoulder.

She entered the bathroom and locked the other door that entered his bedroom. It was imperative that she cool down before she ended up throwing herself at the big bastard and begging him to fuck her. It was a real possibility.

She turned on the shower, stomped over to the sink, and twisted the tap. The water was cold when she cupped her hands and leaned in, drinking some of it, hoping to erase the sweet taste of his kiss. *It must be some natural sex chemical GarLycans secrete to make defenseless women horny as hell.*

The door she'd just locked came crashing open. She jerked upward and spun, gaping at Aveoth. He stopped at the doorway from his bedroom into the bathroom. "What in the hell is wrong with you? Did you say *drugs?*"

She shoved back against the sink and watched as his nostrils flared. A look of surprise widened his eyes and his gaze lowered to her thighs. "Shit."

"What did you do to me?"

His gaze lifted, holding hers. "It wasn't intentional. I swear on my honor."

"Bullshit!" She wasn't buying it. Sweat beaded on her skin, the heat coming back. She'd heard about hot flashes but these seemed worse. Her clit throbbed painfully again and her breasts actually hurt.

The color of Aveoth's eyes swirled to mostly silver. "I swear I didn't do this on purpose."

"What did you dose me with?" She leaned heavily against the counter and clutched it to keep upright. Her knees didn't want to support her weight and her legs shook. "Make it stop!"

"Damn it." He gripped the doorframe and it creaked, the wood sounding as if were being crushed. "I'm different from other GarLycans.

This has never happened before. Well, not like this. I'm so sorry, Jill. You must believe me."

"Give me something to counteract whatever the hell this is!" She spun, bending over the sink since her legs trembled harder. The need was turning into pure agony. "I'm not having your bat babies, goddamn you."

"Listen to me. I told you there's this thing that happens to Gargoyles every thirty years. It's called the ravage. It's not my time, but I think you somehow triggered my hormones and you...you must have swallowed some when we kissed."

She squeezed her eyes closed, leaning more on the counter. "You're blaming this on me? *Really?* Are you kidding me?"

"No! Of course not. I'm shocked by this. The ravage is complicated."

"So you're in heat like that stray cat I fed. Goddamn you, Wings."

"I'm not the one in heat, but I think I've put *you* into it. It wasn't intentional, Jill. I swear on my life. As I said, I'm different. I really wanted you, and for whatever reason, my hormones levels must have increased since I met you. I somehow transferred them to you by kiss. I didn't even know this could happen."

She groaned and started to crumple. Aveoth was there instantly and picked her up. She would have fought, but she'd have only ended up on the floor if he hadn't gotten to her. He spun, carrying her through the broken door and to his bed. He took a seat on the large mattress, cradling her in his arms.

"I really didn't know this was possible. I swear. Let me help you."

"Right. By putting a youngling in my womb? Fuck off." She tried to climb off his lap and he turned, helping her. She rolled onto his bed and curled into a ball on her side. She was burning up, aching, and could feel wetness between her thighs. It was more than that. She was soaked.

"Am I bleeding?"

"No." His voice deepened. "It's not your period causing that. It's lust."

"Get away from me."

"That's not going to help, Jill."

"Put me in the shower. Cold water will."

"It won't."

The bed moved, and she turned her head, peeking at him. Aveoth started to get naked by shoving his pants down.

"Don't you dare."

"I'm going to help you."

"By fucking me? Pass!"

"No, sweetheart. I'm just going to get you through this. It's my fault. I apologize."

She tried to roll away when he put his knee on the bed and it dipped. He was faster, and grabbed her. She gasped as he flipped her onto her back and began to strip her. It was tempting to fight, but getting rid of his T-shirt seemed to help the aches a bit. She stared at him as he lay on his stomach, pushed her legs apart with his strong hands, and slid down the bed. Her eyes widened when she realized what he was about to do, and her mouth opened.

He moved fast, and suddenly his head dipped between her thighs. Hot breath fanned her pussy, and then his mouth opened up and his tongue was on her clit.

She threw her head back and clawed at the bedding as he licked her. Pleasure hit so hard, she saw spots, and then a climax ripped through her. She cried out, her body jerking.

Aveoth snarled and burrowed his face closer, his tongue merciless on her clit. She bucked but couldn't get away as another wave of ecstasy rolled through her.

Jill lost the ability to think. It was just pleasure, her heart pounding so hard she felt as if it might beat right out of her chest, and yet another climax hit. He was going to kill her with his tongue. There was no slow descent after she came. Just need and bursts of extreme rapture.

She moaned, cried out, and climaxed again.

Chapter Nine

Aveoth had jacked off in the shower. He entered his bedroom and stared at Jill sleeping in his bed. Guilt, disbelief, and shock still echoed through him. His ravage was years away but his body had betrayed him *and* Jill. She'd never forgive him.

His dick stiffened and he glared down at it. "I deserve sainthood." He'd only used his mouth on Jill until she'd passed out from exhaustion. There was no way he'd take advantage of her in that condition. He strode over to the nightstand and removed his personal phone before he returned to the bathroom. He called Kelzeb.

His friend answered on the second ring. "Is something wrong?"

"Where are you?"

"Between meetings. I'm walking." Kelzeb paused. "No one is near me. What is wrong? You sound pissed."

"I kissed Jill."

"That's progress."

"And it sent her into heat as if I'd withdrawn my hormone fluid from the back of my very neck while suffering the ravage."

His friend inhaled sharply. "What?"

"You heard me."

"That's not possible. It's not the right time for you."

"I also didn't use a needle to withdraw the fluid buildup that I don't even have." He closed his eyes and reached behind his neck, feeling for a lump. There wasn't one. "There's no sign of the ravage but that's what happened."

"I'm coming to you."

"No. I couldn't stand you being near her right now. I'm feeling overprotective and aggressive as hell."

"Is she okay?"

"She's passed out in my bed."

"Did you mate her?"

"Hell no. I kept my dick away from her."

"You just let her suffer through it?" Kelzeb sounded shocked.

"No. I got her through it with oral sex. She's never going to forgive me. Her reaction...shit. I can't even blame her for thinking I did this with purpose. She accused me of drugging her like humans do in clubs. What do they call it? Date-rape drugging?"

"You're going to have to tell her the truth about you when she wakes."

"I can't. Not yet. She was already mistrustful but now she's going to hate me. I can't share my deepest secret with her, Kelzeb. What if she betrays me?"

"There's never been anything like you that we know of. And this hasn't happened to you before. Why now?"

"Maybe it's because I'd decided to mate her? I don't know." His shoulders slumped.

"Look, I'm going to put it out there. You either need to tell her you're a bit different so she has a chance to understand what happened, or she probably *will* think you're a dishonorable asshole who'd unleash a chemical bomb on her sex drive. You said it. You want her to be your mate. This isn't something you'll be able to hide from her if your body reacts to her this way. It's likely to happen again."

"Fuck." He wanted to punch something.

"Whatever you do, the rumors are growing stronger amongst the clan. Everyone seems to know about you having a human living in your quarters. Hawk came to me."

Aveoth got a handle on his emotions. "What did he say?"

"The Gargoyle Council held a secret meeting today. I sure as hell wasn't informed. He saw them grouped together heading toward their chambers. He wanted you to know."

"Do you think we can trust Hawk?"

"I do. Hawk loves Chaz and Fray. He had to have heard the rumors that circulated about Abotorus. Can you see him complying if an order came down to eradicate GarLycans in our clan?"

The answer was simple. "Fuck no. He'd have fought alongside his sons to the death."

"Exactly. He would kill anyone to protect them," Kelzeb said.

"You're right. Hawk would never side with the pure-bloods, since most of them agreed with Abotorus that GarLycans have weaknesses they can't abide."

"I'm wondering what those ancient fucks are plotting."

"A flat-out attack would be stupid but I wouldn't put anything past the council. Quietly alert GarLycans to be vigilant."

177

"Already done."

"You should have called me right away, Kelzeb."

"I said I would only interrupt your time with Jill if there was something I couldn't handle." Humor bled into Kelzeb's voice. "As much as I hate the council for the way they fuck with us, they are just a pain in our asses. I'm certain they've never inspired loyalty to anyone except other full-bloods, considering the way they make no secret about looking down on GarLycans. Their numbers are far fewer than ours these days."

"I never want it to come to GarLycans fighting Gargoyles in our clan. It would be all kinds of fucked up. Father against son. Never," Aveoth swore. "I'll talk to Kado."

Kelzeb snorted. "He won't listen. That's the cold bastard who swore years of service from his own son just to score points with Abotorus. He made Creed a servant to our old lord. I've always wondered why he chose Creed and not one of the first three sons."

"I pondered that myself, and spoke to Nebulas after we discovered the assignments the council had given Creed. Fucking bastards had him out in the dead zone, patrolling far beyond what was considered sane."

"I remember. What did Kado's eldest son say? Did he defend his father?"

Aveoth remembered his anger. "No. Nebulas was furious at his father over his brother's mistreatment. Creed's wasn't a planned birth. Kado's mate went into heat and she got pregnant."

"Lycans don't accidently get pregnant."

Aveoth sighed. "My guess is she wanted another child but Kado didn't. She probably didn't care about his wishes. Would *you* want to take orders from him? I can't blame her. He gave his son's life to Abotorus as punishment to his mate and to the son he never wanted."

"Prick."

"My opinion of Kado has never been high. Nebulas said he was aware his father had been angry over the matter, but he didn't know his brother was still paying the price. I promised him that I'd never allow the council to assign Creed duties again. That's why I had you send him to be a Lycan pack guardian. It keeps him far from his father's reach."

Kelzeb grunted. "I wish we could send Kado away. But we'll deal with whatever the council's planning."

"I'll set up a meeting with him."

"At least we know that coward won't challenge you."

"True." Aveoth thought about his current problem. "My main issue right now is Jill and what I'm going to do when she wakes."

"Tell her as much of the truth as you can. Hopefully it will be enough if you don't want to share your history just yet."

"I'll contact Kado now."

"Don't meet with him without me there."

"Of course not. I'm thinking this evening. Are you free?"

"I'll make sure of it. Good luck with Jill."

"Thanks. I'm going to need it." Aveoth disconnected the call and crept back into his bedroom. Jill still slept. He left his bedroom and began to prepare food for her. She'd be hungry. He just hoped she'd give him a chance to explain.

* * * * *

Jill sat up in bed, gripping the thick bedspread covering her body. A light had been left on. It wasn't the room Aveoth had given her but instead his bedroom. Memories returned and heat warmed her cheeks. He'd gone down on her, gotten her off several times, until she'd passed out from exhaustion.

She glanced around, seeing that she was alone. Her gaze went to where the opening should be to the ledge, but he'd sealed it off. "Of course he did," she muttered. "So I can't escape."

She pushed back the bedspread and stared at her naked body. A quick assessment told her she'd been washed. Nothing hurt but she felt her throat, not feeling any bite marks. Wings had drugged her though. His kiss had turned her on so strongly that she hadn't even put up a fight.

She stood and let her hand wander down to the V of her thighs. It didn't hurt there, either, so she was pretty sure he hadn't done more than use his mouth.

Anger filled her. It had been unfair, what he'd done to her. He talked about honor, but a nice whatever-the-hell he was wouldn't have dosed her.

The bathroom door lock was still broken but she entered it and stared at her reflection. She again scanned her body, twisting and turning to see if he'd bitten her. There were no marks or bruises. She washed her face, brushed her teeth, and entered her bedroom. A clean shirt had been

180

left on top of the bed. She hesitated but then put it on. It beat walking around naked. The thing had to be Aveoth's, of course, and it hung to her thighs.

She opened the hallway door and the scent of food hit. Her stomach growled. Part of her wanted to barricade herself inside the bedroom but she was too angry. Hiding wasn't who she was. Her life had always been hard, and she faced things straight on. Including freaky men with wings. Her and Aveoth were going to talk.

She stormed barefoot toward the kitchen and found him sitting with his back to her at the counter.

"I hope you slept well."

His deep voice startled her, since he didn't move on the barstool. He had probably heard or smelled her coming. She crossed her arms over her chest as she came to a halt. "So much for your talk of honor and all that bullshit. You drugged me."

"It wasn't intentional."

"Bullshit." She wasn't buying it.

He slowly turned on the stool and stood. His features surprised her. He looked tired, and his normally stimulating eyes were just blue now, no sign of silver. "That has never happened before, Jill. I wasn't even aware I had the ability to put you into heat with just a kiss. I'm a lot of things, but I'm not a liar."

"I'm not a cat. I don't go into heat."

"I'm mostly Gargoyle, and under certain circumstances we can trigger heat with humans, Lycans, and even other Gargoyles. This truly wasn't planned. Will you please at least listen to me?"

"Do I have a choice? You have me trapped here."

"Are you hungry?"

"As if I'd trust you to prepare me anything. You drugged me once. You could do it again."

He sat back down. "Every thirty years, a Gargoyle experiences the ravage. We usually get a day or two warning before it hits. Our emotions are unstable and a lump forms at the back of our necks. It's a chemical buildup of sexual hormones. We find a woman to agree to share our ravage with us."

"I didn't agree to that shit."

He nodded. "I'm aware. May I continue?"

She kept silent, staring at him.

"We use a syringe to remove some of that chemical, or hormone, whatever you want to call it, and put it in a glass. The woman will drink it. It affects her quickly, just the way my kiss did to you yesterday. You may feel the back of my neck. There's no lump. My emotion levels haven't spiked. I'm not in the ravage, nor is it due, but for whatever reason my body somehow produced that chemical inside my mouth when I kissed you. I swear to you that I don't know why or even how it happened. This was a first."

"I still call bullshit."

His eyes swirled silver but they calmed quickly, returning to a bright blue. "I understand your mistrust but I'm telling you the truth. Don't you think I would have fully bedded you if this had been planned? You certainly would have let me fuck you." His voice deepened. "Instead, I tended to you orally and suffered the most painful hard-on of my life. I tended to my own needs afterward in the shower."

She still didn't trust him. "Maybe you did things to me after I blacked out."

His eyebrows rose and he actually had the nerve to smile. "You'd feel it if I'd fucked you. You're dainty, Jill. I'm not." He stood and reached for the front of his pants.

"What are you doing?"

It shocked her when he opened them, shoving the black material down. The sight of his straining, thick cock freed wasn't something she could unsee. He was really big and really hard.

He yanked his pants up, adjusting his hard-on, and sat back down. "You'd know it with certainty if I'd been inside you."

She recovered, glaring at him. "That was crude."

"Effective though." He sighed, breaking eye contact momentarily but quickly looking back at her. "I'm trying to get you to trust and like me, goddamn it. What happened was detrimental to gaining that goal. All I can do is apologize and tell you the truth. I didn't know that would happen. When it did, I tended to you in the least traumatizing way I could."

"You think going down on me wasn't traumatizing?" She knew her cheeks were burning. It was embarrassing to remember how much she'd enjoyed it. "You put your face where it shouldn't have been!"

He glanced down her body. "You would have suffered if I hadn't done that." His gaze returned to hers. "It was either pain or pleasure. I never want to see you hurting, Jill."

"So that was you doing me a favor?"

He stood and rounded the counter. "I don't want to fight with you. It was an accident. You don't seem willing to believe me but I did my best to get you through the end result." He bent, taking something out of the oven.

She noticed his hands turning gray before he lifted a glass dish and set it on the stovetop. She wondered if that was his version of pot holders, partially shelling.

He turned to face her. "Please eat."

She was hungry. "Fine, but it better not be drugged."

He got out plates and a large spoon, dishing what she assumed was some kind of breakfast casserole. It smelled good. He put both of them down on the counter by the barstools, then gathered silverware. "I would never purposely hurt you in any way."

He looked so defeated and, despite her anger, his voice bothered her. He was usually confident but now he seemed defeated. Even…sad.

What if he *was* telling the truth? It didn't excuse what happened. Though she was a little more open to listening and asking questions.

"So you're telling me that you didn't know us kissing could drug me?"

He held her gaze. "I did not. I swear on my life."

"How is that possible?"

He took a seat beside her. "GarLycans and VampLycans are a young race, Jill. There was never any recorded history of our races breeding until after VampLycans came to be. We still are learning what we're capable of and don't have answers for everything, like lifespans. For example, will a VampLycan die of old age the way a Lycan would after so many hundreds of years, or will they endure agelessness the way Vampires do, as long as they drink blood? It's the same for GarLycans, although we do tend to inherit most of our traits from our Gargoyle blood. I can't tell you what my lifespan will be with certainty. I can guess it will be thousands of years, but who really knows? We don't. I can do things Gargoyles can't because I'm not a full-blood. What happened when I kissed you wasn't planned, nor did I suspect it was a possibility. It's never happened to me before, or been reported by any other GarLycan."

She took a bite of the casserole. It was good but slightly odd tasting. She refused to ask him what meat was inside it. With her luck, it might be sheep or maybe even a rabbit. She thought both animals were cute. It was best not to know. His words replayed in her head as she considered everything he'd said.

"I won't risk kissing you again, Jill. I'm afraid to. I never want a repeat of what happened and the fear I saw in your eyes. You must hate me."

She glanced over at him and discovered his shoulders slumped, his focus on the food in front of him. He looked depressed, and his tone sounded the same. It made her feel bad...and a little guilty. He certainly seemed sincere.

But her anger returned. It was possible he was telling the truth, but it was *still* really screwed up that *her* body had been out of control because of some freaky hormone thing going on with *him*.

She decided to stay silent and just eat.

They finished their meal and Aveoth stood, carrying their dishes to the sink. "I am going to leave soon and deal with some problems in the clan. A guard will be assigned outside the door but it will be for your protection. I don't trust Winalin or anyone like her to not try to harm you while I'm gone."

That surprised her. "You're actually going to leave me alone and not drag me with you this time?"

He faced her, and the normal sparks of color in his eyes remained absent. "Yes. I believe you've had enough of my company recently. I am truly sorry, Jill. I never meant for that to happen."

Damn. She felt really guilty. He'd been nice to her since they'd met. She couldn't deny it. The possibility of him telling her the truth about that kiss seemed more likely than not. It might suck that he wouldn't allow her to go home, but he'd sworn to keep her safe. He also could have nailed her while she was drugged out of her head, but he hadn't. She believed that too. The guy was hung. She'd have felt that afterward if he'd fucked her.

"I'll leave you now. I have calls to make to two trusted GarLycans I wish to guard you, and I have the head of the Gargoyle Council to confront. He's an asshole who loves to cause trouble."

"Because I'm here?" She'd heard everything that Winalin had said.

"Kado needs no real excuse to be a thorn in my side. He hates me and every other GarLycan, including one of his own sons. I'm not even certain he likes his other three, since they're GarLycans, but he at least didn't give *them* away to that bastard Abotorus. He is cruel."

"He gave away his own kid? Like, put him up for adoption?"

Aveoth shook his head. "Are you familiar with an indentured servant? Kado signed away his son's life for a certain amount of years to work for the clan right after his birth. Abotorus allowed it. I never would have. There have been a few times when clan members offered one of their sons to me in that way. I refused."

She remembered her history. "So this guy is like a slave?" It horrified her. "Can you set him free?"

"It's a fucked-up tradition I inherited when I became a lord." He reached up and scrubbed his face with his hand. "I can't dishonor Creed that way by outright giving him his freedom until the time expires. It would embarrass him and injure his pride." He dropped his hand, staring at her. "I did, however, assign him a job he wanted that is far from here, so he's not under the command of the Gargoyle Council. They abused him as a youth with harsh assignments."

She felt sorry for whoever this Creed was.

The silver flared in his eyes but he looked furious. "I must leave. I hope you will forgive me at some point, Jill." He bowed and walked toward the hallway.

She stood and reached out as he passed, touching his arm. He froze, his head swiveling to stare at her hand lightly gripping his forearm. His gaze lifted to hers.

"I believe that you didn't mean to drug me but I can't say I'm happy about what happened, either."

Relief showed on his face. "Thank you."

"Be careful."

"Always. I have something to protect now." He pulled away, walking down the hallway and out of sight to his bedroom.

She sighed and closed her eyes. *Why does he have to be so damn hot? And sweet?* The memory of his face between her thighs—and what he could do with his tongue—had her opening her eyes and taking a seat on the barstool again.

She wanted him, even if he wasn't human, but they'd be a train wreck. "Damn. I'm in trouble."

Chapter Ten

Aveoth closely watched Chaz and Fray. "You do not enter my home unless you feel someone has broken in. Jill is under my protection. She's mine. Keep her safe at all costs. I don't give a fuck who you have to kill, but no one harms her."

Fray grinned. "She must be super-hot. Good for you, my lord. We won't let anything happen to your woman."

Chaz growled. "Respect, brother. Chill your ass out."

Aveoth fought a smile. He liked and trusted the two GarLycans. The older twin, Chaz, tended to be more serious. Fray constantly said what was on his mind, even if it wasn't appropriate. They amused him with their laid-back personalities. He'd read a lot of complaints about both until he'd put them under Kelzeb's sole command. His best friend encouraged them, and Aveoth understood why. They were a breath of fresh air in the mostly stagnant attitudes at the cliffs.

"I'm totally being respectful." Fray grinned wider. "Lord Aveoth has a woman and he wants to keep her. I'm down with that. Plus, he just said we have permission to slay any assholes who would attack her. Only snobby Gargoyles are butt hurt right now about her being here. They treat us like shit most of the time, so we have a license to kill. That's high-five time." He lifted one of his palms up.

Chaz shook his head. "Knock it off. I apologize, my lord. My younger brother must have missed out on some oxygen at birth since he was in the womb longer."

"You're like one minute older."

Aveoth chuckled. "Enough. Protect Jill. No one is to visit her, especially Winalin." That killed his humor. "She's a threat."

"I bet." Fray snorted. "She's been after you forever and thinks her shit doesn't stink. The fact that you'd pick someone with human blood must sting her stuck-up ass big time."

"Goddamn it," Chaz rasped. "I apologize again, my lord. Perhaps I hit him in the head too hard while we were sparring this morning."

"I'll be back soon. Make certain nothing happens to Jill." Aveoth strode off, but heard Chaz hissing at his brother as he went down the corridor away from his home.

"You're such a dumbass, Fray. I can't take you anywhere."

"Lord Aveoth is cool. He wasn't pissed. He knows Winalin is a snobby bitch. Who doesn't?"

Aveoth grinned, turning the corner. He masked his features fast though, and found Kelzeb waiting for him at the top of the stairs. His best friend arched an eyebrow.

"The twins," Aveoth whispered.

Kelzeb winked. "My favorite guys. Good choice for protection duty. They'll defend her with their lives and both of them are excellent fighters."

"I'm aware. Let's go see Kado."

"How much of a pain in the ass was he when you demanded to speak to him?"

"He's predictable. I'll give him that."

"So he whined like an infant?"

"Pretty much."

Aveoth's phone buzzed and he took it out of his pocket. He cursed, coming to a halt. A female voice began to speak as soon as he accepted the call.

"Why is it that I had to hear you have a woman from Renna? She overheard it being spoken about."

Kelzeb turned, giving him a curious look.

"I would have called you but I've been busy, Mother. Right now isn't a good time. I'll return your call soon."

"I want to meet her."

"You will. I have a meeting to attend."

"You always have meetings. Are you dragging that poor girl with you? It's cruel, Aveoth. That's why I rarely leave my quarters. I heard she is human. The poor dear must be terrified. Bring her to me and I'll entertain her."

"I left her in my home with guards."

"She's trying to escape? I can't say I blame her."

He gritted his teeth. "Thank you."

"I didn't mean it that way. I know you'd be on your best behavior, but she must be terrified as a human here. You never planned to introduce her to me, did you?"

"That's not true. I meant to ask Renna to fit her for a wardrobe. You would have come along with her. Perhaps tomorrow would be a good time for that."

"The poor girl doesn't have any clothing? Are you keeping her chained naked to your bed?" Her voice became cold, and he heard her rage.

"Of course not! She has nothing appropriate for the cliffs. It's a long story. I really need to go." He lowered his voice. "Kado is making waves. I have to deal with him."

She growled. "Of course he is. Call me later."

He disconnected and shoved his phone back inside his pocket.

Kelzeb resumed walking down the stairs. "Are her feelings hurt?"

"Probably. I'll deal with that later."

They reached the council floor and Kelzeb stepped ahead of him, one hand gripping his sword. Aveoth did the same as they paused, preparing for a confrontation. He didn't trust Kado or any of the council members. It was possible they'd attack without warning.

"I'll apologize in advance for whatever Domb says," Kelzeb muttered.

Aveoth held his friend's gaze. "You are nothing like your father, nor are you close to him. We've been over this."

"The bastard is an embarrassment."

"So was Lord Abotorus while he lived. I will never hold you accountable for Domb or his actions."

"Let's do this." Kelzeb sighed. "I'm ready for the dirty looks from the old bastard."

"I'm ready for a fight if they demand one."

"Me too." Kelzeb took the lead, striding down the hallway once more.

The double doors were open, copious amounts of candles lit in the chambers, and it came as no surprise that every chair around the squared table was taken when they stepped inside. The four-member council had assembled.

"You may enter," Kado called out.

Aveoth noticed the way Kelzeb's shoulders stiffened as he stopped. He stepped next to him and glared at Kado. "As if I need your permission. You'd be amusing to me if you weren't so offensive. Bow—*now*." He cut his angry gaze to every face around the table, daring them to refuse.

The four rose quickly, Kado the last to stand, and lowered their heads. Kado glanced up first, his eyes unable to hide his outrage. He opened his mouth to speak but Aveoth cut him off.

"I've warned you before that I won't stand for any plotting you do together outside of the scheduled meetings I'm notified of in advance. I'm aware you gathered today in private." He stepped forward, pulling his sword. "Does anyone wish to challenge me? I'm prepared."

Heads lowered and remained there. Kado wouldn't meet his gaze anymore.

Long minutes passed. Aveoth wanted them to be uncomfortable and worried. The bastards were up to something, and he wasn't about to pretend otherwise.

"I had planned to discuss the breach of protocol with Kado, but I'm glad he overextended his authority once again by calling you together. I won't have to trust him to twist my words. I'll say it directly to you. Look at me."

Their heads rose, and he saw that none of them could avoid showing emotion. It ranged from anger, to resentment, to fear. Domb shot hateful glances at Kelzeb but his friend seemed to ignore them. Aveoth despised that Kelzeb had to suffer those looks from his own father. It pissed him off more though.

He glared at each of them, settling on Kado last.

"I am your lord, and I do not answer to you. Whatever you discussed today is irrelevant. Your duties do not include gossiping about why I brought a woman into my home. I'll assume that's what caused you to secretly hold a session today. Don't let it happen again—or prepare to raise your swords to the death."

"You *are* our lord," Kado ground out. "It is our duty to think of the clan's future. There is talk that you have a human breeding vessel. With all respect, we would like to discuss the possibility of you breeding with a Gargoyle instead."

Milgo glanced up. "Elco has offered Winalin in the human's place. It would be more appropriate. Your youngling would be a fine, strong addition to our clan."

Domb jumped on that. "She's fitting of a lord. Not some human breeder."

Aveoth was done. "Elco craves power, yet has never lifted his sword or performed duties to earn a place in our clan. He is here only because he was born at the cliffs, leaching off us like an infant at his mother's teat. That was acceptable until he became old enough to act like a responsible clansman. I refuse to promise him favors or status in exchange for the use

194

of his sister's body." He glared at each of them. "It's disgraceful for him to barter his own flesh and blood in that manner.

"Precious daughters and sisters, rare they may be, are to be mated to men who are excellent protectors and who will value their worth. They *will not* be bred and passed around to many, the way it was done in the old clan you fled from. That's why so few women survived in the old times. And it's a shame I have to explain this to the council. You better think long and hard about where you lost your honor—and try to find it once again. I'm done here. No more secret meetings. You're adjourned. Get your asses up and out of this room within thirty seconds of my exit."

He spun, storming out.

Kelzeb followed on his heels. They went up two flights of stairs before his friend whispered, "Would you like me to go back and make certain they emptied the chamber?"

"Fuck them. I made my point." He was furious. "I hope they challenge me or outright disregard my decree. I'm in the mood to make some heads roll."

"Sexual frustration will do that."

Aveoth growled.

Kelzeb quickened his steps and joined him at his side as they moved through the corridors. "Why are we heading toward one of the scout tunnels?"

"I need fresh air to clear my head before I return to Jill."

"I'll stick with you. Are you thinking about finding a VampLycan to kiss to see if she reacts the way Jill did?"

Aveoth halted, stunned by the question. "No."

"It might be a good idea. You need to discover if this is something new you're experiencing or if it's just a Jill thing."

"I don't want anyone else."

Understanding dawned in Kelzeb's steady gaze. "You are starting to care for her."

"Jill is going to be my mate."

"What if you can't convince her to agree?"

Aveoth inhaled deeply and exhaled. "I'm determined."

"What if that takes weeks or months? She seems like a strong-willed person."

"I'll wait for as long as it takes. I'm not letting her go. She's mine."

"This will be interesting. Just don't take off any of my body parts while we spar when you go crazy from wanting her and being denied."

A smile curved his lips. "Deal. Let's stretch our wings."

* * * * *

Jill turned the page of the book she'd taken from Aveoth's library. It was a classic she'd loved as a child about a magical city by the sea. The fantasy aspect of it appealed to her, since her reality had drastically changed in a matter of days.

Her mind kept drifting to the tall GarLycan lord, though.

She wished she could hate Aveoth, but her memories kept replaying only his good points. He'd beat up her kidnappers, saved her from plummeting to her death, chose her over a gorgeous Gargoyle woman...and she *liked* the way he looked at her most of the time. He seemed like a good man, albeit a scary one. The fact that he wasn't human was becoming less of a deterrent in terms of attraction.

Maybe I've lost my mind.

"Hello? Please don't be frightened," a woman's voice called out sweetly. "I'm Aveoth's mother. I'm going to open your door."

Jill gasped, turning her head as the bedroom door slowly opened.

A tall, regal-looking woman sporting a gown entered but immediately paused at the threshold. Her silky black hair was coiled atop her head in some intricate twists. She was pale-skinned, beautiful, and didn't look old enough to have an adult son.

The woman smiled and clasped her hands in front of her trim waist. "My name is Galihia. I'll stay here so I don't frighten you, child. May I ask your name?"

Jill put the book down and stood. "Jill." She swallowed hard. "You only look about twenty-five."

"You're too kind. I'm much older than that. Please sit and be comfortable, as you were. I wanted to meet the woman my only son has brought to live with him. My curiosity got the best of me. You're so pretty." Her gaze lowered, seeming to take in Jill down to her feet. "And dainty! You're adorable."

"Thank you?" Jill wasn't sure if that was a good thing or not.

"I am so happy to find you in this room."

"I'm not sure how to respond to that."

"My son put you next to his bedroom. That tells me that you're very special to him." She beamed, her beauty nearly radiant. "I am very happy for you both."

She remembered what he'd said about Lane. He'd kept his lover in a room on the lower floor. Maybe the woman thought they had gotten married or something. "Oh no." She shook her head. "I think you've got the wrong idea."

Galihia's smile faded. "Perhaps so. I'm still glad to meet you."

Good going. Jill hated to see the look of sadness her denial had put on Aveoth's mother's face. "I mean, I only just met your son very recently. I sleep in here and he's in there." She jerked her thumb toward the adjoining bathroom that linked their rooms. "We, um…" She closed her mouth. "I'm making a mess of this. I'm not like Lane. Is that a delicate enough way to put it? I don't want to shock you or something."

Galihia cocked her head, smiled, and then laughed. "I'm not a woman who shocks easily. I'm Aveoth's mother. He tends to be brutally honest and frank."

"Of course." Jill relaxed and took a seat. "Would you like to sit?"

"No thank you. I can't stay that long. Renna and I have plans in a bit. We're watching a movie together."

The name rang a bell. "That's the woman who's supposed to make me clothes. Aveoth mentioned her."

"She is family to myself and Aveoth. I don't know what I'd do without her. She takes care of me."

"Is she an indentured servant?"

Galihia appeared horrified. "Never! Her mate died, and she knew how lonely I was, so she came to live with me. She's my best friend, as well as my blood. You'll like her, and she will love you. She asked to come with me but I didn't want her to face my son's wrath."

Jill arched her eyebrows.

"I didn't get permission from him first to enter his chambers. It's not that he's mean. My son has a huge heart and he's a good man. It's just that he probably wanted to wait a bit longer before we were introduced. I hope I don't frighten you. We must seem so strange to you. Do you know anything?"

It took her a second to figure out what Aveoth's mother was probably hinting at. "You mean that he's a GarLycan? I do."

A smile returned to her face. "I'm so relieved to hear that. I didn't want to give any secrets away but I'm so glad, and also that he mentioned Lane to you. She was a sweet woman but they didn't have a spark. Do you understand?"

"I think I do. Aveoth said they got along but weren't close."

"It broke my heart because I had hoped he'd be less lonely when she came here, but that didn't happen. Did he tell you much about his childhood?"

"A little," she admitted. "I know he was taken and kept away from you by his father. He said he flew to you when he was young, just to see you, since it wasn't allowed."

She nodded, sadness entering her gaze again. "My mate was a cruel, heartless rock of a man." Tears filled her blue eyes. "My son was such a happy baby, always smiling, and he loved to be held. Then I watched the life drain out of him a day at a time as my mate destroyed the happiness around him, until he took him from my arms to live apart from me. You can't imagine the hope and fear I saw in his eyes when he flew to me that first time, as if I'd reject him too. My poor baby. I wanted to escape with him but there was nowhere to go. Abotorus would have tracked us to the ends of the Earth." She reached up and wiped at her tears. "He would have killed us both; he'd accused me of tainting our son with the *pathetic* emotion of love. The best day of my life was when Aveoth killed him. I know that might make you think poorly of me, but I lived for years worrying that he'd murder my son. Imagine that."

Jill bit her lip and stood. "My biological father is a piece of shit. I don't think badly of you. I used to dream up scenarios where he was dying and needed a kidney or something. I so wanted to watch him die, since I sure wouldn't give up a body part for him. He abandoned my mother when she was pregnant, and sent thugs to threaten her since he was so embarrassed that she'd given birth to me."

"You poor dear." Galihia approached, walking very slowly. "Where is your mother?"

"She died."

"I'm so sorry. Do you have siblings? Close family?" Aveoth's mother reached out her hand to her.

Jill took it. "No. It was just me and my mom. I'm alone now."

"No, you aren't. You have Aveoth and his family. I always wanted a daughter, and now I have one."

Jill let her go. "It's really not that way between us. We're not, um...we haven't... Crap. This is awkward."

200

Galihia was a tall woman, probably nearly six feet. She leaned down a little, bending at the waist to do so. "This room is for my son's mate. He put you here. That means he must have strong feelings, dear Jill."

"I barely know him."

"I watch a lot of television. There's not much else for Renna and I to entertain ourselves with. Human men are finicky creatures, seeming prone to stupidity, infidelity, and telling untruths. My son is nothing similar to them. He's intelligent, loyal, and honest. Did he explain what a mate is?" She went on before giving Jill time to answer. "He'll be faithful and loving to you until he takes his last breath. He knows what he wants, and that is you, dear Jill. He doesn't need months or years to decide. His choice was made the moment he brought you to this bedroom. You're no longer a part of the human world, so you need to open your eyes to see the differences. Do you understand?"

"I feel like I fell down the rabbit hole."

Galihia grinned. "I read that tale to my son when he was a child."

"He got the reference when I said it to him just after we met."

"Don't let the fear of the unknown dissuade you from seeing what is before you. I am biased as his mother, but I'm also truthful. Aveoth is an amazing man with a tender heart that beats beneath his breastbone. He hides his emotions in front of others because he must, but to you, he's the emotionally fragile boy who longed so much to be loved and held. Give yourself to him, and I promise he'd cherish you forever. Open up to him, and he will give you everything he is."

Tears filled Jill's eyes. "We're just so different."

201

"Are you truly? You're alone in this world. He feels that way because of his place in the clan and the expectations he's under as a lord." Galihia reached out and touched Jill's cheek. "He's longed for someone like you, dear Jill. He's the one who is truly afraid you'll reject *him*. Please don't hurt my son. You're his one chance at happiness."

"Why me?"

"I don't understand." Galihia frowned.

"I saw that Winalin Gargoyle person. She undressed in front of Aveoth and threw herself at him. I can't compare to her looks. I mean, she's a bitch. I get why he hates her, but he could have anyone. A Victoria's Secret model would be all over Aveoth. I'm not putting myself down, but I'm a realist. My looks draw men's attentions. I'm fit but I don't have any super-cool physical tricks up my sleeve or some supernatural beauty going on. I take after my mother. I can't shift or grow fangs. I was shocked when I found out my father wasn't human."

Galihia frowned. "What was your father?"

"A VampLycan."

The woman before her paled. It instantly alarmed Jill.

"I didn't know him. As I said, he was a piece of shit who abandoned my mom when she told him she was pregnant, and he sent thugs to threaten her every few years so she'd never tell anyone I was his. He was probably afraid she'd go after child support money, too."

"It's not that." Galihia's smile reappeared, but it didn't meet her eyes and looked forced. "Does my son know?"

"Aveoth got me from Decker Filmore. That asshole is my biological grandfather. He had jerks kidnap me from my work and they flew me to Alaska. I *really* hate that family."

"Never tell anyone else that your father is a VampLycan. Promise me."

"No problem. I'm not exactly thrilled about it."

Aveoth's mother clutched Jill's hands. "It will put you in danger. No wonder my son hasn't introduced us yet. He must be working on a solution to deal with this development. The full-blooded Gargoyles in our clan will outright reject having someone with any Vampire heritage as his mate. He's going to have to kill some of them." Her features softened. "He must love you deeply." Her full smile returned. "Don't you see? He's chosen you despite how much trouble it will cause him."

"It makes you happy that Aveoth is going to have to kill people?"

"We live in a violent world. Death is a part of it. My son will take out any threat to you or to your future. Never spare a moment of pity for those deaths. His father needed to die. There are cruel ones like Abotorus here. Appreciate my son's dedication to you, my dear. How many women can claim a man will do anything to keep her safe? He'd wage a war with his own clan for you."

Jill was quiet, thinking about that for several moments. "That's grim, but I get the point. Are you upset that I'm part VampLycan?"

"No. I'm happy that he found you, dear Jill. All that matters is that you are the one my son wants. I'm thrilled he's found you, and that you're his mate."

"I'm not his anything. It's too crazy to think it could ever work between your son and I."

"Why?"

Her mouth fell open but she closed it, swallowed, and freed her hands from Aveoth's mother's again. "I don't belong here."

"Was your life where you came from a very happy place? Were all your needs met? Was there a man who you loved with all your heart, who made you feel as if your life was complete?"

Jill was tempted to lie but that wasn't her. "No. My life sucked but I didn't feel like I'd been dropped in another universe." She eyed the woman's formal gown. "I'm not dressing like you. No offense. It's beautiful but aren't you hot? Uncomfortable?"

"You are to become the mate of our lord. That means you can demand change for our women. My mate never gave me any standing in the clan besides his official breeder. Aveoth won't do that to you. He'll listen to you and want you to be happy. Make that your first official decree after my son announces you to the clan. Demand we dress more casual in public."

"I'm sure that will go over well." Jill rolled her eyes.

Galihia laughed. "Probably not, but I know *I* would appreciate it. So would Renna. The most difficult thing for her to adjust to since moving to the cliffs has been the formal dress code women endure. I'm afraid that was my mate's doing. He felt it was indecent to reveal our limbs to his clansmen, and he decided pants decreased our femininity. Aveoth just hasn't changed it, but you could convince him to do so. He'll be a caring and devoted mate to you."

Jill sighed and sat down. "It's not that simple."

"It could be. Aveoth is an amazing man, as I said. I know I'm his mother but he has so much love to give if you'd only allow him the opportunity. Life here might be different from the one you left behind, but change is sometimes the best thing that can happen to us. May I give you some advice?"

Jill held her gaze, considering it. It wasn't as if she had a lot of friends here, and Aveoth's mother had been nice to her. "Please."

"Stop thinking so much and allow yourself to feel, dear Jill. Take a chance. Allow my son to bed you. Lycan blood runs through your veins. One trait that is *always* passed down is good instincts. Listen to yours. Are you attracted to him?"

"Yes."

"Are you afraid of him?"

"No."

"Do you think he'd harm you in any way?"

Jill shook her head.

"Why have you kept him distanced?"

"He has wings and can turn to stone. Plus, the whole we-have-nothing-in-common thing." She thought about mentioning the drugged kiss but decided not to, in case she also had to explain the afterward part. There was no way she'd admit Aveoth had gone down on her to his mother.

"Would you disqualify a human man because he had a scar or a limp?"

Jill frowned. "I see where you're going with this, but there's no real comparison between someone who limps and someone who can fly. They wouldn't give me bat babies if they knocked me up." She regretted saying that as soon as the words were out. "I mean—"

A snort of laughter came from Galihia. "Bat babies? That's funny. Our children don't have wings at birth."

"I'm so sorry. I didn't mean to insult you. You have wings too, right?"

"I do have the ability to fly, although I'm a bit rusty. I never leave the cliffs. Your lack of wings isn't an issue. They don't allow women to leave."

"Don't you feel like a prisoner?"

"No, dear. I'm protected and safe. I could ask for scouts to escort me for a flight over our territory if I really wanted to stretch my wings. You're so young, and you have no idea of the kinds of danger lurking out there in the world. I do."

"Aveoth said I was lucky to have survived as long as I have, since I don't smell human if I'm bleeding."

"You were hurt?"

"I ran into something and got a small cut. It was fine."

"You *are* very lucky to be alive. The danger to you is great without protection."

"I was raised in bad places. I know how dangerous the world can be."

"Humans are nothing." Galihia waved her hand. "I mean that on a danger scale. I watch your television. I could take dozens of bullets and survive, even if I didn't shell my body first. They'd bounce off if I hardened my skin. I can be hurt unshelled but I'd recover. I'm also stronger by far. Six of your humans could attack me and I'd win in a fight."

Jill glanced down her. "Not in that dress."

Galihia laughed. "Even so, dear. My wings are trapped in this gown, so I'd have to fight without them, but imagine a shelled fist slamming into a human attacking me. He'd feel as if he were hit with a sledgehammer." Her smile faded. "You are fragile and could be killed so easily. You're safer here."

"Even though Aveoth worries about his clan rising against him?"

"He shared that with you?"

She nodded.

"My son is a strong leader and the best swordsman in this clan. No one ever won against my mate, yet Aveoth did. He's a very skilled fighter. That alone has made many rethink challenging him, and the stupid die quickly here. He will never allow anyone to hurt you. Have faith in him. It's well placed if you give him a chance. I feel in my heart that you won't regret it. What do you have to lose? Your life has already changed. You won't be able to forget my son, or look at things the way you did before your eyes were opened to more than just the human world. Consider that carefully. Would you really be happier returning to where you were taken from? Or would you wonder what might have happened, and all the possibilities if you gave my son a chance?

"You did fall into your own rabbit hole." Galihia slightly bowed, lifted her head, and winked. "Enjoy the adventure. I must bid you my leave now."

Jill watched the woman turn and gracefully exit her room, closing the door behind her. She fell back on the bed and stared up at the ceiling, deep in thought.

Chapter Eleven

Aveoth reached the twin brothers and smiled. "Thank you for guarding Jill."

Chaz nodded. "Lady Galihia visited."

Aveoth stiffened. "I'll call her and see what she wanted."

"She asked to talk to your woman inside." Fray took a step back. "We couldn't tell her no, so we let her pass."

"Fuck." Anger gripped Aveoth.

"Sorry." Fray didn't look it. "She gave her word she wouldn't frighten, harm, or upset your guest. You know your mother. Could *you* turn her away?"

"She was here for about twenty minutes and left smiling." Chaz shrugged. "She claimed she adores your Jill and told us to let you know she expects you both for dinner soon."

"You have her approval," Fray added.

"You two may go. I appreciate you ensuring Jill's safety."

He opened the door, locked it behind him, and ran up the stairs. Jill's bedroom door was closed. He hesitated there, heart pounding. Had his mother upset Jill? He didn't believe she would, but after Winalin, Jill might be leery of all women at the cliffs. He raised his fist and tapped. "It's Aveoth."

"Come in."

He didn't hesitate. Jill sat up on the bed. The visit couldn't have been too bad. She didn't appear frightened or angry. "The guards I assigned outside said my mother came to see you."

"She's really nice, but it was a shock when she told me who she was."

He relaxed and leaned against the wall just inside the door. "I wasn't hatched from an egg. I mentioned having a mother."

Jill smiled. "It was the fact that she looks so young. She's really beautiful, Aveoth. I like her."

"I'm grateful." He wanted to go to her but stayed back. "May I ask what you two discussed?"

"A lot of things."

He cringed. "I hope it wasn't something embarrassing."

"Ah. Like that you drooled constantly as a baby and crossed your eyes a lot?"

Heat flushed his cheeks. "I did?"

Jill laughed. "I have no clue. You should see your face."

He pushed off the wall and slowly approached her. "I like it when you tease me."

She stood. "Your eyes are swirling silver and the blue is sparking up big time. They're beautiful. What are you thinking about?"

He halted. "You're the one who is beautiful, Jill."

"That's what happens to your eyes when you're turned on, isn't it? Your voice just deepened too."

"I could mask my emotions if you wish. I don't want to frighten you."

"Nice avoidance on answering my question there, Wings. Your eyes are mesmerizing when the colors are changing. I like them. I just wanted to know what you were thinking about to cause that reaction. How was your meeting?"

"As expected. I went flying with Kelzeb and Duster afterward to cool down. Gargoyles on the council tend to piss me off."

"Is Duster a man?"

"Yes. He's a GarLycan scout and a friend."

"How did the Gargoyles piss you off?"

"Political bullshit. They love to pretend they wield more power than they actually do. I had to remind them I'm in charge."

"Did you have to kill anyone?" She glanced down his body.

"No."

"That's a relief. Your clothes are black, but now I can stop imagining blood on them."

She amused him, and he grinned. "Not this evening." He noticed the book on her bed. "You were reading. I'm glad you found a way to spend your time."

"You really need a television and cable, Aveoth."

"I'll arrange it for you."

"Thank you. I like books but your collection is mostly classics or manly stuff I'm not really interested in. You have a ton of westerns and murder mysteries."

"I can order you books. The scouts go pick up the mail once a week, weather permitting."

"Winters are harsh here, aren't they?"

"Outside, yes. Inside, we're protected."

She got a strange look on her face.

"What is it?"

"Don't you go stir crazy?"

He shook his head. "We're a city built inside this mountain. You've been outside and seen how high we are. There are stairwells and levels from here all the way to the base. A lot of my clan consider the winter months a vacation."

"How is that possible? They're stuck indoors, right?"

"They are during bad storms, but that also means it's impossible for others to attack us. The scouts don't have to patrol as often, and I don't send anyone back and forth on missions."

"What kinds of missions?"

"I mentioned there are some Lycan packs I've assigned guardians to. They live there year-round to keep them protected from Vampire nests, human poachers, and to keep other packs from starting territory wars. Occasionally they request additional, help, so I send reinforcements. I also assign some of my clan to assist the VampLycans. For instance, recently a nest of Vampires came into this area. We helped deal with them."

"You didn't want them to be your neighbors?"

He decided to be completely truthful. "They broke laws, Jill. Kidnapped a VampLycan, and many human lives were lost. They wanted a war, and got one. My men also assist in rescues when we hear about lost humans in surrounding areas."

"Aren't you afraid they'll realize something is different about your people?"

"No. I have scouts fly over the area when it's dark, after the human rescue teams have had to call their search to a halt until daylight. We're able to locate the lost and then one of my men will land, pretend to be human, and lead them to the nearest group."

"I like that you care about humans." She took a step closer, stopped, then took another. "I think that's enough small talk." Jill crossed her arms over her chest and stared up at him.

"You appear nervous. What do you really want to talk about?"

"Your mom said some things that made a lot of sense."

"Like what?" He was more than curious. "Did she try to help you plot a way to talk me into returning you to your old life? It's too dangerous, Jill." His emotions ranged from anger at his mother to dread. He'd been certain his mother would like Jill, but knew she'd still be afraid of how the clan would react to her being human. His mother knew him too well, and knew that he'd absolutely refuse to have Jill sterilized to prevent an accidental pregnancy. "Please don't ask me again. I believe I could make you happy here if you stayed. Give me time and get to know me."

"That's kind of what your mother said."

He was surprised. "She did?"

"My life is never going to be the same, now that I am aware of people with extras and super powers."

He tried not to laugh. "Superpowers?"

"You fly and turn to stone, Wings. I'd consider those superpowers."

213

"Fair enough. Are you willing to give us time? Is that what you're trying to say?"

"I have questions, and I need you to straight-up answer them. No avoidance. Can you do that?"

"Yes." He motioned to the bed. "May we sit? Or would you prefer we go into the living area?"

"I'm good here." She sat on the bed, scooted over, and pointed for him to take a seat a few feet down the mattress.

He sat. "Ask."

"I thought you just wanted to hook up for a while. I even considered that maybe you wanted me just to have your baby, after you mentioned we could breed. What Winalin said implied you just planned to keep me long enough to give birth, then dump me, but your mom is convinced you want to make me your forever mate. Is that true?"

He groaned. His mother had ruined his plan of slowly gaining Jill's trust, making her care for him, and then breaking it to her. Jill wanted the truth but he worried she'd hate him if he gave it to her. They'd made progress. All that might be wiped away.

Her eyebrows arched. "Your face right now. I can't tell if you're pissed or panicking. Was she wrong?"

He refused to look away from her. "No, Jill. She wasn't. I wanted us to have more time before I brought up being mates."

"Wow. Okay." She glanced away then back at him. "You don't know anything about me."

"You're wrong. You're intelligent, strong-willed, have a quick wit, and you're compassionate. You're also beautiful, courageous, and I've never been so drawn to another woman in my life. I've wanted to protect and keep you since the moment you stepped off that jet and negotiated with me to beat on Decker's men." He grinned, still fond of that memory. "Most women would have cried after what they'd endured but you wanted to see both of them bleed. What's more, you meant it. Not once did you flinch away or beg me to halt hurting them. You're magnificent, Jill. I immediately began to fall in love."

She said nothing for long moments. "You know that's a little bit disturbing, right? I have anger issues. Most people don't think that's a good trait to have."

He chuckled. "Whatever you want to call it, it's extremely sexy to me."

Her lips curved upward a little and her eyes showed a spark of humor. "You said fall in love. I heard that."

He shrugged. "I'm part Lycan. We go with our instincts. Mine want to make our relationship a permanent one. My heart immediately opened to you." He reached up and placed his hand over his chest. "You're already in here, Jill."

Her gaze lingered on his hand before she peered into his eyes again. She sucked in a sharp breath. "Here's the deal. You're incredibly hot. And sweet. I've tried really hard to hate you but I'm failing to make it stick. I believe that what happened last night with that kiss wasn't something you did on purpose. You could have taken full advantage of me, but you didn't. I can't think of any other guy who wouldn't have gone all the way, considering the state I was in. It makes me like you even more. It's a big deal that you're not human...but I'm getting over that fairly quickly the more time I spend around you."

Finished, she sealed her lips.

"Are you going to give us a chance, Jill? Is that what you're saying?" He lowered his hand to his thigh, gripping it. He had hope.

She nodded. "I'm not ready to do this mate thing yet or have a bat baby, but the overriding desire to leave you isn't there anymore. Your mother said a lot of stuff that made me really rethink things."

"What did she say?" He silently promised to thank his mother at the first opportunity.

Jill took another deep breath and blew it out. She moved closer. "There's no way I'm ever going to forget you. I thought about the life I had, and what it would be like if you actually let me go. I'm pretty sure I'd regret not taking a chance to see what's between us." She scooted a little closer still.

He wanted to reach out, grab her, and put her on his lap, but refrained. She was coming to him. He just needed patience. He would find it for his Jill. She'd stopped with merely inches between them. She lowered her head, seeming to be staring at her lap.

"May I hold you?" He really wanted to.

She lifted her head, and he couldn't look away from her pale blue eyes. "My life wasn't easy because of Decon Filmore. My mom and I would move every time he found us. She was always afraid those thugs would kill me. End of problem. You see it on the news. Some men murder their own kids to avoid paying child support or because they get married.

216

Having a bastard kid causes issues in their new marriage. It's cold-blooded, but we're talking about a jerk who swore he loved my mom then dropped her like a bag of trash at the curb when she got pregnant. He wasn't a good guy.

"It was tough on us both, living that way. I'd make friends but then didn't dare contact them again once we'd fled. What if those thugs talked to them, lied to get them to give up our new address? They always found us eventually, but we could usually relax for a while in a new place. You know? After a while, making good friends just wasn't worth the pain it caused, knowing I'd lose them. I had people I worked with, neighbors, but I kept them emotionally distanced since caring meant pain."

He couldn't imagine the utter loneliness she spoke of. He'd always had Kelzeb. His childhood had been harsh but his best friend had always been at his side. There were others as well, who he'd trusted and grown bonds with. Duster. Fray. Chaz.

He reached out and put his arm around her. She didn't resist as he drew her closer until she leaned against him, her cheek pressed to his chest. He lowered his chin to the top of her head and placed a kiss there.

"I thought life couldn't get any worse...until my mom died. It hit me like a ton of bricks. I had no one. I had her cremated since it was all I could afford. I brought her ashes home to our shitty apartment and thought, one day I'm going to die too. No one is going to pay for me to be cremated. Her ashes would probably be thrown in the garbage, since I couldn't afford to encase them in some mausoleum. You can never get ahead and save money when you're on the run. Every dime might mean life or death if you have to move suddenly, so you don't waste it. Not to mention, if I put her somewhere permanent, who knew if I'd ever get to visit her since I had to keep moving. I had no clue if Decon would kill me once he'd found out she'd died. Like maybe he would feel he'd lost control, now that I had nothing to lose by legally going after him for money."

He hated the way her voice choked up, and he could smell her tears. He wrapped both of his arms around her, holding her tight. "Do you still have her ashes?"

"Yes."

"We'll retrieve them and bring them here, Jill. We entomb our dead. She'll have an honored place in our mausoleum that will be safe for you to visit whenever you wish." They didn't call it that, but he knew humans did. It was a resting place for the dead.

She sniffed. "Thank you. What I'm trying to say is that I've always wanted to find someone to love, and hoped they'd love me too. But a life partner was just a hopeless fantasy since I knew any sane person would dump me as soon as they found out about the sperm donor and his thugs. Instead, you beat their asses and sent them running away. So...I'll be damned if I'm going to blow any chance I finally have of being happy just because I'm afraid. I've faced every other challenge in life head on, so I can do it again. So what if you aren't human? I don't care about that anymore. Just don't break my heart, Wings. I'm willing to stick around and discover what we can be together."

"You won't regret it." He smiled. "I give you my word of honor."

She turned into him and slid her arms around his waist, holding on tight. He closed his eyes and felt his own tears flood behind his eyelids. They were rare. But Jill was going to stay with him.

"I'll make you happy, Jill."

She sniffed. "We need to have sex."

His eyes popped open and his body instantly responded. "I'm very willing to agree to that."

She laughed, keeping her head tucked. "I bet you are. We should figure out if we're compatible. Sex is important in a relationship if it's going to work."

"We're compatible." He had no doubt.

She finally lifted her head and peeked up at him. Her cheeks were a little pink. She was adorable. Discussing sex made her blush. He liked that a *hell* of a lot.

"You're big, Aveoth. I'm never going to forget you flashing me your goods to make your point. I definitely would have felt that."

He loved hearing his name on her lips. "I'll be gentle."

"A gentle giant, big guy?"

"I'll be whatever you need, Jill."

She licked her lips. "Will I be drugged again if you kiss me?"

"I don't know. I can avoid kissing you."

"I'd welcome a repeat of what happened when you kissed me; at least this time I know what I'm getting into. Besides, sex is always awkward the first time. At least in my experience. I'm not a virgin, but I admit I haven't had any long-term relationships. My record was dating the

219

same guy for a month before Mom and I were found, and I had to move. That drug will help break the ice. This time we'll go all the way."

He searched her eyes. "Are you certain?"

"Yes. Absolutely. Just don't forget I don't want to get pregnant, and um, I don't know how you mate but I've read shifter books. Is it sex and biting at the same time?"

"A bit."

She nodded. "No biting then."

"I can do that. Are you on any human contraceptives?"

"No. I haven't been able to afford health care in over a year, and I didn't exactly have the time to spend a day at a free clinic. Do you have condoms? Do those work with GarLycans?"

"I don't have any but I'm sure Kelzeb can find some for me."

She blushed again. "You have to tell him?"

He thought about it. "I know someone discreet. I'll call and ask him."

"Thank you."

He carefully released her and stood, hating to let her go. "Condoms. I'll be right back. Please don't change your mind."

"I won't. I'll shower real fast, though, and be waiting for you in my bed. How's that?"

"*My* bed. I want you there."

She smiled. "Your bed then."

"I'll hurry. This shouldn't take long."

He strode toward her door, yanking out his cell phone. He heard her laugh but just smiled. He was a man with a mission and Jill wanted him. His day had just vastly improved.

He went to the living area and contacted the one GarLycan he figured would have condoms.

"My lord, do you need Chaz and I to guard your quarters again?"

He cleared his throat. "Do you have condoms?"

Fray didn't hesitate. "I do."

"I need them."

"I'll grab a box and be right there."

"Don't tell anyone. I need your silence."

"No problem, my lord. I'll be at your lower door in five."

Aveoth ended the call and grinned. Jill would be his. He'd seduce her, convince her he was the right man for her and, when she was ready, he'd make her his mate. He'd deal with the clan later. It wouldn't matter who he had to kill to keep her.

He hurried down the stairs and unbolted the door, pacing outside as he waited. Minutes passed before he heard soft foot treads on stone. He faced Fray as he came around the corner. A huge grin adorned the man's features. He stopped near Aveoth, opened the cloak he wore, and offered him a black box with gold lettering.

Aveoth accepted it. "Thank you."

"You're welcome. Have you ever used them?"

"It's been a long while."

"Just open the foil, take out the condom, roll it down your shaft, and toss it away right afterward. Don't allow yourself to soften or the contents spill."

Aveoth nodded. "So not much has changed over the years."

Fray put his hands on his hips. "They come in different sizes now. These fit us better."

"That's good to know."

"I'll get you more. I can make a trip to Velder's gas station. They always keep them in stock there."

"I appreciate it. It won't draw much attention?"

"Not with *me* buying them. I like humans, so it's not unusual for me to keep a supply of condoms. They get pregnant easily."

An emotion Aveoth couldn't read flashed across Fray's features.

"What are you thinking?"

"Nothing, my lord."

Aveoth narrowed his eyes. "Answer." It was a demand.

"I was kind of hoping you'd found your mate."

"I have—but that's between just us."

"Then why the condoms? Ah shit. It's none of my business. Sorry."

"Our relationship is new. Jill just learned about our kind. She needs more time before we add a youngling into the mix."

"That's smart."

Aveoth cocked his head.

Fray shrugged. "Sorry again. My mouth gets me into trouble every time." He bowed.

"Don't worry about it. I always know where I stand with you and your brother. I appreciate your bluntness."

Fray lifted his head and winked. "I'm happy for you, my lord. Enjoy your evening."

Aveoth watched the GarLycan walk away and then turned, entering his home. He bolted the door and took a deep breath. A lot rested on the next few hours. He'd never felt pressure before regarding his sexual performance. Of course, if he was still secreting the hormones, that would make things smoother.

He ran his tongue over the roof of his mouth but he couldn't taste anything in his saliva. Then again, he hadn't the evening before, either. "Damn." He straightened his posture and headed upstairs. "Let this go perfectly."

Chapter Twelve

Jill felt extremely nervous. She had showered, dried off as quickly as possible, and then climbed into the middle of Aveoth's huge bed. There was a pile of pillows behind her where she sat, leaning against them. At first she'd thrown the covers back, exposing her nude body, but then she'd flashed to the memory of Winalin—the bitch. That flawlessness she'd seen had her under the covers and drawing them to her breasts.

"Not a competition and I'm better. I'm not a conceited cunt."

"Who are you talking to?"

Jill jumped and turned her head. "You didn't make any sound. I didn't hear you coming."

Aveoth walked to the side of the bed. His eyes were doing that swirling thing, turning mostly silver. They were sexy as hell.

"Who called you a conceited cunt?" He looked angry.

"No one. I was thinking about Winalin."

"Why?" He scowled.

"She might be a horrible person but she's got a seriously rocking body."

"I didn't notice." His gaze lowered to her chest, where she clutched at the bedding to hide her breasts. "There's no need to hide yourself."

"I like honesty in a man, Aveoth. There's no way you didn't notice that Winalin is perfect. She's got that supernatural beauty going for her. Porn producers would kill to get her on their payroll. Guys would pay a fortune to watch her getting bent by some plumber."

He laughed. "I am ashamed to say I understood that. She'd do it for humans, huh?"

"Yes."

"Good thing I'm not one." He moved over to the night table and set down a big box of condoms. "She only annoys me." His gaze swung to her. "Don't compare yourself to her. It's an insult that I won't allow. You're a thousand times more attractive in every way."

She glanced at the condoms. "You got them."

"Of course." He turned toward her. "What would make this more comfortable for you, Jill?"

"Kiss me."

"I plan to." He suddenly spun away and strode across the room. "Mood lighting."

She watched him as he bent near the fireplace in the corner and lit it. The flames grew as the logs caught fire, and then he stood, quickly moving to turn off most of the lights in the room. He went to a cupboard along one wall, opened it, and took out candles. She smiled as he lit them, placing them on various surfaces near the bed.

He was a romantic. That surprised and delighted her.

He finally came back to the bed. She could see him well enough but had to admit the dim lighting helped her relax a bit.

"Better?"

"Yes."

"Relax, Jill. You almost look frightened. I promise you pleasure."

"All guys say that."

"I'm not a guy."

He was her badass GarLycan. A lord of his clan. Her Wings. She nodded. "Strip." She pushed the covers down to reveal her breasts.

He growled low, his fascinating gaze fixing on them. "Beautiful."

"I'm pretty attached to them," she teased.

"I am as well." His voice deepened as he almost tore his shirt off.

She admired his bare chest. The guy had a lot of muscles. He was total eye candy, and the sight of him turned her on. He bent, tearing at his boots. He just tossed them aside, then straightened, both hands going to the front of his pants. Then he was the one teasing, as he very slowly unfastened them.

She glanced up, his heated, silver and blue flashing gaze locked on her face. He pushed them down and she broke eye contact.

The guy was hung. She'd seen it before, when he'd flashed her that morning, but he looked even bigger now, thicker, and she swallowed hard. There was that saying about bigger being better. She really hoped that was true.

He kicked away his pants and bent again, putting his hands on the bed. She stared into his eyes as he crawled to her.

"Don't be frightened," he rasped. "We'll take things slow."

She licked her lips and shoved the covers totally out of the way so they weren't between them. "I'm not afraid. Remember what I said about the first time being awkward?"

"How can I remedy that?" He stretched out beside her, the mattress dipping with his weight.

She had to lean back a little to not fall against him. "Kiss me. That should do it. You're really great with your mouth." Her memory flashed to his face between her legs. That helped turn her on more. The man had nearly licked her into a coma of climaxes.

"I'd like to avoid that in case the ravage hormones are still present. I want your mind clear when I make love to you, Jill."

"That's sweet. Really." She reached up and slid her hand along his cheek, then into his hair. His skin was warm and his black hair silky to the touch. "But it was hot in more ways than just my body feeling as if I were burning alive inside. My mind is clear right now when I say I want you, Aveoth. Please kiss me. I'm not one to do drugs, but I could get addicted to the one you produce. I want it...*and* you."

"I can't resist you, Jill." He sat up a little, leaned closer, and stared deeply into her eyes. "Are you certain?"

"Yes. Just remember the condom. I couldn't put a sentence together last night. It was all about my body craving for you to touch me. I wanted you inside me so much. I might actually beg, but take that minute to protect me, okay? No bat baby."

A smile ghosted his lips. "You have my word."

He leaned in and Jill closed her eyes. His lips lightly brushed hers. She reached up, clutching his shoulders, and parted her lips. He slid his tongue between them, deepening the kiss. He also wrapped his hand around her waist and tugged her down the bed a little. He put her flat on her back and moved her farther, off the mound of pillows. Then he came down partially on top of her.

Sensations swamped her. His chest was hot, firm against her breasts. Her nipples grew taut and sensitive. He shifted his weight and she was pretty sure he'd used his free arm to shove the pillows away from them. The telltale signs of the drug hit fast. Her body became inflamed from the inside, as if she had a fever. Her clit began to throb and she spread her legs, aware that the feeling would just increase. She moaned against his tongue and slid her hands to his back, raking her fingernails along his supple skin.

He growled, his chest vibrating against hers.

She turned her body a little, throwing one leg over his ass and trying to tell him she wanted him fully on top of her, not just partially pressing against her. He seemed to understand and broke the kiss, lifting up. Jill opened her eyes.

Aveoth's eyes were pure silver now, glowing, and they reminded her of liquid being melted in a pot. The light and darker silver swirled, as if being stirred.

"You're amazing."

"The drug is still present. I'm sorry."

"I'm not." Staring into his eyes helped her focus on them instead of her body's reactions. "I'm aching for you. We won't need foreplay if this keeps happening." She arched her hips, spread her legs wider. "I'm ready."

He put his hand on her thigh and lightly trailed upward. "Let me see."

She moaned but kept staring into his eyes. He hesitated before cupping her mound...but he just rested his hand over her pussy, not doing anything else.

"Please! Don't make me beg, Wings. That will piss me off." She bucked her hips.

He smiled. "I would never want that, my beautiful Jill." He rubbed, sliding his hand over her clit and slit. His expression changed in an instant and a deep rumble came from his chest. "You're not ready for me yet."

"I'm soaked. I ache. I need you!" Panting, she closed her eyes. The second she did, her body burned hotter. She dug her nails into him, pumping her hips against his hand in desperation to come.

He growled and slid his hand higher up her mound, then down. One of his fingers entered her and drove in deep. She moaned louder. It felt wonderful. She squirmed, wanting more. Aveoth gave it to her. He moved his hand, fucking her with his finger and using the pad of his palm to press against her clit. He quickened the pace until she arched her back, crying out his name as she came hard.

He tore his hand away and suddenly wasn't on her anymore. She panted, trying to catch her breath. She opened her eyes and turned her head, seeing his back to her. He was fumbling with the box on the night table. She heard him curse, the sound of cardboard ripping, and then he was back. She opened her body to him as he moved back over her. His eyes were still silver, alive with all those swirls, and bright blue flashed too. Streaks of them flared through. He caged her under him and she lifted her legs, wrapping them around his hips. He was such a huge guy. She might have found that more alarming if the need to be fucked wasn't so strong.

He slid a hand between them. She didn't look down, unwilling to break eye contact. Those eyes of his were mesmerizing. *Beautiful.*

Magical. Amazing. He could be one of the wonders of the world, all because of his eyes.

"You're mine, Jill. I won't bite—but you're mine," he rasped.

She felt the thick tip of his cock press against her pussy. He pushed forward, entering her with care. She closed her eyes, moaning. He was so big. She could feel her body taking him but it was a tight fit.

Aveoth had broken out in a sweat. Jill felt so fragile under him, and he was terrified he'd hurt her if he went too fast. He pushed his dick in a little more and groaned. She was small but she sheathed his shaft perfectly. He was careful to keep most of his weight off her, using just enough to keep her pinned. He needed to be in control of her movements and his own.

He withdrew a little and pushed in deeper. She was so wet, hot, and welcoming. All those Lycan instincts he kept leashed beat at his insides to be freed. *My mate. Bite. Mark her so everyone knows she's mine!*

Her moans and the way she wrapped her legs around him, combined with the pleasure of being inside her, almost snapped his control. His gums ached as his fangs lengthened and the skin over his wing seams swelled, threatening to split open to allow them to come out. Every inch of his skin tingled as he worked his way inside her pussy deeper, fucking her slowly. Inch by inch her body adjusted to him, until he was fully seated inside her snug confines. He froze there.

"Yes!" She dug her nails into the skin along his back, near his shoulders. She bucked her hips, urging him to move. "Aveoth!"

He withdrew and began to thrust in slow, long lengths. She was perfect, pure pleasure, and his seed threatened to spill at the sound of her moans growing louder. Her short fingernails were kneading his skin, her hard nipples rubbing against his chest as he rocked a little faster against her.

Her muscles clenched even tighter around his shaft and she cried out, climaxing. He stopped trying to hold off his own release and let himself follow her. He lost his mind in the blinding, hot ecstasy that ripped through his body.

All control slipped, good intentions gone.

The haze lifted when he stopped shooting his seed into the condom protecting his Jill from pregnancy. The delectable taste of her blood was on his tongue…and he realized his face was buried in the crook of her throat.

Aveoth was horrified, and he gently withdrew the tips of his fangs from her skin. He licked frantically, hoping like hell he hadn't damaged her, and that he was healing her skin. He lifted his head enough to glance down at the wound, relieved it was just two puncture marks and that he hadn't done worse.

He bit his tongue, not caring how it hurt, and licked at her again to cover the bites with his blood. It had worked on her forehead. He pulled back again, watching them closely.

Jill stroked his hair with one hand, her legs still locked around him, and she was breathing heavily under him. She made a slight noise but it didn't sound pained. He dared to look at her face then. Relief swept through him a second time when she smiled. Her pupils were a little dilated, her skin flush, and her other hand brushed against his wing, her fingertips caressing the area where they connected to his body...

Fuck! He broke eye contact with her to glance at his arm. His skin was a little grayish in color but he hadn't shelled overly much. He panicked further until he remembered the condom. Jill was at least safe in that regard.

Instincts won't be denied, no matter how strong-willed you are.

His mother's warning, one she'd told him countless times, echoed inside his head.

No shit, Mom. He'd tried to mate Jill, despite planning to put that off until the timing was right.

Jill rolled her hips and moaned. "More."

She was under the influence of the ravage hormone he was secreting. That was probably why she wasn't raging at him for biting her or fucking her with his wings out. He stared into her eyes. Lust and desire were there. She clawed at him with her fingernails and tightened her hold around his shoulders, grinding her pussy against him.

"Please, Aveoth." She struggled under him, frantically trying to urge him to keep fucking her.

He wanted to, but fear that the condom would break and release the mating chemicals that would be present in his sperm had him withdrawing his dick from her body.

She protested, fighting him. He was afraid to bruise her if he had to manually force her to unwind her limbs from him. He stared into her eyes, using his gifts in a way he rarely did. He focused hard on her and pushed toward her mind to reach her.

"Let me go, Jill."

She went still under him. Slowly, she opened her legs so they weren't tangled with his, and her arms fell back so they were splayed on the bed next to her head.

He hated the way her breathing slowed as she peered into his eyes, all emotion wiped from her face.

Aveoth moved fast, sliding down her body, and he knew the moment the thrall was broken, when he looked away from her. She tried to sit up, grabbing at his arms.

He gripped her legs in his hands and pinned them open on the bed, burying his face between her thighs. She cried out as he placed his mouth against her clit and licked. Her hands tangled in his hair and she moaned loudly.

He made her come over and over, until she went lax in his hold.

Aveoth lifted his head, licking his lips. Her taste was addictive as hell. He was almost sorry that she'd passed out. He studied her peaceful face while she slept, and then sat up. The condom was still on since his dick hadn't softened. The sight of it made him grimace as he reached down to carefully remove it. It was messy as hell, since he'd filled the damn thing with his seed.

He climbed off the bed but took a moment to cover Jill, since her legs were still splayed open. She looked vulnerable without him over her, and he couldn't walk away, even just into the bathroom with her in that state. He hurried in there to throw the condom in the trash and wash off his stiff shaft. He could smell the difference in his semen, needed to remove all trace of it from his body. There was no doubt now that he'd secreted the mating chemicals.

He sheathed his wings inside his body and wet a towel to wash the blood from his back, from his wings ripping out in the first place.

He hurried back to the bedroom to check on Jill's throat. The only evidence of the bite left was his bloodied saliva drying on her skin. He studied her completion, sure he hadn't taken much of her blood, since her coloring was good. He adjusted her body under the sheet he'd thrown over her, then lay down atop the cover, rolling her onto her side and curling around her, holding her tight.

He could have hurt her. It dampened his lust and his throbbing dick calmed, eventually softening. "I'm so sorry, baby. I promised not to bite."

She slept peacefully, breathing slow and steady.

He kissed the top of her head. She felt small and fragile curled into his arms. He probably should clean her while she slept so she'd be more comfortable, but he just needed to hold his mate. It bothered him that material was between them so he carefully pulled it out, plastering his skin against hers. He wanted to keep her warm and safe. He also hoped the hormone stopped being produced every time he kissed her.

The phone on the nightstand vibrated a while later and he rolled, reaching for it. A quick glance at the caller ID revealed it was Kelzeb. "What?"

"I just beat the shit out of Elco. I thought you'd want to know."

Aveoth sighed. "What did he do to piss you off?"

"He came to me about you denying his sister over a human, since I'm your advisor. I kept calm until he started throwing out threats and mentioned the Gargoyle Council is on his side. The prick has been talking to them."

Aveoth wasn't surprised. "How angry were you?"

"He'll live, but he won't be leaving his quarters for a few days. Your little chat with the council didn't do much good." Kelzeb sighed. "They are plotting trouble, Aveoth. *They* might be close-lipped, but Elco is a loudmouthed idiot. He implied they're going to force you to step down in public. And Tork's newly birthed son is being introduced to the clan tomorrow…"

Aveoth ground his teeth together. "I forgot about that with everything that's been going on."

"I figured. I've handled all the last-minute details. It's at three o'clock. I hope you don't mind, but I stopped by Renna's home earlier and gave her a general description of your Jill. A gown will be ready for the event, but she'd like to actually measure her. Can you take her there now?"

He turned his head, staring at Jill slumbering. "No. I will first thing in the morning."

"Now would be better."

"She's sleeping beside me. I'm still giving off the hormones when I kiss her. I'm hoping it stops, now that my body believes I've mated her."

Kelzeb hesitated. "What does that mean?"

"Use your imagination. I was wearing a condom, though, so the bond didn't take."

"Shit. That good, huh?" Amusement laced his voice. "I'll assume you got carried away, since I doubt you wanted to go mostly Gargoyle during sex with her. Did it frighten her?"

"No. The hormone helped. She was focused on other things."

His friend chuckled. "Bond with her. Shit is already hitting the fan. Make it official tomorrow after the ceremony for the baby. We'll have two new clan instead of one. That way, no one can whine about her anymore. It will be a done deal."

"They'll still whine."

Kelzeb laughed outright. "True, my friend. But I won't have to hear anyone asking me to make you rethink having Jill in your home. I've warned our trusted to expect some trouble. We stand with you if the council decides to challenge you."

"I appreciate it."

"Nobody wants Kado and his group in charge. One more thing."

"What?" Aveoth rolled, watching Jill sleep. She looked peaceful.

"Hawk stopped me in the hallway on my way home from beating Elco's ass. It seems Gorzak was approached by the council to challenge you for leadership."

Aveoth felt sadness. The Gargoyle had lost his Lycan mate some years ago, and had become remote. They'd taken him off work rotation. "That was low of them to go to a man who feels he has nothing to lose."

"Hawk was pissed. They are good friends, and he felt they were trying to take advantage of his grief. Gorzak ordered them to leave his home."

"He doesn't care enough to fight for anything. Did they approach Hawk too?"

"He thinks they knew better. He says he would have challenged whoever approached him...and would have handed you their head as a gift. I see where Chaz and Fray get their twisted sense of humor. He appeared disappointed that they didn't pull him into their plotting so he could kill someone."

"He's still dealing with his own grief of a lost mate."

"True. I'll let you go. We'll speak in the morning."

"Thanks." Aveoth hung up. He went to put the phone on the night table but then made another call. His mother answered on the fifth ring.

"I hate this invention. Couldn't my son speak to me face to face?"

He smiled but his humor faded fast. "You came to see my Jill. Why?"

"You hadn't brought her to me. I approve of her. Not that it would matter, but I do. She's sweet and brave."

"She is so much more than that. The time wasn't right for you to meet her though."

"You're wrong. My timing was perfect. She needed a woman to speak to."

He would concede to her wisdom. "Thank you. She's giving me a chance to show her we're right for each other."

"I'm glad, my son. Renna and I are sewing a dress for her right now for tomorrow's welcoming event. We're making it extra special, in case you announce her as your mate."

He couldn't help but smile. "Thank you. I need to go. I love you."

"I love you too, but we need to discuss one more thing before you end this call."

"What?"

"Tell her the truth about you, my son. All of it. I know her secret. She should know yours as well."

His heart sped up and he gently eased out of bed, striding to the bathroom. He closed the door. "She told you who her father is?"

"Yes. It came out in conversation. She promised me that she wouldn't tell anyone else. I explained Gargoyles hate anything with even a drop of Vampire blood. Did you choose her because you feel real emotions for her, or are you using her?" Her voice grew cold. "Tell me you're not like Abotorus."

"I'm *nothing* like him." Rage tightened his chest enough to make it difficult to breathe. "How could you ask that? Even think it?"

"It's something he would have done. He would have used her to hide his own secrets." Her voice softened. "I apologize but I had to speak my concern. She's a tender woman who has seen a lot of pain. Protect her heart. It's delicate."

"I would never hurt her. I treasure Jill."

"I'm glad. Some will challenge you. Kill them all, and be brutal enough to spread fear throughout the clan to anyone who even *thinks* of

238

using your mate against you. They respect savagery. In that regard, I encourage you to be similar to my mate where the clan is concerned. You must survive and thrive. You're my heart, Aveoth."

He closed his eyes and his anger dissipated. "I know. You've done everything to protect me and sacrificed so much."

"I wanted us both to live. You need to mate her and tell her everything, Aveoth. All of it. Make it a true mating of the heart. She'll protect your secret. In order for her to love all of the man, she needs to know who you truly are."

"I know."

"Go be with her. Show her how amazing my son is."

The line clicked and the call ended.

Aveoth returned to the bedroom, placed the phone on the night table, and got back into bed to hold Jill. Tomorrow they'd talk. His mother was right. He needed to tell Jill everything.

Chapter Thirteen

Jill woke warm and happy. Aveoth's big body radiated heat along her back and the weight of his arm anchored around her waist made her smile. Memories of the night before left no morning-after regrets. They had sexual chemistry by the truckload.

She wiggled a little to get onto her back to be able to see him, staring at his handsome face on the pillow they shared. He looked younger while he slept and his short hair was messy. The bedding was lowered to their waists so she got to take in his chest and shoulders. He had the best body. Overall, she decided she was one lucky woman. Everything about Aveoth was sexy.

He'd bitten her, but she wasn't mad. The sex had been off-the-charts hot and amazing. Capital A. Maybe O, since he'd made her have a lot of orgasms. She grinned thinking about that. There was a lot to be said for a supernatural being. He was fantastic at a lot of things, sex included. Part of her wanted to watch him sleep but her bladder urged her to get out of bed.

He stirred and a low growl came from his throat when she carefully extricated herself from him and climbed out of bed. "Where are you going?"

"Bathroom. I'll be right back."

She streaked naked across his room and closed the door, grinning. She hurried but took a minute to brush her teeth. A check of her throat amazed her. The skin was tender to the touch where he'd bitten her but there wasn't even a bruise remaining. It seemed he had magical healing abilities when he licked her.

It was tempting to wrap a towel around her body but then she decided against it. They had passed the modesty phase after he'd spent a lot of time with his face between her legs two nights in a row. She just opened the door.

And there stood Aveoth, in all his naked glory, inches from the door.

She allowed her gaze to wander down him.

"Go get in bed. I'll join you in a minute. Don't get dressed. I'm not done with you yet." His voice came out a little raspy and a whole lot seductive.

She looked up and found him smiling. She couldn't help but return it with one of her own. "I think I'm really going to become a morning person, living with you, if you keep ordering me to get back into bed."

"Good. I will have to reschedule my life to start meetings later in the day. I look forward to it. Now let me pass and I'll be right back."

She stepped around him and heard the bathroom door close behind her as she got back into bed. This time she didn't cover up. He was in there for a few minutes and when he came out, he joined her by spreading out on the bed next to her. Then he rolled, startling her and taking her flat to her back. He adjusted his body, pinning her under him. She laughed, opening her thighs to fit his hips between them.

"You feel happy to see me," she teased. "Do you always wake up hard?"

He chuckled. "I do when I'm with you."

241

She reached up and slid her fingers into his hair, lifting her head to go for his mouth. He pulled back a little to avoid kissing her.

"What's wrong? I brushed my teeth."

"So did I. It's just that I don't want you taken over by my hormones."

She understood. "I can still kiss you though. Let me have your neck."

He hesitated, and the color changes in his irises flashed a lot of silver. "I'm not sorry I bit you, but I will apologize for losing control."

"It made me come really hard. I was afraid your fangs would hurt but it turns out the biting does it for me."

Brighter silver burst in his eyes like mini fireworks, overshadowing the blue. "I treasure you, Jill."

"I think I feel the same way about you. I remember the wings you sprouted, too. They're so soft to the touch."

"Again, I lost control. I apologize."

"Don't." She meant it. "They're a part of you. Of course, I probably should ask if that's going to be a problem if I'm ever on top while we're having sex. Does it hurt you if you're on your back with your wings out?"

He grinned. "If you're on top, I won't care if I feel a little discomfort at my wing joints. Last night was special. I don't usually lose control of my body that way."

She stared into his eyes. "You're confusing me again. Total honesty, remember?"

"I got the urge to mate you, and it was so strong I lost control. The condom protected us from bonding though."

"How do GarLycans mate?"

He hesitated.

"Is it terrifying? Horrible? Painful? Traumatic?"

"No."

"Then spit it out."

He chuckled. "We should discuss this later." He caressed her with his hand.

"Avoidance. You chose not to kiss me so I can still think. Answer."

His expression grew serious. "We softly shell our skin, our wings come out, and we bite during sex. The taste of your blood, along with my partially shifted state, will trigger my body to producing mating hormones. The condom prevented them from reaching you. Otherwise your body would be changing right now."

"How?"

"It's difficult to explain, but those hormones alter a woman on a DNA level. You'll carry my scent. Gargoyle sperm is also strongest when we're partially shifted, so it increases the chances of pregnancy."

She carefully considered his words, trying to remain calm. "DNA level? You mean my body physically changes? Do I eventually turn into what you are?"

"No. You'll never have wings or the ability to shell. Mating sperm will mark you as mine." He hesitated, seeming to think. "Your scent will change, so you smell like me. It won't be temporary or something you can wash away. Your cells will modify enough to carry parts of my DNA so the scent stays."

"Like a disease?"

He frowned. "No. Diseases make you ill. A mate makes you stronger. When we do mate, I'll feed you my blood from time to time. We slice our skin and have our mates drink it, usually from a cup. My blood will give you a better immune system and your ability to heal will increase. Your lifespan will vastly lengthen, too. Drinking from me will repair you on a cellular level, to prevent aging the way you are now."

Shock coursed through her. "Wow. *That* doesn't sound bad."

He smiled. "I'm glad."

"So I won't turn into an old lady if I stay with you?"

"No. I should tell you that Gargoyles live for millennia."

She was glad to be pinned under him at the moment. "Thousands of years? Is that right?"

He nodded. "The clan some of the Gargoyles here left to form ours had a lord who was nine millennia old."

That shocked her again. "Nine thousand years old? Shit! Can *you* live that long?"

He shrugged. "I'm a GarLycan. Our race has only been in existence for two centuries. My mother was one of the first babies born from the union of a Gargoyle and a Lycan. I swore to never reveal her age. You've seen how young she looks. We age almost like humans until we hit adulthood, when it slows. Of course, we're larger than typical human children are."

A thought hit her. "How much did you weigh at birth?"

"I think nine pounds, my mother said."

"That's pretty big but not terrifying."

He smiled. "Your being so human might help with a smaller birth weight. The child will be half yours. I bet you were petite at birth."

"Five pounds, six ounces."

He raised his hand, looking at it.

She laughed. "You're imagining how tiny that is, aren't you?"

He nodded, staring into her eyes.

"You have big hands...along with big everything else. Let's stop talking about babies. I'm not ready for that. What's the lifespan on a Lycan?"

"We'll go over all this later. I promise not to die on you within the next thousand years at least. I want to spend a lot of intimate time with you."

She smiled. A thousand years should have scared her but it didn't. Her entire life had been all about temporary homes, friends, and jobs. He was offering her what seemed like forever. "Kiss me."

He avoided her lips. "I don't want you drugged. Today we have an event to go to."

Wariness and dread filled her in equal measure. "What kind of an event? More judging?"

"A celebration. A GarLycan named Tork mated to a Lycan while he served as a guardian over her pack. He brought her here during her pregnancy and their son was born last week. I will formally introduce and welcome him as a member of my clan. There will be food served and social niceties."

She laughed.

"What's amusing?"

"Social niceties? That's an odd way to put it. Kind of funny. As opposed to what? Violence and death?"

He grinned. "Not during a welcoming ceremony. Everyone is expected to be on their best behavior since mates and children will be present."

Her humor died. "Shit. I'm going to have to put on one of those old-fashioned dresses, aren't I?"

"I apologize now, but yes."

"We need to talk about that."

"Later." He nuzzled her face, going for her throat.

She moaned as his lips lightly teased the sensitive skin under her ear. "Yes."

His hand stroked her thigh and lifted it. She curled it around his waist, feeling the hard length of his cock nudge her pussy. It didn't take much for Aveoth to get her hot. The feel of him over her, his teeth raking her skin, had her hurting for him to be inside her.

"Lose the old-fashioned dresses for something more modern for women and I'll be your mate," she teased.

A rumble came from his throat, his chest vibrating against hers. His scent filled her nose and the ache between her thighs increased. Not only could the guy make some magical aphrodisiac drug with his mouth, but he smelled like sex and sin. His lips left her throat.

"I'd make that deal if you were serious."

She stroked his warm skin, loving touching him. "I'm all about negotiations in bed."

"You're going to drive me insane, Jill." He nipped her throat with his fangs.

It didn't hurt. Instead, a jolt of pleasure radiated straight to her clit. "Bite," she encouraged.

"You're going to make me lose control again." He lifted his head, staring into her eyes. His were molten silver, their light and dark shades moving fluidly. "Don't say things like that right now, with you naked under me. You're being playful. My mind knows that, but my instincts don't. You tempt me too much, Jill. Don't fool around with my heart."

It hit her then like a ton of bricks. She was falling in love with him.

He was a bit scary, there were a lot of unknowns about how life would be with him...but she already knew she never wanted to let him go. Her instincts were riding her to make their union a permanent one. He could belong to her forever.

"I always face things head on," she said, as much to herself as to him. "Do it, Wings. Make me yours."

Blue flooded his eyes, wiping out the silver. "Don't joke."

"I'm not." She arched her neck to expose her throat. "I hope I don't get pregnant. I'm not ready for that...but you explained how the mating happens. It's a risk I'm willing to take. I'm in it for the long haul, Aveoth. Are you? Just promise not to break my heart. No cheating."

"I give you my solemn vow. You'll be my everything, Jill." Silver sparked in his eyes, overtaking the blue. "I will protect and love you until my dying breath, and even beyond that."

Tears filled her eyes. "I swear to do my best to make you happy. I already can't see life without you, and I don't think I ever want to. We're so different...but we'll face whatever comes together."

"Put your hands over my shoulder blade," he rasped. "I need to slightly shift. Are you ready?"

"Yes."

She slid her hands into place and felt smooth, supple skin. It swelled a little under her fingertips and then seemed to part, soft velvety wings slowly sprouting outward. She smiled as she brushed her fingers over their velvety surface. God, he was amazing. She watched over his shoulders as they grew outward, spreading wide.

"Look at me."

She tore her attention from his black wings to study his face. The tan skin paled a little, getting a slightly gray tinge. She reached up with one hand, caressing his cheek. He was still warm and soft but the texture of his skin had become slightly smoother.

"Are you certain? This is what I need to look like when I mate you."

She was falling for him even deeper. He looked concerned about scaring her. "You're so sexy." A thought hit, and she grinned. "This gives new meaning to the phrase rock hard, doesn't it?"

He chuckled. "I'll be gentle."

"I know you will."

She adjusted her legs, hooking him better around his waist. She rubbed her calves along his ass. The exposed skin there was warm but felt a little similar to soft plaster. It wasn't an unpleasant sensation, just strange. She trusted Aveoth though. He wouldn't hurt her.

"Do it, Aveoth. Make me yours."

"Are you absolutely certain? There's no undoing this."

A small part of her panicked, but then a calmness spread through her, taking the panic away as she stared into his eyes. "I'm sure. I'm never going to feel this way about anyone else. I want to grow old with you, for however long that takes. Life won't be boring."

He adjusted his hips and his hand teased her clit. Pleasure spread through her limbs. She was wet, ready, and wanted him. "Now, Wings. I don't need foreplay."

He gripped his shaft and pressed the tip against her pussy. "I'll treasure you forever, keep you safe, and love you, Jill."

"I promise the same."

He released himself and came down on her, his hips surging forward as he entered her. Jill threw her head back and moaned. He was big and really hard. That joke about him having a rock dick suddenly felt like reality, but it didn't hurt. He slowly began to move in and out of her, gentle and slow.

"I'm not that delicate," she got out, using her fingernails to dig into his shoulders to urge him on. She wanted to kiss him but remembered how he didn't want her exposed to the chemical. She bit her lip instead as he thrust into her deeper, moving over her faster. "Yes!"

Aveoth tried to keep some control. Jill *was* delicate, despite what she claimed. His instincts were riding him to drive into her welcoming body and bite her. She tossed her head and he struck when her throat was exposed.

He kissed her, his fangs raking over her skin. She moaned louder, her legs locking tighter around his waist. He ground his hips in a way that had him riding against her clit as he fucked her harder. She clawed at him, her vaginal muscles clenching around his shaft. His balls seemed to swell and he knew it was time.

He licked her skin, then bit.

She cried out when his fangs punctured her and he felt her climaxing. He fought to keep moving, driving into her as the taste of her blood filled his mouth. She was so sweet, so incredible. His skin tightened, tingled all over his body. He was shelling a little more but he couldn't stop as he started to come. He pounded into her deeper, stilled and released his semen. All thought ceased as ecstasy took over.

He wasn't certain how long he remained in the haze of rapture, but when he stirred, he instantly adjusted his weight to take some off Jill. She was clinging to him, panting. He withdrew his fangs, licking the bite, and used a fang to tear at his tongue and induce his own bleeding. He kept licking her until the puncture wounds healed.

My mate. My Jill. Mine forever.

"Damn," Jill chuckled. "That was so hot. I just came like two or three times."

He smiled and lifted his head, checking on her throat first. It was healed. He stared into her eyes and unshelled his body, his skin softening. "Did I hurt you at all?"

"Nope. Next time I'm on top though. You get heavier when you shell."

"I apologize."

"Don't. I'm not complaining. It was only an observation. Your mattress is really soft and I just sank into it a little more."

She was amazing. He'd been taught that humans lost their sanity when they discovered Gargoyles existed, and she'd been raised believing she was completely human. But Jill made jokes and didn't seem frightened at all by the way he'd just claimed her. She wasn't terrified of him with his wings and partially shelled. He reached up and stroked her hair back from her face.

"We're mated."

"I don't feel any different."

"It takes time." He lifted up and carefully eased off her, sliding his wings into his skin. He lay to the side of her and placed his palm over her stomach.

She turned toward him and placed her hand over his. "What are you thinking about? Do you feel regret?"

He hated to see the doubt in her gaze. "Never. I want our bond to be strong. Will you drink some of my blood? I don't want the calling to hit you."

"What's that?"

"It's something that happens when a mating bond isn't strong. If you begin to sweat, tell me right away. To you, it'll just feel like a spike in temperature, but you'll put off a scent that will draw unmated males to want to have sex with you." Rage burned through him at the thought of anyone attempting to touch his mate. "You need to drink my blood. My entire clan will be around you today. You won't leave my side, but I would hate to have to kill someone with children present."

She curled up on her side, her legs resting against his own. "You didn't mention this calling thing before."

"I just thought of it. I'm taking you out of my home today, around other males."

She crinkled her nose. "Blood, huh?"

"Yes. It won't be too terrible. You *are* part VampLycan."

"Don't remind me of the sperm donor. Not now. Today is amazing so far."

Aveoth noted the teasing way she looked at him, and he smiled at her. "Stay here."

He let her go and rolled out of bed, strode to his kitchen, and got a goblet from the cupboard. He took the time to wash and dry it since they'd sat for decades untouched. He reentered the bedroom, grabbed one of his daggers, and approached the bed. Jill had sat up in bed and had the covers over her lap. Her expression amused him.

"It won't be that bad, Jill. I promise."

"Do I have the liver-and-onions face? My mom used to make them sometimes because she was a freak who loved them." She grimaced. "So gross."

He sat next to her and grinned. "Liver and onions?"

"Never had that?"

"I can't say I have."

"Lucky you. Trust me. If someone ever offers that to you for dinner, just say no."

He gripped his dagger and crossed his legs, placing the goblet against his ankles to keep it upright and steady. His gaze held hers. "I'll cut, bleed into the cup, and then you drink it."

"I almost wish I had fangs right now. You biting me was sexy." She glanced down. "Although that goblet is beautiful, those designs in the glass. It looks expensive."

He shrugged. "They're very old. That's all I know. I inherited them from Lord Abotorus after his death. This is the first time I've used one."

"Is it like the official blood-drinking glass?"

She always amused him, and he laughed. "It is for us. Are you ready?"

"Never, but go for it anyway. It can't be worse than my twenty-first birthday. I hit a bar with some work friends and each of them bought me a different drink, since I was legal. Some of them were downright gross, and man was I sick the next day. Lesson learned."

He sliced into the meaty part of his arm with the dagger tip and held it over the goblet as he bled. He glanced at Jill, hoping she handled the sight of blood well in the daylight. She watched, looking a little pale, but didn't move away. His Jill had courage. He put down the dagger, filling the cup a fourth of the way before his wound healed enough to stop bleeding. He held it out to her, peering into her eyes.

She accepted it with both hands. They trembled slightly so he gently cupped them. "My blood is yours, mate."

She nodded. "Um, thank you."

He chuckled. "Just down it. You should handle it well. You're not fully human and you're already changing."

"So your super-sperm will help my body take blood?"

He laughed again, loving her sense of humor. "Yes."

"Down the hatch, then."

He released her and watched as she lifted the goblet to her lips. She closed her eyes, took a deep breath, blew it out, and then began to drink his blood.

A warmth spread through Aveoth's chest as she kept swallowing. His mate was accepting his blood. It was as it should be.

She finished, and had a dazed look on her face when she opened her eyes. A little blood remained on her upper lip and he leaned forward, kissing her. She stiffened for a moment but then kissed him back. He pulled away before deepening the kiss, even though he wanted to make love to his mate. They didn't have time. He needed to take her to his mother and Renna to be fitted for her gown.

"Are you well?"

She held his gaze. "Yeah. That was weird. Blood is thicker than water, for real, but I'm fine."

"Let's shower, and then I'll take you to my mother's chambers."

"Why?"

"You need something to wear."

"I was totally serious about the old-fashioned dresses. They have to go."

"We'll work on it together. I promise."

"Okay. I'm not wearing a corset. That's final."

"Agreed. Go jump in the shower and I'll join you in a minute." He sat up and climbed off the bed, taking the goblet and dagger with him. He also snagged his cell phone on his way back to the kitchen.

He contacted Kelzeb first. His friend answered slightly out of breath.

"What are you doing?"

"Sparring with Fray. What's up?"

"I'm mated."

His friend was silent for a long second, then exclaimed, "Congratulations! I'm happy for you."

"They'll know the moment I expose Jill to our clan today and they pick up her scent. Prepare for the worst."

"I'm on it. We'll be ready."

"Thank you, my friend."

"I always have your back. Hey, Fray, we're done. Looks like we might have some actual fighting to do later so I don't want to wear you out."

Aveoth heard Fray laughing in the background. "The big guy claimed her, huh? Awesome."

"I'll see you later today." Aveoth ended the call and placed the second one to his mother. She let her phone ring six times before answering.

"I hate this thing."

He chuckled. "It was a gift from me."

"Only so you don't have to come see me as much. A small chunk of metal isn't the same as looking into my son's eyes when we speak."

"Jill's my mate. It's done. We'll be there in less than an hour. She's going to need a dress for the welcoming ceremony, something befitting a lady."

His mother inhaled sharply, then laughed. "That's wonderful! Renna and I will go through my closets. Your Jill is much shorter but we can put something together appropriate for her coming out to the clan. How did she take your secret?"

He sighed. "I haven't told her. I will, but the time wasn't right."

"Aveoth..."

"She accepted me as I am. If she can handle the wings, and me shelling to claim her, she can handle the rest."

"True. We'll see you soon."

He hung up, hoping he was right.

Chapter Fourteen

Aveoth had escorted Jill to his mother's door and promised to come back within the hour. She hugged Jill, seeming happy to see her.

Jill couldn't help but gawk a little at Galihia's home. The main living room looked like a mix of something that should have been featured in a magazine called rock mansions. Wooden shelves had been built against the rock of one huge wall, thousands of books lining them. A fireplace stood in the center of that wall, as well. A painted portrait caught her eye and she approached it, staring up. It was Galihia holding a tiny baby. He was wearing a white baby gown but had a tuft of black hair on his head. Striking blue eyes peered at her from the canvas.

"That was Aveoth at two months," the woman said from behind her.

Jill turned. "You haven't aged a day, it seems. And he was adorable." Her gaze went back to the painting. Burning fire logs were in the same fireplace in the background. "How old is Aveoth?"

Galihia laughed. "He hasn't told you?"

"No. He wouldn't tell me how old you are either. I think he worries that I'll have a heart attack or something."

"I'll let my son answer those questions. For now, come with me. Renna is waiting in my bed chambers."

Jill followed the beautiful GarLycan through a kitchen, a smaller living room, and down a hallway. The double doors to the bedroom were wide open, and she spotted another woman who had to be in her late forties.

The woman wore a cream-colored gown similar to Galihia's. She had black hair, dark brown eyes, and smiled when she saw them.

"This is her?" The woman rushed forward. "It's so good to meet you! Welcome to the family."

Jill hugged her back, despite being a bit stunned at the woman's obvious joy. "Thank you."

"Don't crush her, Renna." Galihia pulled Jill out of the other woman's arms. "Meet my aunt, Jill. She's one hundred percent Lycan and will hug you to death if you let her."

"Knock it off, Gali. You'll scare the girl." Renna winked at Jill. "Someone should show her open affection. The people who live in the cliffs are a bit stuffy. It was the hardest thing to adjust to when I came to live here. Lycans are huggers. We're into touching and showing emotions. GarLycans and Gargoyles tend to hide them. You are such a cutie! I'm so proud of Aveoth for choosing you."

Jill wasn't sure what to say, so she went with the first thing that popped into her head. "Thank you again."

Renna assessed Jill's body. "We're going to make you look beautiful when Aveoth presents you to the clan. Not that you don't already look beautiful. I should say more elegant. Gali and I have already hemmed the gown we thought was right while we were waiting for Aveoth to bring you to us." Her gaze lingered on Jill's chest. "We'll have to let out the top a little, though. Your breasts look larger than my niece's. Let's try it on."

Jill grimaced. "Formal attire? I haven't really dressed up to that degree before."

Renna chuckled. "I like you already. I'm into comfortable dressing myself but not in public. You're the new lady, and you should make a fashion statement."

They towed her toward the bed and made her strip. She blushed a bit, not really comfortable with being naked in front of the two women, but then they had her step into a big dress. It was yards of material, an off-white with tons of lace, and they pulled it up her body. The dress covered her from her shoulders to wrists and all the way down to her feet.

"We misjudged," Renna stated, dropping to her knees where Jill stood. "She's shorter. We need to tuck in another inch of skirt."

"The hoop skirt will take care of that," Galihia murmured.

Jill groaned. "Hoop skirt?"

"A small, lightweight, padded skirt. Like a pillow around your hips. Not a cage," Renna announced. "It accents our hips by flaring that area out a bit. I swear to the moon that this clan is full of cavemen." She chuckled. "They do live in caves, so we shouldn't be surprised."

Jill didn't want to know what a cage was, but an image she'd seen in a history book of women wearing wires around their lower bodies flashed in her mind, and she shuddered.

"Renna," Galihia admonished.

"Oh, you know I'm right, Gali."

Jill turned her attention to Aveoth's mother. "Can I ask you some questions, Galihia?"

"Of course you can. You may also call me Gali."

"What's going to happen when Aveoth introduces me to the clan?"

"The Gargoyle Council will have a hissy fit," Renna muttered, tugging on the skirt a little.

Jill knew her eyes widened but Gali just smiled.

"Don't worry. My son will have everything in hand. You'll be safe, and we'll be with you. There is a ceremony room where we hold events. It's a large cave."

"Everything here is in a cave," Renna interjected.

"Renna," Galihia sighed.

"Gali," Renna sighed back. "Just tell the girl the truth. The Gargoyle Council won't be happy, especially if they realize who her father is." The older woman stood and put her hands on her hips. "They're going to be furious when they learn she's half VampLycan. They are fine to fuck but never to mate according to those gas bags." She turned her gaze on Jill. "Fights might break out. We'll protect you if anyone gets past your mate. It won't happen, though. I wanted the three of us to wear black, but my niece said that wouldn't be appropriate."

"Black?" Jill glanced between them.

"Black hides blood splatters so much better." Renna winked. "So we picked cream dresses, since red doesn't clash with it. Families tend to wear the same colors to events. At least the women and children do. It will help you identify who is related."

"Auntie," Gali begged. "Don't scare poor Jill. It will be fine. No one knows." She held Jill's gaze. "Do they? Have you told anyone else what your father is?"

She shook her head. "No."

"Good. I expect the council will posture and make noises but the four of them can't do anything. They wanted my son to mate that horrible Winalin. I can't stand her."

"She *is* pretty," Jill had to admit.

"She's a pretty piece of trash," Renna growled. "She's the only pure-blooded female Gargoyle in the clan who isn't mated, and she's been chasing after our Aveoth since she was old enough to walk. Like it's her birthright to become lady to the clan. She treats me like I'm a servant, and she actually ordered Gali to tell her son to mate her. As if she has any right to tell us what to do. She reminds me of a flower that grew near our village. It was beautiful, but it gave you a bellyache and a case of the runs if you ate it."

Gali chuckled. "My son never considered mating her, Jill. She annoys him to no end."

"She's pretty unpleasant," Jill agreed.

Renna stared at her with a questioning gaze.

"She paid a visit to Aveoth and decided to get naked in front of him, thinking he'd go all sex fiend on her. I was there. She was...disappointed."

Renna snarled. "Trash. Pure trash. I would have slashed her across the face with my claws."

Jill held up her hand. "I don't have any."

"A shame, because marring her a bit would do her some good."

"Winalin might cause a scene today. Ignore her. That's what I do when she comes at me. There's a lot to be said for refusing to engage."

Gali walked to the bed and leaned against the post. "Take off the dress and we'll make the adjustments. Do you sew, Jill?"

She began wiggling out of the gown. "Not really. I can learn."

"I have this." Renna took the gown and walked to a table set up to the side. "You two talk."

Gali offered Jill a silky white robe, which she put on. "Thanks."

"I wanted to give you a history lesson. It's important."

Jill took a seat on the bed. "Okay."

"Abotorus founded this clan. He talked his close friends and some scouts from his old clan into fleeing to Alaska. Their lord had forbidden his clan to breed. They were higher in numbers than he wanted, and Gargoyles live a very long time. Abotorus talked those members into coming by offering to allow them to find mates and have children. It was a dream many of them had given up hope of ever having. The closest people to settle near this territory were the Lycans, who'd survived a war with Vampires."

"They gave birth to VampLycans," Renna added from across the room, where she was working on the dress. "Some of those nasty Vampires had controlled the Lycans' minds, and had gotten them pregnant."

"Yes," Gali sighed. "Abotorus was under pressure to make good on his promises. The Lycan pack had a lot of unmated women who hadn't been victims of the Vampires. A scout wished to mate with one he'd met. There weren't a lot of human women in the area, and most of them were already married or had children. Abotorus reluctantly agreed. He admitted to me years later that he didn't think Lycans were breed-worthy, and was sure a child between Lycans and Gargoyles wouldn't be physically possible. He was wrong. The Lycan conceived right away.

"Other clan members saw it as an opportunity, and they demanded to take Lycan mates as well. They were more mentally stable than humans, according to what they saw from that first couple. Abotorus felt pressured again into agreeing. But as more couples had children, all boys, there were grumblings amongst the clan members. My mate didn't hide his distaste for GarLycans well enough. He felt the children were weak and not worthy of being part of his clan. His men didn't agree. To save himself from a possible uprising, Abotorus demanded to mate me. My mother was Lycan and had birthed the first girl to this clan. I wasn't happy when I learned of my fate. The great Lord Abotorus was cold, looked at me as if I was beneath him, and I dreaded each year as adulthood approached."

Jill frowned. "What do you mean?"

"I was betrothed to Lord Abotorus when I was a year old. It appeased his clan but it gave him years before he actually had to claim me. Eighteen is considered mating age. I wanted to run away so many times but there was nowhere to go."

"You should have come to my pack," Renna whispered.

Gali glanced at her aunt, then back to Jill. "Abotorus would have sent an army to destroy any clan or pack who tried to harbor me. It would have meant the slaughter of every living soul there, just to punish them. I belonged to him, and felt doomed to my fate. Each birthday I grew more wary, terrified of the future I'd face with him."

"He was a nightmare," Renna growled. "Cold. Cruel."

"All true," Gali agreed. She took a deep breath. "I snuck out two days before the mating ceremony, and I wanted to fly away. But I wouldn't have survived on my own for long, and I knew I couldn't seek safety from anyone without causing their deaths. Abotorus was spiteful. I flew over a nearby valley and saw a man hunting." She paused. "You must never repeat any of this, Jill. Give me your word."

Jill nodded.

"He was a VampLycan. He shifted into his animal form, took down an elk, and then a hungry pack of wolves arrived at his kill. I landed on a hill to watch what he'd do. He shifted to skin and just laughed, then backed away to allow them to feast on his kill. He talked to the wolves, and the wind was just right so I could pick up his words. The pack was starving, it showed in their thin bodies, so he told them they needed it more." Tears filled her eyes. "It was so kind. I hadn't experienced that often growing up, except for the way my mother treated me. My father was Gargoyle, and he would have murdered every wolf for daring to try to take what he'd hunted."

"Are you sure you want to tell her all of this story?" Renna left the dress and approached. "It's dangerous."

Jill glanced between the two women as they studied each other.

Gali nodded. "She's my son's mate. She needs to know the truth."

"Fair enough." Renna took a seat near Jill. "Your mate's very life is in your hands, Jill. This is a very dangerous secret she is sharing. That's what my niece won't say. Go on, Gali."

Gali cleared her throat. "I followed this VampLycan to a cabin near a stream and watched him wash the blood from his skin. He was so

264

handsome. It was the first time I'd ever seen a man bare. I kept thinking about how he'd given up his meal for those wolves and how my future mate would never do that. It made me sad, and I wished someone like him could be my mate instead. I crept closer, curious. I know now he must have heard me, but he didn't let on. He finished washing and walked inside the cabin. I got even closer, hoping he'd come back outside. He did...but I didn't know it until he'd grabbed me from behind."

"The sneaky VampLycan had an emergency escape hatch out the back of his cabin and had circled around her," Renna chuckled. "He grabbed her, turned her in his arms, careful of her wings, and told her she was the most beautiful woman he'd ever seen."

Gali's eyes teared up. "He offered to let me come inside to get warm by his fire. He was incredibly kind. He didn't attack me the way I'd been told a man would do if I was ever captured. His words were sweet, and he was so worried about frightening me. He took me inside, made me a meal, and offered me his bed. He thought I was on my own and probably sensed my sadness. I was offered safety and shelter by him. I was attracted to him in a way I've never been before...and it got me thinking. I didn't want my first time with a man to include me chained to a bed by a cruel mate. So I kissed him."

"They did more than kiss," Renna whispered. "She spent the night and all the next day with him."

"It was the evening before my mating ceremony. This VampLycan didn't know that, I never told him my situation or my name. I knew it would mean his death if Abotorus found out I'd let someone else touch me. The VampLycan offered to allow me to stay with him, promised to protect and take care of me for as long as I needed him." She reached up and wiped at her tears. "I knew Abotorus would begin the hunt at first light when it was discovered I was gone. He'd have killed that VampLycan, probably all of them in his rage, so I snuck away while the VampLycan slept. I returned home, bathed myself, and the next morning at dawn, I arrived at the altar to meet my fate."

Jill let everything she'd heard sink in. "It's not a crime to have a lover before mating, right? I'm guilty of that. I wasn't a virgin when I met your son. Did Abotorus figure out he wasn't your first?"

She shook her head. "He was so enraged at feeling pushed into mating me that he drank heavily before chaining me down to the bed to claim me. I'm glad I knew a generous lover before that night."

Jill shuddered at the chaining part. It sounded unpleasant, barbaric, and she imagined the worst.

Renna snarled, and Jill glanced down at the woman's hands, seeing claws had grown out from her fingernails. "He was a monster. He damn near tore out her throat when he bit her and was savage in the claiming."

"Aveoth doesn't know that." Gali stared into Jill's eyes. "Never repeat that part to him. He knows our mating wasn't a happy one but I've smoothed over the abuse I suffered. I discovered weeks later that I was pregnant. Abotorus began pouring his blood down my throat daily to make up for my weak Lycan side, hoping it would make his son more Gargoyle. Aveoth was born with strong Gargoyle bloodlines, but I knew within a day that my mate wasn't his father. My son bit my nipples with tiny fangs, and he took blood as well as milk at my breast. He *needed* blood. That's not a Gargoyle or a Lycan trait."

Jill felt her jaw drop open but closed it fast. She swallowed hard. "Does Aveoth know?"

"He didn't until his seventeenth year." Gali approached and knelt in front of her, taking both of her hands. "The clan will kill my son if they ever realize the great Lord Abotorus isn't his birth father. They loathe all things with Vampire blood. The blood I drank during my pregnancy heightened Aveoth's genes he'd gained through my Gargoyle father. At least that's what I believe. But you and Aveoth both had VampLycan fathers. Do you understand? Vampires are their long-standing enemy."

Jill nodded, totally getting it. "I won't tell. I swear."

"My son plans to tell you, but I wanted you to hear it from me. I'm the one who took a lover before I mated. It's his biggest fear that the truth will come out. Aveoth and Kelzeb overheard my mate and the council making plans. The boys came to me for advice on how to stop them. My mate decided introducing Lycan blood into the clan was a mistake when Aveoth was seventeen. Abotorus was plotting to kill me and Aveoth, taking a pure-blood Gargoyle mate. I told my son the truth that day so he wouldn't feel guilt over having to challenge who he thought was his father to protect my life, his own, and the lives of all other GarLycans."

"And Lycans," Renna added. "He would have killed the mates too."

"The Gargoyle Council can never take leadership of this clan. They were my mate's closest friends, and they still think the way he did. You've met Kelzeb, haven't you?"

"Yes."

"His father is one of the council members who agreed that GarLycans were a mistake. He had planned to murder his own mate and son. That's how deep their hatred runs. Aveoth understands like no other in this clan that mixing bloodlines isn't a sin, and it makes us stronger. He needs to remain our lord. Your bloodlines don't matter to my son. He chose you because you hold his heart. I hope you can do the same for him."

Jill thought about the man she'd fallen for. He'd beaten up bad guys, been sweet to her, and had offered her his heart forever. "I love Aveoth, Gali," she admitted. She wasn't ready to tell Aveoth, but she could ease his mother's mind. "This doesn't change that." If anything, it made them have more in common. "I'll keep your secrets."

"He's going to need your blood from time to time," Renna scooted over, pressing against Jill's side. "Offer it to him. He doesn't have much Vampire but if he's hurt, give him a vein. He'll heal faster. We need to keep our boy strong."

Jill stared at each one of them in turn, and instantly felt a bond with the women. They all wanted to protect Aveoth and keep him alive. They loved him too. "I can do that."

"It's time to get you ready to face the clan." Gali squeezed her hands gently and smiled. "You're going to make a wonderful lady. Aveoth is trying to get rid of old thinking and crush the Gargoyles who still think the way my mate did. He'll succeed with you by his side."

* * * * *

Aveoth checked his weapons and met Kelzeb in the corridor outside his home. It was time to pick up Jill, his mother, and his great-aunt to escort them to the welcoming ceremony. His gaze took in his best friend's formal attire and the weapons strapped to his body.

"I'm ready for this. Are you?"

Kelzeb nodded. "I'll fight my father if he challenges you."

Aveoth inwardly flinched. "Let's hope they take the news better than expected and that it doesn't come down to removing heads."

"Doubtful. I know what you're planning. The council is going to lose their shit."

"We have the support in place. It's time we take a stand."

Kelzeb nodded. "I'm with you."

Aveoth appreciated that, and returned the nod. "Did you request Tork bring his family in a little late?"

"Yes. I warned him that we had a little business to discuss first and you didn't want his new baby and mate anywhere near the chamber until it was finished, in case violence broke out. He wasn't happy that he'd miss a fight, but he agreed."

"Good." His thoughts turned to Jill. He should have warned her of his plans but it was best if she wasn't overly concerned. It would be stressful enough for her to meet the clan.

They reached his mother's and he knocked. The door swung over—and he forgot how to breathe for long seconds.

Jill stood before him in a beautiful gown. The trim over her breasts, near her wrists, and down the flowing skirt were lace. Her blonde hair had been piled upon her head in some sort of bun with tiny braids weaved throughout.

She looked down his body before her chin lifted. "You look so hot in formalwear. The sword and daggers strapped to your body make you extra badass."

"You're beautiful."

A blush stained her cheeks. "I feel like I should formally curtsy in this thing. I never went to prom but I feel like that's what I'm dressed up for."

"What's a prom?" Kelzeb frowned.

Her gaze cut to his best friend. "A formal dance kids go to in high school."

"Curious," he replied.

Aveoth stepped toward Jill and took her hand. He lifted it to his lips and kissed her. "I would dance with you anytime, my lovely Jill."

She smiled. "You're just being so charming so you can talk me out of changing how women dress here. Keep it up. I like it."

He loved her sense of humor. His mother and great-aunt strolled into the room, and he noticed how their gown colors matched Jill's. A warmth spread through his chest. It was his mother's way of telling the clan she'd accepted Jill into their family.

"Don't mess her up," Renna chided. "I see that glint in your eye, Aveoth. Wait until after the ceremony to destroy all the work we put into your mate."

Jill glanced back at them with a confused expression.

"They fear I'll rip your dress off and take you to our bed," he whispered.

She swung her head back to him and outright grinned. "Anything to get out of this dress. I do mean that, Wings. *Any. Thing.*"

He pulled her toward the door by her hand he refused to release. "Let's go, ladies. The clan awaits." He led Jill into the corridor and placed her on his left, folding her hand over his arm. "Stay at my side unless there's trouble. Then get behind me and put a safe distance between us."

Her expression sobered. "We should have worn black after all, huh?"

"I don't understand."

She squeezed his arm. "I do, though. Blood is really going to show up on cream. Black absorbs it. I'll try to avoid getting splattered if any goes flying about."

He stiffened his spine, wondering what his mother and great-aunt had spoken to Jill about. "I won't allow anything to happen to you."

"I believe it. I trust you."

The warmth returned to his chest. He wouldn't let Jill down. His mate would change his world, and he needed to make sure she was accepted. No matter what the cost. She'd be safe at the cliffs—or he'd tear the damn mountain apart.

Chapter Fifteen

Aveoth entered the ceremony chamber and scanned the faces in the gathering crowd. Kelzeb walked behind him, escorting his mother and great-aunt. Bodies parted, giving him wide berth as he strolled with Jill at his side across the room to his rightful place at the royal couch. It was a custom Lord Abotorus had kept from his previous clan. Aveoth wanted to burn the damn thing. It had been placed six steps up from the main floor so everyone could clearly view it, as though it were a throne. He faced the room from his perch but didn't take a seat.

Kelzeb climbed the steps with the women of his family and motioned for his mother and great-aunt to take a seat. They hesitated until both looked at Aveoth for permission. He gave them a nod. His mother appeared confused, and he understood why. Only the lord was allowed to sit there, and his mate, if any. At all the other ceremonies, he'd sat alone while his mother and great-aunt had stood at the sides of the couch.

It was time for customs to change. Both women did his bidding.

His gaze scanned the room again and he saw surprise on some faces. They'd noticed the exchange and where the women were seated. He smiled when their gazes jerked to him but he allowed his anger to show in his eyes.

Jill kept still and silent at his side but her hold on him tightened. He placed his palm over hers, gently rubbing her skin to assure her things were fine. Whispers circulated and more gazes turned his way, to his mother and great-aunt, and to Jill. Then the room grew silent quickly without him giving the order.

He tracked the four council members as they moved around the room, coming together near the front. Kelzeb stepped to his right but kept a few feet of space between them. His best friend put his hand on the hilt of his sword. Aveoth didn't have to look at his face to know that Kelzeb glared at those four Gargoyles.

"Thank you for assembling this day." Aveoth used a louder voice than normal so the sound would carry to every part of the room. "As we all are aware, Tork and his mate had a son, and they will share his name when I accept him into the clan. They'll be along shortly...but I wanted to make an official statement while I have you all gathered." He took a deep breath. "I'd like to introduce you to my mate. This is Lady Jill."

Shock and surprise registered on some faces. He noticed a male near the back was pushed, and wasn't surprised when he identified the culprits. Elco and Winalin were rudely making their way forward. Elco's face was badly bruised and one arm hung uselessly at his side, the hand clearly bandaged.

Aveoth also spotted smiles on the faces of most GarLycans loyal to him.

"I protest!" Kado sputtered.

"Shut up," Aveoth snapped. "I'm not done." He deepened his voice further. "You will listen to what I have to say before anyone else interrupts." He eased Jill's hand off his arm, not taking his attention off Kado and the advancing siblings. He lowered his voice. "Go sit with my mother," he urged Jill. "Please."

She did as he asked, leaving his peripheral vision. He didn't dare track her movements but knew she was safe.

He gripped his own sword handle and raised his voice again. "No one has ever dared ask me why I challenged Lord Abotorus." Instant silence fell over the room. Aveoth continued. "He and the council, all those years ago, determined adding Lycan blood into our clan was a mistake. They were plotting to annihilate each and every one of you with a drop of Lycan blood running through your veins. Lord Abotorus had decided to murder his own mate, the Lady Galihia, and myself so he could breed with a pure-blooded Gargoyle."

Shock crossed many faces, followed by rage, but a group of his most loyal nodded in agreement, already aware of the past that had been avoided.

Kado opened his mouth, but Aveoth drew his sword and pointed the tip at him, holding his gaze, daring him to say a word. The Gargoyle clamped his lips together.

He lowered his sword. "I challenged Lord Abotorus to prevent that tragedy from happening. It would have destroyed this clan. No lord should have the right to demand any of his people kill their own children and mates. It's an abhorrent abuse of power. Yet...that was their plan.

"We're stronger than ever as a clan with our mixed bloodlines. We've thrived and grown in numbers. I keep track of the Gargoyle clans who are our enemies. Not a single member of those clans will ever have the option of claiming a mate, or holding a child in their arms. It's the very reason the first group of Gargoyles fled Europe and settled in this mountain. They wanted a future—and we've become that future. I will *never* allow GarLycans to be called a mistake, or to be wiped out."

He glared at each face of the council. "The slaughter of younglings and mates will never happen in my clan. I will no longer tolerate the prejudiced belief that pure-bloods are better than half-bloods."

He let his words sink in to the assembled.

"I've waited a long time for this day...and it's time to make a point. I want every GarLycan and Lycan mate to go to the left side of the room, and pure-blood Gargoyles to step to the right side. Now," he thundered.

His clan divided, the vast majority of them on the left side, with just over a dozen on the right. He waited until they were done positioning themselves and peered at the Gargoyles. "Hawk, would you kill your own sons?"

The Gargoyle flashed a look of pure rage. "Never!"

"It wasn't an insult. I already knew what your answer would be, and of your love for Fray and Chaz. As I said, I'm making a point. Some of the men around you can't say the same." He lifted his sword to the council members, one at a time pointing them out. "They plotted with Lord Abotorus to demand that you kill your mate and sons. Council members, look to your right. Your clansmen are never going to allow you to do that."

"You're lying!" Kado roared.

Aveoth jumped, clearing the stairs and landing near the four council members. "How *dare* you. You don't even have enough honor to be truthful to your own clan. You slink behind closed doors and plot like snakes, yet think *we're* beneath you! You four conspired with Lord Abotorus to murder every Lycan mate and GarLycan in this clan, and you don't even have the balls to admit the mistake you made." He eyed the other three members. "Do any of you have the honor to admit the truth? Or are you as spineless as your leader?"

Domb raised his chin. "I have honor. Lord Abotorus was correct in stating Lycan blood poisoned our clan and needs to be cleansed. The council agreed—and we still do." He shot a look of contempt to the other side of the room. "Your feelings make you *weak*," he sneered. "I hear you laughing and making light of things with your jokes. You gather in your little groups to have fun. It's pathetic!" Then he turned to look up at Kelzeb. "My son is my greatest disappointment. He chose friendship over his own father and has defied me on too many occasions. There's no honor in that. My mate is an annoyance I've had to deal with on a daily basis, and for what? To gain *him* in my life? I regret allowing her to birth him!"

Kelzeb jumped from the dais to land next to Aveoth.

Aveoth prevented him from attacking by making a low growl, trying hard to avoid bloodshed.

"Protect the women," Aveoth demanded.

Kelzeb made a grumbling sound deep in his throat but backed up, returning to his previous spot.

Aveoth glared at Domb and allowed his wings to slide out. He spread them wide and slightly shelled his body. "Do I look weak to you? I could take on all four of you, kill you the way I did Lord Abotorus. I refuse to call that traitor to the clan my father. *He* was the disappointment, and so are you."

None of the four members reached for their swords and most of the Gargoyles backed away from them, distancing themselves from the council. Only Elco and Winalin remained close. It told Aveoth who remained loyal to the four. That didn't come as a surprise.

"You recently held a secret meeting and plotted to force me to mate Winalin. That will never happen. Your dreams of turning this clan into what *you* wish are over. It ends today."

He backed up a few steps so he could see more of his clan, staring at the faces of the GarLycans and their mates. "You're alive today because I refused to allow you to be slaughtered in the name of prejudice. You're strong, valiant, and I am proud to call each of you my clansmen and women."

He turned his head, addressing the council and the two siblings backing them. "I mated Jill. Mixed-bloods are what made this clan strong. My mate his half human and half VampLycan."

Someone softly gasped from the crowd, but that was the extent of the reaction from the GarLycans. Pure rage showed on the council members' faces, though. Domb even reached for his sword.

"Do it," Aveoth dared him. "I'd take pleasure in killing you."

Domb withdrew his hand and placed it behind his back.

"I will not lie about her bloodlines. The VampLycan is very weak in her, but it's there. She is my mate, will one day birth my younglings, and I will reign down hell to protect her and them, just as I did to safeguard the lives of GarLycans and their mates in this clan. No more prejudice will be allowed. No more plotting deaths over bloodlines. Today ends in celebrating our differences. Anyone who has a problem with that, draw your swords and challenge me." He pointed in the clear dividing area between the right and left. "The line will start here."

The four council members didn't move, but they shelled their bodies and reached for their swords. They glanced at each other, and Aveoth could almost read their minds. The cowards didn't plan to take him on one at a time.

They stepped forward as one to form a line, facing him and drawing their blades.

Kado was the one to speak. "You are no longer our lord. You mated the enemy! We demand your death or banishment. Decide now."

The council was too focused on him to notice what was taking place behind them. Aveoth grinned as he scanned the room again. His clan hadn't let him down. He'd hoped telling them the truth once and for all, and bringing the facts of the past into the open, would achieve unity.

The women and children were easing to the back of the room to get out of the way, but the rest of his clan were glaring at the council members, their own weapons drawn.

"You think that's funny?" Kado thundered. "We'll have your head!"

"You have to go through us first," Fray advanced with his twin brother, taking positions to Aveoth's left. "You want to be cowards and fight against him en masse? Look around you, shitheads. You advance on our lord and the biggest chunks left of you will be your heads."

Duster unleashed his wings, flew over the council, and landed at Aveoth's right. He fisted daggers in both hands and shelled his body. "I think fingers are going to be the biggest pieces. We all want to partake in cutting them apart, so we can whack at their heads a bit. I call ears!"

"Noses," Chaz chuckled.

"I need a new rug in my bathroom," Hawk called out. "Milgo's got a lot of hair. Dibs."

Pride surged through Aveoth as more voices rose in his clan, announcing they'd attack the council to defend him, his mate, and his family. The council members formed a circle to protect their backs, and he saw fear flash in their eyes.

"I'm done taking your shit," Aveoth stated loud and clear. "So are they. I'm disbanding the council as of this moment. You've punished and tormented GarLycans by assigning them shit duties and talking down to them, thinking you're superior. You huddle in your secret meetings while you plot to harm this clan. *No more.*"

Gorzak was staring at something behind Aveoth, a wide grin curving his lips. Aveoth dared to glance back and noticed that Kelzeb had his cell phone out, a gleeful expression on his face. His friend was recording his father's downfall, and seemed to be enjoying it. Aveoth didn't order him to put the phone away, instead facing the council again.

"You can't disband the council!" Elco stepped forward but he didn't go for his weapons.

"I just did." Aveoth narrowed his gaze on the jerk. "If they—or you—don't like it, I'd be more than happy to send you back to Europe. *They* have a council that would love to bring charges against these four for treason from when they fled."

"They'd execute us," Kado protested.

"Damn straight they would. Now fucking *bow*, and pledge your allegiance to me and my mate. Otherwise—fight."

Kado dropped his sword and knelt. The other three followed his lead, unarming themselves and bowing their heads.

"Apologize to the clan for being shitheads who planned to murder most of them."

Each muttered the words but he knew they didn't mean a single one. It was tempting to force them to fight but they wouldn't. All four were cowards.

"You have no authority anymore. You hold no rank." He shot a glare at the siblings. "Have Elco and Winalin teach you how to be useless and do nothing in a clan. They are experts at it."

Some laughter filled the air.

"If you defy me, if you plot, hold meetings, or show any intent to do harm to this clan, I will personally put each one of you in a box and drop you off with your old clan gift-wrapped, since you're too cowardly to fight. Be *grateful* I'm nothing like Lord Abotorus, or I'd take your heads regardless of your unwillingness to hold a blade. He had no problem murdering unarmed clan members. Get out of my sight now."

The four clan members rose up, didn't touch their weapons, and fled.

He watched them leave before turning his attention to the siblings. "Go with them. Either find your place in this clan by accepting you're not above everyone else, or get the hell out. I'm sure we can hunt up two more boxes if you need to be dropped off at another clan. They'd be more than happy to find use for a full-blooded Gargoyle female. Of course, you won't find them willing to make you any deals for her, Elco. They'd just murder you and use her as a breeder. Old clans love to chain and abuse their women."

Winalin paled and grabbed hold of her brother. He put his arm around her and led her out of the room.

Aveoth sighed and sheathed his sword. "Anyone remaining have a problem with my mate being part VampLycan?"

Heads shook, many of the clan giving him bows and smiles. He completely relaxed. "We're a stronger clan by mixing our bloodlines. Everyone has the right to take a mate and have younglings here if you wish. Human. VampLycan. Lycan. I don't give a shit, as long as you're happy and so is your mate. Is that clear?"

They nodded, some of them calling out agreements.

"Tork, his mate, and their son should be here at any moment." He smiled wide. "Let's celebrate."

* * * * *

Jill's face hurt two hours later from smiling. At first it had been forced as Aveoth introduced her to what seemed like dozens of people one by one. They were friendly, seemed to be okay with her as their new lady, and no one had made her overly nervous.

Tork and his mate Benla smiled as she carefully took their son into her arms. Torris was adorable and the scent of baby powder filled her nose. "It's an honor that you trust me," she told the couple.

Aveoth had instructed her to say that before the couple approached, explaining that allowing her to hold their son showed their faith that she wouldn't harm their baby. It was tradition when a new clan member was introduced to allow the lord and lady to accept their child.

281

"Are you okay?" Benla asked kindly, her tone soft. "You look nervous."

"I don't have much experience with babies," Jill admitted. "He's so darn cute."

The Lycan grinned. "He is. My mate and I make pretty babies." She looked up at Tork with love in her eyes. "We should have many more."

Tork put his arm around her. "I agree." He turned his attention on Aveoth. "I was told what happened and what you shared before we arrived. Everyone is talking about it. You've always had my loyalty, but now you also have my gratitude. I do have something to ask."

Jill stared down at the baby and admired his big golden eyes. He gazed back at her, and she felt her heart melting. Bat babies looked just like human ones, only their eye color was a bit different. Some darker browns bled into the boy's irises, then lightened in spots. The colors were fluid and constantly changing. Like Aveoth's, it was amazing.

"*What?*" Aveoth snapped, drawing her from her musings. She looked up to see that his skin had grown a little ashen and he seemed pissed.

"The council," Tork repeated. "They said I wasn't allowed to have another baby with my mate until they gave permission. You didn't know? They've been doing it for a while." Tork looked concerned.

"Goddamn them," Aveoth grumbled. "I had no idea. They loved to do shit behind my back. Why didn't you or anyone else come to me with this? Did you talk to Kelzeb?"

His friend was at his side in an instant. "This is the first I've heard of denying permission to breed, or I would have told you. You know I don't

282

have a mate, or they probably would have tried to pull that bullshit on me too."

"You can have another baby whenever you're ready. That's a choice between you and your mate. No one else has the right to say otherwise." Aveoth drew closer to Jill and his features softened as he admired the baby. "Younglings are a joy to all. May I?"

Jill carefully transferred the baby into his arms, and Aveoth grinned outright. She would swear her ovaries ached watching his features grow animated as he made soft baby noises. Maybe she *was* ready for a bat baby after all in the near future. There was something very appealing about Aveoth with that baby.

"Take care of that, Kelzeb. Talk to other mated couples and see what else the council did. Tell me and we'll clear up any matters."

"I had to get permission to mate," Tork offered. "They only agreed after I begged and pleaded. They said I'd owe them favors."

Aveoth's head snapped up and he growled in a scary way. The infant in his arms reacted by jerking in his hold, and then began to fuss softly. Aveoth instantly calmed his temper and handed the baby over to Benla.

"I'm going to kill those cowards. Why did you even ask them? They had no say in the matter."

"It's what all of us have been told. That we had to go to them for permission." Tork kept his head down. "Each of us were summoned to their chambers while we were in training and given rules as youths."

Jill leaned against Aveoth's side and gripped his arm because he looked enraged and about to lose his shit. It didn't take much to guess that was news to him. "They're just assholes. Simply tell everyone that's bullshit."

"I wish those four weren't such cowards. Did you see how fast they dropped their swords to avoid me killing them?" He held her gaze.

"I'll take care of it immediately," Kelzeb swore. He walked away, mingling with the nearest group.

"Congratulations on your adorable son," Jill told the couple. She jerked her head, giving them a signal to get lost, and hoped they understood. They did, leaving her alone with Aveoth.

She stepped in front of him. "You look ready to kill somebody, Wings. Deep breaths. We've avoided bloodshed so far and I'd hate to have to return your mother's dress all stained. I mean, it wouldn't be a loss. This thing should be turned into curtains anyway. There's enough of it."

He put his hands on her hips. "I want to kill the council."

"What council?" She winked. "You disbanded them."

The tension seemed to leave him. "They'll always cause us trouble."

"Assholes never change. True enough. It was pretty clear, though, that there aren't any village idiots here to follow them, except that guy with the battered face and the porn queen clinging to him when they left."

His lips twitched. "Village idiots?"

"Yeah. You know. Grab the ropes and torches to lynch someone and only the stupid people go along with it. They're outnumbered, and the only ones in fear of being hung from a tree to be set on fire is *them*.

284

Maybe the five of them can spend their time pretending to be plumbers while Winalin shows them the leak in her body where her soul escaped."

"The battered one is Winalin's brother."

"Eww. Okay. Maybe he can hold the camera."

He tugged her closer and pressed a kiss on her forehead. "You always amuse me. I never know what you're going to say next."

"I'm special that way and no take-backs now. You're stuck with me. That mate thing sounded pretty solid and forever."

"It is and I'm grateful." He lowered his head, peering into her eyes. "How are you holding up?"

"I'm intimidated by your clan. I won't lie. I'm hanging in though. Everyone who's approached seems to be okay with me."

"They are or I'd have drawn my sword."

"You're kind of hot when you get all murdery."

"Is that an actual word?"

"It is when you knew what it meant. Plus, you're the ruler of this place and I'm your mate. It's a real word. I said so."

"I love you, mate."

"I love you, too. Now feed me. I'm starving."

"I can do that. They are serving a buffet on the other side of the room."

"Do we have to sit on that couch? Because I have to say that it feels like bricks are under those cushions. It's the most uncomfortable thing ever."

"I'll have it burned."

"Good. I'll throw the match."

"We're a perfect pairing." Aveoth released her and offered his arm. "Come with me."

"Lead on, Wings."

Chapter Sixteen

Jill stared out of the window of the taxi, feeling exhausted. The man sitting a few feet from her in the backseat cleared his throat, drawing her attention. Chaz seemed to be holding her gaze when she looked at him, but it was hard to tell. The dark sunglasses he wore didn't show his eyes at all.

"Why are you wearing those? It's not that bright of a day."

He reached up and lowered them. "Why do you think?"

He and his brother had silver eyes. They weren't human-looking in the least. She'd noticed that about them before.

"Can't you mask your emotions and go to a more normal color the way Aveoth does?"

He shook his head. "Nope. They're always this way." He shoved the sunglasses back up. "Are you okay?"

"Not really."

"I'll keep you safe."

"I have no doubt you will. It's just that I didn't expect this when Aveoth said he had a surprise for me last night. I was thinking kinky sex or something."

Chaz smiled and averted his face. "Be happy it wasn't my brother assigned to you. He'd have made some smartass remark to that statement."

"Where are Aveoth and Fray?"

"Shopping."

"How in the hell did Aveoth manage to get use of a jet? And who was that big guy waiting for us on it? Aveoth wouldn't answer my questions."

"Your mate was stressed, taking you around an unfamiliar male who kept looking at you in a way that made Aveoth want to kill him. Garson is a bit of a flirt."

"Well, I'm still ticked. Aveoth practically dragged me into the bedroom on the jet, refused to answer my questions, and distracted me until I fell asleep." The sex had been great but she wasn't about to admit that to her guard. "By the time I woke up, we were landing and he just ordered me to shower and get dressed. Then he was gone and you were shoving me in this taxi."

"We'll talk when we reach your address." He turned his head forward, nodding in the direction of the driver.

She sighed, understanding. The guy in front could hear every word they said.

Some of her bad mood faded when she spotted the familiar area. A few blocks later, the taxi stopped in front of Mack's metal shop.

"Go first," Chaz insisted.

She opened the door and got out. He slid across the seat, paid the driver, and climbed out the same door she had. He was careful not to touch her but kept close. The car drove off, leaving them on the sidewalk.

"Why'd you do that?"

"I wasn't about to get out before you, in case the driver took off with you still inside."

"Taxi drivers don't abduct people, and especially since you were with me. That would be all kinds of stupid, since you'd seen his face and knew the number of the taxi. It was clearly marked on that card where the opening was to pay."

"I don't trust humans."

"Tell me what's going on, Chaz." She glanced up and down the road. "Nobody's around."

"Lord Aveoth wanted to take you home so you could get your mother's ashes. He called the VampLycans for help to arrange it, since they owe us a few favors. It turned out that one of Lorn's enforcers happened to be in Anchorage and was en route to the airport, on his way home. The timing was there for the VampLycan to hire a jet instead of a bush pilot and divert it to pick us up. And Lord Aveoth wants to give you a gift for your mating, so he's shopping while we go pack up your apartment. That's *all* I'm saying."

It was kind of romantic. "It was just so fast and unexpected."

"It was either go last night or possibly wait weeks until we could find another opportunity for a VampLycan to be at a large airport."

"And that makes sense...why?"

"VampLycans have the ability to erase memories and control humans. No sane pilot would have landed a jet on an airstrip that isn't even on a map. Garson handled paying them and keeping them under his control. Neither pilot will remember being there. We weren't aware that landing strip could even handle a jet until you were brought there in one by Decker. Normally when we travel long distances, we'll hire a bush pilot in a small plane to fly us to larger airports, and then travel commercial."

"But you have wings."

"Radar can be a bitch to avoid in populated areas. And imagine having to fly almost two thousand miles." He rolled his shoulders. "I'm fit, but that would be rough, especially if I were carrying someone in my arms. It would also take us days, since we can only fly at night outside of safe territories controlled by us or the VampLycans. Lord Aveoth didn't tell anyone he was leaving, since the clan is still unsettled after yesterday. This way, we'll be back before anyone notices we're gone. Jets are faster."

She sighed. "You know what? Let's just get my things and get back at the airport. I'm tired, a bit cranky, and out of sorts." She walked over to the main door and tried to turn the handle. It was locked. "Shit. Mack isn't here. Come on."

"Who's Mack?" Suspicion laced Chaz's voice. "Lord Aveoth won't like it if you had a romantic attachment to a human."

"Mack is like a father figure to me. I worked for him and rented the place over this shop for dirt cheap. He's probably with his boyfriend today or at a show for his newest pieces. He's an artist. This is a metal shop. Want to guess what kind of works he creates?"

Chaz just chuckled.

She led him around the building to a gate and reached over it, feeling for the latch. Her fingers caught it and she tugged it open. Metal creaked as she shoved it open to ease into the backyard space.

"Close that behind you. Mack doesn't want anyone to wander back here."

The gate slammed and she went to the back door, bending and lifting a stone. The emergency key was a little muddy but she knocked it against the wall and shoved it inside the lock. She put the key back and returned the rock to cover it. "Come on in."

Chaz gripped her arm and jerked her back. "I go in first."

Right. He's my bodyguard. She meekly stepped out of his way. "The worst thing you're going to find is a mouse or spider. Take the stairs to the left. My apartment is up there."

"What is that smell?" He sounded disgusted.

She entered behind him and inhaled. "Spray-paint primer. This is the area where Mack does that, and from how strong it is, I'm guessing he wasn't here long ago. We leave the back door open to air the place out while he's spraying."

"I'm going to check this area over here."

"The door on the left is the office." She jerked her head. "To the right is the shop. I wouldn't go into that area. Mack will have turned on the fans to help his sculptures dry after painting, but it still reeks to high heaven. Come on." She took the stairs quickly and reached her apartment. The door wasn't locked, but then, it never was.

"I said I'd go first," Chaz demanded from behind her. He gently pushed her aside and stepped forward. He stopped dead right inside the door. "Someone has been here. They tossed your belongings. Do you know what they were looking for?"

Jill didn't know if she should laugh or feel embarrassed. The drawers of the dresser were partially open, clothes hanging out of them. The laundry hamper was overturned in the corner, the contents spilled in a messy pile. The blankets were wadded up at the end of her bed and the pillow was on the nightstand, covering most of her alarm clock. The lamp had been knocked over next to it and was broken.

"Um, stand down, Chaz. This is how I left it."

He gaped a little at her over his shoulder, appearing stunned.

"Don't judge me. I had overslept the day I was kidnapped because I went to bed too late, and I kind of bashed my alarm with my pillow while I was still out of it. The lamp breaking was an accident. Then I couldn't find anything to wear." She nodded toward her dresser before pointing at her hamper. "I realized what I wanted was probably in there. Mack gets bitchy if I'm really late, and I didn't want to hear him rant at me again. I would have cleaned it up after my shift."

He masked his expression. "I see." Humor sounded in his voice though. "Do you own a suitcase?"

"Boy, do I. I'm the queen of moving." She strode over to the closet and opened it, pulling out an already-packed duffle. "This is the emergency go-bag I keep ready. Give me a few minutes and I'll collect the rest of my stuff. She yanked a backpack off the top shelf of the closet and walked into the tiny bathroom.

"Emergency go-bag?"

"Long story, but let's just say I've had to grab shit and leave fast before. My nice clothes are always packed." She took her makeup bag out of the only drawer in the bathroom, returned to her small living/bedroom, and carefully placed her mother's urn inside the backpack from on top of the dresser. "I'm ready."

He seemed surprised. "That's it?"

"I'm not taking my dirty clothes or what's in the dresser. They all have holes from sparks flying. I do a lot of the welding for Mack. I have everything I need."

"What about personal possessions? Humans tend to have pictures and things."

"In the go-bag already. It's kind of heavy. Do you mind carrying it?"

Chaz lifted the duffle and slung it on his shoulder. "Lord Aveoth believed this would take a few hours."

"He was wrong. I do need to leave Mack a note, though. I feel bad about just taking off on him. He'll have paper and pens in his office." She went to walk out of the apartment but Chaz blocked her way.

"I go first."

"Right. Okay. After you."

He stepped out the door—but then halted so fast she almost slammed into his back.

Five quick, loud blasts sounded, nearly deafening her.

Chaz's big body jerked repeatedly with those noises then pitched to the side, falling down the stairs.

Jill heard every thud. It shocked her so much that it took her seconds to react and understand those were gunshots.

"Fuck!" Survival instincts kicked in. She lunged, grabbed the door, and slammed it. Guilt ate at her over leaving Chaz, but he was a superhero, body-wise. Gali had said they could survive gunshots. She hoped that was true. Being mostly human meant she'd be dead if she were shot, too.

She stepped to the side, her fingers curling around the top edge of the dresser, and she yanked on it hard. It fell over, blocking the door. She spun and ran into the bathroom.

That door was thinner, but she slammed and locked it. She jumped into the shower/tub combo, put her foot on the corner of the tub, and yanked at the window latch. The window groaned in protest as it swung out. She threw out the backpack first, and then clasped the edges to jump up into the small hole.

The sound of wood smashing came from the other room, and she figured whoever had shot Chaz had just realized breaking down the door wasn't their only obstacle, as an animalistic snarl followed. Two resounding booms indicated they were perhaps trying to kick the dresser out of the way, but Jill was halfway out of the open window by then, ignoring the pain of having her stomach dig into the thick windowsill.

She looked down at the double Dumpster beside the building, cursing because she knew the landing was going to hurt.

She kicked her legs wildly and bucked, lifting both arms to protect her head as gravity worked to make her fall out the window. She hit the plastic lids below.

Agony shot through one shoulder and her body flipped on impact. She rolled right off the Dumpster before she could recover by trying to grab hold of something, anything, to stay on top of it.

Her side took most of the impact when she slammed into the pavement. Jill lay there panting, hurting, but a noise from above made her turn her head to stare up.

The sight of Fido, his scarred face filled with rage, scared the hell out of her. He was trying to fit his bulky body out of the window, growling at her.

She groaned, favoring her right arm as she stood. The backpack lay a few feet away, and she snatched one of the shoulder straps with her fingers. There was no way she'd leave her mom's ashes behind. Her legs felt okay but she was limping from her hip feeling out of whack. She headed as quickly as she could toward the gate to escape the backyard.

A man in a suit suddenly opened it before she got there, and she froze.

"Hello, Jillian." It was the shark.

He pulled something from his breast pocket. She stared in dread as he uncapped the syringe and threw the cap on the ground.

"Your grandfather would like to have a word with you."

"Fuck you." She backed up, heart pounding. "Stay away from me!"

A body pressed against her back, stopping her retreat. She twisted her head, staring up at someone new and terrifying. He was tall, bulky, and his big hands clamped down on her shoulders. A cry escaped her at the feeling of excruciating pain. She was pretty sure he'd just dug claws into her skin.

"We knew you'd come back for your mother's remains, and you didn't disappoint us." Shark came at her, looking smug and pleased. "You appear surprised. Your father has had men watching you all your life, Jillian. Your mother was important to you, and Decon had searched your homes many times. He knows her ashes are your most prized possession."

"That's a shitty way to put it," she muttered. "Heartless bastard."

"It's true. We gave you to Aveoth knowing you'd come back for that urn, or he'd send someone he trusts to retrieve it for you. Then it was just a waiting game to grab whoever came. But you were our ultimate hope...and here you are."

"What the hell does that mean?"

"Decker needed a way to control Aveoth. Now we have it. He'll do whatever we want to get you back." He waved the syringe. "It's time for you to sleep."

"Wait!" She dropped the backpack as her mind worked fast. "Aveoth won't give a shit if you have me. He's not the one who just got shot by your people. Do you want to know why?"

Shark's eyes narrowed.

"Fido was right. Aveoth wanted to kill me because I'm so mouthy. I seduced the goon you idiots shot to get the hell out of there." She forced a wide grin. "You are *so* dumb."

He leaned in close and inhaled. "You smell like Lord Aveoth."

"Only because the bastard bit me—and I bit him back. He didn't like that. The scent will fade in a week or so after that nasty blood of his leaves my system. At least that's what my new boyfriend said. Aveoth was furious that I wasn't some demure moron ready to bow down to his every whim. He tossed me out of his home so I flirted with..." She jerked her head toward the building. "I can't even remember his name."

Fido came rushing at them from the back of the building. He must have given up on fitting through the window. He snarled, flashing fangs at her. She met his glare but then smirked at the shark.

"Cole, isn't it? Sorry to disappoint, but all you've done is rid me of a pain in the ass. Or at least he probably *would* have been if you hadn't killed him. He made me promise to mate him if he brought me home."

"I don't believe you." Cole didn't seem sure though.

"Don't you think Aveoth would be here if I mattered to him? Do you see him? No. Maybe logic is too complicated for you, but try it for once."

He jabbed the needle into her arm. She tried to jerk away but the bastard holding her shoulders wouldn't permit her to move much. A coldness spread up her arm and into her chest.

"I'm taking you to Decker," the shark hissed. "Those were my orders."

"Fuck you."

Spots danced before her eyes and her knees collapsed under her. Everything went dark.

* * * * *

Aveoth grinned and showed Fray what he'd just purchased. "What do you think?"

"Your mate will love it."

"She was raised human so I wanted to buy her a ring. My mother told me what size to get. I hope she's right."

297

"Resizing a ring would be a bitch once we get home. You ready to return to the airport?"

"Yes."

Aveoth's phone rang and he withdrew it, seeing Chaz's number. "They must have beat us to the jet." He answered. "We're on our way now."

"They took her," the GarLycan rasped.

"What?" Instant fear and rage poured through him. "*Who* took her?"

"VampLycans. They shot me. I didn't have time to shell first." Chaz coughed, and it sounded wet. "Get to her place. I haven't recovered enough to stand yet. They might still be near."

"We're on our way." He hung up.

Fray was already at the curb, and he opened the back door of the cab they'd had waiting for them in front of the jewelry store. The GarLycan appeared furious. "I heard. Let's go."

Aveoth nearly dove into the backseat and seethed as Fray climbed in the other side, giving the driver the address. His mate had been taken. The idea seemed surreal but he knew it was a fact. Chaz would never play such a twisted prank on him.

Fray withdrew a wad of cash. "Break every speed limit to get us there and this is yours."

The driver glanced back, and then the vehicle lurched forward, tires squealing as he punched his foot down on the gas.

"Remain calm, my lord. We'll track them and get her back."

"Who would dare do this?" He immediately answered his own question. "Decker."

"You don't know that for sure. There's no way he'd know we'd brought her here."

"Unless Garson betrayed us. I'll tear him apart a piece at a time."

Fray grasped his arm tight. "Breathe in and out. I have spent time with Garson. He wouldn't do this. I don't know how they tracked our movements, but watch your skin," he murmured.

Aveoth glanced down and saw the warning signs of partial shelling. It took every ounce of control to force his body into submission. Fray whipped out a spare pair of sunglasses from his jacket and held them out.

Aveoth took them and covered his eyes. "I'm going to—"

"Not here. Not now. Just breathe, my lord. In. Out. We'll get her back."

Every minute seemed like an eternity until the cab screeched to a halt in front of an old gray building. Aveoth almost ripped the door open to get out, breathing in every scent around him. He picked up VampLycans right away. One glance back showed Fray giving the driver money. Aveoth rushed to the front door of the building, only to find it locked. He viciously twisted the handle and threw his shoulder into it. The lock broke and he shoved inside.

Aveoth stared at the shop, his nose burning from the strong stench of chemicals. Metals and paint fumes. He stormed across the room to another door and threw it open. Chaz lay on the floor in a pool of blood but the enforcer's eyes were open. His sunglasses were lying feet away.

"I'm sorry."

Aveoth assessed Chaz's severe injuries at a glance. He'd suffered two blasts to the chest, and additional shots to his shoulder, stomach, and hip. Blood coated his lips and ran down his chin to his throat. Aveoth stepped over the male, staring at the open back door and up the stairs where blood was smeared on the steps.

"Outside," Chaz got out, coughing up more blood. "She escaped from upstairs and they rushed out the door after her."

Aveoth ran and picked up more scents once he'd left the stench of the building's interior. Fray was right on his heels and they separated.

His enforcer crouched near a Dumpster and touched the ground. "She was here." He looked up. "The window is open. She must have jumped out that way and fallen to the ground."

Aveoth tracked the scents he recognized. They were from the two VampLycans he'd beaten for Jill after meeting her for the first time. There was an unfamiliar scent, too, by an abandoned backpack. He followed his nose out an open gate, where all the scents disappeared at the street. Fray grabbed his arm again.

"We'll get her back. Don't lose your shit, my lord. It's broad daylight. You can't fly in the city to search for her."

"Decker has her again!"

"He'll want something then. He always does. It means he won't dare hurt her. Think. I know it's rough right now because she's your mate, but you must."

He closed his eyes and tried to clear his thoughts. "I can track her."

"Shit. I forgot. What direction?"

Aveoth mentally reached out to Jill but couldn't get a sense of where she was. "I'm getting nothing."

"You bonded to her, you can, you're just upset. Concentrate, my lord."

Aveoth tried again, then felt more rage and frustration. "I sense nothing. They've killed her!" He crashed to his knees, his heart feeling as if someone had ripped it out.

Fray bent and hooked his arms around him, lifted, and nearly dragged him back into the yard they'd just left before putting him down. He kicked the gate closed and began prowling the yard. Aveoth stayed down and grew cold inside, dead. His skin throbbed and he knew he had begun to shell. It didn't matter anymore. Nothing did.

Fray came back to him and knelt. "I found a topper thing to a needle. Don't shut down, Aveoth." Fray gripped the back of his neck and squeezed hard. "Do you hear me, damn it? Decker wants something. He needs your mate alive. You're not sensing her because she must be drugged. You know it can block your ability to get her location if her mind is shut down."

He latched onto the words and fought to breathe again. To soften his skin.

"That's it," Fray encouraged. "Come on, Aveoth. If nothing else, get mad at me for being informal with you."

Aveoth opened his eyes and saw the red syringe cap Fray held in his palm. He took it and sniffed. It did smell of some form of drug, even if it was slight.

301

"She's carrying your scent." Fray released his neck. "Decker wants his clan back. He'll use Jill to force you to help him do that. Are you thinking clearer now? I'd like to check on my twin. He looked like shit when I glanced at him."

"Go to Chaz."

"I'll be right back."

Aveoth slowly stood—and silently promised to reign hell down on Decker and any of his loyal to get Jill back. He checked his phone but he hadn't missed any calls. Decker would be contacting him, though. The bastard had taken his mate.

He entered the building, watching as Fray helped his brother stand.

Chaz refused to meet his eyes. "I'm so sorry, my lord."

"Stop." Aveoth came forward and put his hands on the GarLycan's chest, examining the wounds. They were bad but the holes were very slowly closing and the bleeding had slowed. "Punctured lung?"

"Yes. It doesn't matter. I failed you." Chaz leaned heavily on Fray. "I failed your mate."

Aveoth glanced at Fray, seeing the twin's fear flash across his features. He could guess why.

"Not another word, Chaz. I know what you're going to say. I refuse to take your life as punishment. The bastards used the stench in here to hide their scents and they attacked you with human weapons before you could react." He'd noticed the three shotguns, discarded on the floor by an open door that revealed an office with a desk inside. "It was a trap.

Anyone could have walked into it. None of us suspected Decker would come after my mate here."

Aveoth took off the sunglasses to get them out of the way and withdrew a dagger from the hidden thigh pocket of his leather pants. "You want to make it up to me?"

Chaz lifted his head. "My life is yours, my lord. I'll do anything for you."

Aveoth stared hard at each twin. "I need you both to swear secrecy and loyalty to me forever—right now."

Both appeared confused but it was Fray who spoke. "You've always had that, and forever will."

"Good. Then do exactly what I say." He sliced his skin on the meaty part of his inner forearm and lifted it to Chaz's face. "Drink my blood now. That's an order."

Chaz's eyes widened, uncertainty showing in them.

"My father was a VampLycan. My blood will heal you. Drink it."

Chaz only hesitated for an instant, then sealed his mouth over the cut. Aveoth focused on Fray. The VampLycan removed his sunglasses, their gazes locking over Chaz's head, and Fray gave a sharp nod, silently telling him he meant the vow.

"I'll explain later. Decker will want to return to Alaska. Let's get there first. That means we need to get the fuck out of here and back on the jet. We can't do that with Chaz bleeding out and looking the way he currently does. Humans would stop us and call their law enforcement."

"VampLycan. I'm blown away." Fray whistled. "I never would have guessed that about you in a million years."

"We'd all better hope no one else ever does in our clan."

"No shit. We won't tell anyone. Does Kelzeb know?"

Aveoth peered into Chaz's eyes, which were still locked onto him. "Yes."

Chaz surprised him by winking. Then the GarLycan stopped drinking his blood and took a step back before reaching down and tearing open his destroyed shirt. The holes in his chest were rapidly sealing before their eyes.

"Fuck!" Chaz touched one of the wounds, already closed. "Amazing."

"I'll find you something else to wear. You're covered in blood." Fray strode into the office.

"I hope the jet can be flown with one pilot instead of two."

"Why is that, my lord?" Chaz removed the rest of his shirt and began to undress.

"I need to drink blood now. That's the down side to being part VampLycan."

Fray returned carrying a T-shirt and shorts. "It's the best I could find in there." He held them out to his brother. "It was that, or I could go upstairs to Jill's apartment to get you a dress or something."

"Hurry up and get dressed, Chaz. We need to go." Aveoth was desperate to get back to Alaska.

Fray stepped forward. "I heard what you said." He offered his arm. "You need blood."

Aveoth was touched. The brothers truly accepted what he was. "I appreciate that but two of us are weaker than normal right now. Let's not make it three. I'll take blood once we reach the jet."

Chaz had put on the human's clothing. They were too small and he looked ridiculous in shorts with boots. It didn't matter. "That's your mate's duffle bag there and she had a backpack with her mother' ashes. Did they get that too?"

"It's outside. I'll grab it." Fray exited the building, putting his sunglasses back on.

Aveoth tried hard to hang on to his sanity. His mate had been taken—and VampLycans would die.

Chapter Seventeen

Jill woke up in the same jet she'd been in before when she'd been kidnapped, only now it wasn't just Shark and Fido she had to deal with. The quiet man who'd clawed her shoulders was also present, still at her back in one of the seats behind her.

She glared at the remaining jerk in a chair across from her, who she suspected was half the reason her sperm donor even existed. He confirmed her suspicions when he introduced himself as Decker Filmore.

"You're going to get my clan back for me, and help me accomplish a lifetime goal."

They had her tied like a mummy, with ropes encircling both her and the chair she sat in, winding from chest to ankles. "You know, for a jacked-up family who never wanted anything to do with me my entire life, this is all kinds of fucked. You understand that, right?"

Decker just placidly smiled. "I didn't know about you, or I would have killed your mother right after your birth and brought you home. You wouldn't be the foul-mouthed woman you are today. I'd have taught you to respect me."

"He'd have beaten you into submission," Fido growled.

She didn't spare him a glance since he sat somewhere behind her. "Did you hear that? I think a dog is talking. Someone grab a camera, hit record, and we'll be trending on Twitter if you post it. It's a miracle."

"Goddamn bitch!" Fido snarled.

"Sit down," Decker commanded. "She knows what buttons to push. What is Twitter?" He looked to the shark for clarification.

"Ignore her remarks. Jillian is rude, and she tends to say things that don't make sense in her sad attempts to make one feel stupid."

"I don't have to attempt anything. Stupidity is a done deal in your case." She flashed him a smile, since he sat in front of her.

Decker glanced at his watch. "How long until we land? I want to call Aveoth and get this over with. I almost wish I could watch him kill my enemies."

"We'll finally make those traitors pay...and do it from the comfort of the jet." Shark also glanced at his watch. "Soon. We've already crossed the border into Alaska."

"Aveoth won't do what you want." Jill wiggled, trying to loosen the ropes, but they had no give in them.

"We should drug her again." Shark flashed his white teeth in his own evil version of a smile.

"I agree. Anything to avoid staring at you two." She tensed her legs, pushing on the ropes. "I noticed you're not doing a chimney impression this time. I take it the jerk you serve doesn't like smoking?"

"Do not call Decker a jerk!" Shark snapped.

Decker leaned forward in his chair, his gaze fixed on her. "Aveoth might want me to prove she's still alive. No more drugs. You remind me of your grandmother. My mate had no respect for me either—and I killed her. I'd keep that in mind."

"I'd say I'm shocked but…so not. All you Filmores are losers. Too bad you didn't extend that murder streak to the rest of your family so none of you are left."

Deep growling sounded from behind her.

She put her head against the seat and sighed. "Your doggy sounds like it might piss all over or chew up your expensive plane. I vote that we open a door and toss Fido out."

"I'm going to fucking kill her," Fido snarled.

"Sit down and shut up, Boon!" Decker ordered him. "I won't allow you to fuck up my plans because you have no control over your temper. This bastard child is going to be the downfall of our VampLycan enemies. All four clans will bow to me or they will die. Aveoth will do whatever I say because he wants her blood."

She swallowed hard, not liking the pure bliss that crossed Decker's face with that little rant. He really wanted to kill a bunch of people. It sickened her that they were related by blood. "You're wrong. Dimwitted and delusional, too."

Decker cocked his head, studying her too close for her comfort. "I don't believe what you told Cole. I do, however, think that you probably *did* seduce one of his GarLycans into running away with you. That will make Aveoth want you even more. He and I are a lot alike in regards to seeking vengeance against those who've done us wrong. He'll make your life a living hell, Jillian, and enjoy every moment he pays you back for betraying him with one of his own enforcers."

There was no way she could allow Decker to use her against Aveoth. He had a lot of pride and honor. To do the bidding of a heartless prick would kill him inside. Aveoth had offered her everything he had by mating her. She needed to do everything in her power to outthink these bastards.

They were in the air, and VampLycans didn't have wings. One glance assured her the cockpit door was closed. It meant the pilots would be safe if she could somehow get the cabin to decompress and force them to make an emergency landing. That couldn't happen unless she got out of the ropes.

A plan formed, and Jill tried to look terrified over Decker's words, even purposely making her hands shake.

Decker noticed, and smirked. "I almost pity you. I hear GarLycans love to chain women and keep them locked up in dark caves."

Fido barked out a laugh.

She turned her head and arched her back enough to spot him over the headrest. "What do you think is funny, dog breath? I'd prefer being kept in chains inside a dungeon any day over being near *you*. At least a real man would be fucking me. You're never going to be able to touch me. What a poor, sad puppy you are."

He lunged out of his seat, right at her. She automatically flinched but expected the attack. Fido really did have anger issues and no control. He'd want to make her pay for that taunt...which hopefully meant getting her out of the chair first.

"Goddamn it, Boon!"

The infuriated VampLycan ignored Decker, his claws slashing at the ropes. His other hand dug into her arm, trying to drag her out of the seat at the same time. It happened to be the arm attached to her injured shoulder.

309

Agony ripped through her and she fought not to pass out. That wasn't part of her plan.

* * * * *

Aveoth paced in his office, ignoring the steady gazes of Kelzeb, Fray, and Chaz. They'd arrived back at the cliffs an hour before but Decker hadn't called. He should have.

"What if they've killed my Jill? She's so human. What do they know of drugs? They could have overdosed her. I smelled the VampLycan who had threatened to rape her. What if Decker couldn't keep him leashed? She'd have fought him, and she's so fragile!"

"Don't torment yourself, Aveoth." Kelzeb stepped in his path. "Decker is too much of a greedy fuck to harm her. He needs your mate to get what he wants."

"He's insane and has no honor," Aveoth shot back.

"I'd go with Kelzeb's theory here," Fray said. "We all know Decker will stop at nothing to get payback on the VampLycans he hates. He'll treat your mate as if her ass is made of glass."

"We'll get her back," Chaz stated firmly. "Decker is toying with us. He'll contact you."

Aveoth pushed Kelzeb out of his way and resumed pacing. "His demands are going to be unreasonable."

"They always are." Kelzeb snorted. "He'll want his clan back, and he'll try to push you to go to war with the other clans to take out his competition. Same as always. It might be a good idea if you put them on alert and let them know he has your mate."

"No." Aveoth shook his head. "Some of the VampLycans in Lorn's clan are still loyal to Decker. We keep this between the four of us and do whatever is necessary to get my mate back."

"She's not giving off the calling. That's the good news."

Aveoth stopped pacing and glowered at Chaz.

"I apologize. I was just thinking about how things could be worse. Not all of Decker's enforcers are mated. She'd drive them insane with her needy scent if you hadn't strengthened the bond."

Aveoth suddenly stilled and closed his eyes. "I feel her!" He rushed to the open balcony. "I can sense her. She's getting closer."

The three GarLycans had followed him outside. Kelzeb moved in front of him. "How far?"

Aveoth had to concentrate hard. "It's difficult to tell, but at this stage of our mating, she has to be less than five hundred miles away."

"It means she survived the drugs they gave her." Fray raised his hand. "High five. That's something to celebrate."

Aveoth rumbled at him. The enforcer dropped his arm to his side.

"Sorry, my lord. One worry down though. Always look for a bright side. She's alive, and closer than we thought."

Chaz punched his twin's arm. "Shut up. You're not helping."

"Close your eyes and try to focus on her. I know this is new but you can do it, Aveoth."

He listened to Kelzeb and tried to clear his mind, closed his eyes, and mentally reached out toward Jill. He wouldn't be able to pick up her thoughts, but Gargoyles had the ability to link to a mate's location if they were within range. The distance varied by the strength of the bond. He regretted not having her drink more of his blood, silently promising to fix that mistake once he safely got her back home.

"She's closer." He turned slowly to the right but then stopped, adjusting to the left a tiny bit. His eyes snapped open and he pointed. "She's in that direction."

Fray nodded. "Decker is bringing her back here. He'll probably use the landing strip. We should go there and be waiting."

"Attack them when they land and take Jill," Chaz added.

"I can call twenty of our men to go with us. We'll take down anyone Decker has brought with him while you go after your mate."

He nodded at Kelzeb. "It sounds like a good plan."

Aveoth's phone rang and he snatched it from his pocket. Kelzeb stopped him from accepting the call. Aveoth growled at him.

"Don't seem too eager. They believe we're cold, that we don't bond to mates as strongly as they do. Remember what they presume to know about us and use it to your advantage."

He hated everything his best friend said but it was solid advice. He gave a sharp nod and cleared his throat before answering the call. "Lord Aveoth here."

"I have something that you lost."

Aveoth allowed the cold to seep into his bones. He'd played this game plenty of times in the past with Lord Abotorus and the council. "I told you to never call me again, Decker. You don't learn."

"I'll kill Jillian if you threaten me with death again. I can put it on speakerphone and make you listen as she draws her last breath."

His wings ripped out of his back. The pain helped to keep him from threatening to tear out Decker's throat for even saying those words. "You don't have her."

"I do. I'm sending you a photo by text."

"Let me talk to her if you really have her."

Decker snorted. "I'm not giving you that satisfaction. I want a face-to-face meeting with you and we'll negotiate her return."

"Put her on the phone now or I'll assume you're a liar. Prove that you have her or I hang up."

The silence drove Aveoth crazy.

Decker finally sighed. "I would, but she pissed off Boon. He struck her before I could stop him. My granddaughter has quite a mouth on her. She's alive but unconscious. I sent the picture. Look at it. That's your proof. I want to meet with you face to face. You try anything and Jillian is dead. You might be able to fly but you don't have the ability to heal someone who's torn to pieces. That's how you'll get her back if you don't do exactly what I demand. Are you listening?"

Aveoth had to relax his hand so he didn't crush the phone he held. "I am."

The spiteful prick had the nerve to laugh and sound happy. "There's a set of large boulders to the northwest of the landing strip, about a mile into your territory next to a clearing. Do you know where I speak of?"

"I do." Aveoth ground his teeth together.

"We meet there in twenty minutes. You go there. She's dead if you aren't on top of that boulder. I see an aerial attack coming and she dies. You try anything and—"

"She dies. I am not a moron, Decker."

"Whatever you're planning won't work, Aveoth."

"That's *Lord* Aveoth to you."

Decker chuckled. "Perhaps I should have you call me Lord Decker, since I have what you want. We'll be at the clearing in twenty minutes. Any aggression and you'll never get your hands on Jillian." He ended the call.

Aveoth handed the cell phone to Kelzeb so he wouldn't smash it. "Did you hear all that?"

"We did." Kelzeb tapped the screen and grimaced at whatever he saw.

Aveoth had forgotten about the photo, and he wasn't certain he wanted to see it. "Is it Jill?"

His friend turned the phone—and Aveoth stared at his mate. She was tied to a plush leather chair, her head tilted to one side, and a red mark showed on her cheek where she'd been struck. A little blood stained her lower lip.

"I'm going to kill them all."

"We *will* kill those fuckers." Kelzeb sounded just as furious as he felt.

"He's going to force me to do his bidding. I can't risk Jill's life."

"Decker will underestimate what the four of us can do. We'll think of a way to save her before it reaches that point." Kelzeb held his gaze. "We're smarter."

"I feel sick from worrying about her," Aveoth admitted.

"That's natural. We'll meet with Decker and get her back. Whatever it takes."

"Yes."

"They aren't going to play fair so we lie our asses off if need be," Fray chuckled. "I'm down with that. It might not be the most GarLycan thing to do, but look who we're dealing with."

* * * * *

Jill had woken again while she was being dragged off the jet. It was daylight now, the sun high and bright, and she got a clear view of the landing strip. It was a long, paved road with trees lining both sides about sixty feet from the pavement.

It was Cole who kept hold of her, forcing her to move. She struggled to lift her feet as she shook herself further awake...and then a heavy weight on her chest finally caught her attention, and she looked down. "What the *fuck*?"

The shark's tone implied he wasn't any happier about her predicament than she was when he confirmed, "It's a bomb."

"Have you idiots totally lost your minds?" Her hands were tied behind her back and she struggled to catch her breath. She had a *bomb* strapped to her chest. "You'll *all* die if this thing goes off."

315

She twisted her head, looking back to find Decker. He kept about ten feet of space between them.

"I don't think that's far enough. Want to come closer? I'm taking you with me if I go boom."

"Shut up." He waved what looked like a TV remote in his hand. "It won't go off unless I push this button."

"Why don't *you* wear this stupid thing if you want to commit suicide? That's what you're doing. Who was the idiot who built it? Did they even know what they are doing?" She really hoped it was just for show, but one glance at Shark's grim expression made her feel even more fear. He looked scared...which mean it was probably real.

"It's the only way Lord Aveoth won't attack us. He does and you end up dead," Decker snapped.

"I've been kidnapped by clowns and their crazy ringleader."

"Shut up," Decker repeated. "Or do you want Boon to hit you again? I wouldn't mind letting my enforcer drag you to our meeting place. Keep your legs moving and your mouth closed."

I have a bomb strapped to my chest. Oh my God. Jill wasn't one to panic, but then again, she'd never thought she'd be a walking explosion, either. "Are you terrorists now? Maybe you watched too many Road Runner cartoons as a child, you think things blowing up isn't as dangerous as it seems?"

"Be quiet!" Shark hissed. "Everyone is already on edge. We're meeting with Aveoth soon. If he wants you, he'll agree to our terms."

She studied his face instead of where she was going, and it almost made her trip on a clump of dirt, causing her to stumble. Cole caught her, and the fear he couldn't hide seemed to notch up higher.

It gave her an idea.

"You're the smartest one of the bunch, aren't you?" She kept her voice low. "Grab the stupid remote before that moron gets us both killed."

He ignored her and kept forcing her forward.

"This day has completely turned to shit and it's just getting started." She just hoped it wouldn't be her last. The trees thickened as they walked through the wooded area. Her hip still hurt enough to make her limp and she was pretty sure she'd dislocated her shoulder, from the way sharp pains jabbed through her every time she moved it. *Yeah. This is definitely making my top ten list of absolute worst days ever in my life.*

Four shapes came into view as they left the trees and entered a clearing. Jill locked her gaze on Aveoth as he and three other winged men from his clan waited on a massive boulder above them. She felt a little safer seeing all those faces. Kelzeb and Fray were with him, as well as Chaz. Relief hit hard and fast. Chaz looked pretty great for someone who'd been shot and fallen down stairs.

The shark released her but Boon took hold of the straps at her back, effectively keeping her in place when they came to a stop. He leaned in and spoke close to her ear. "Don't try to escape. You wouldn't get very far before he pushed that button."

"I'm not a moron. There's nowhere to go that the signal won't reach. We're in an open field with big boulders in front of us."

"Bitches are stupid," he huffed.

"And you have bad breath. Back off, Fido."

She closed her eyes for a moment, wishing more than anything that her hands were free. She'd love to scratch out his eyes. He wouldn't dare hit her back. One punch and she'd go down, possibly triggering an explosion. He would die in the blast with her.

"I'm here," Aveoth thundered, his voice deep and loud.

"Don't try anything," Decker shouted back. "If any of those GarLycans attack us, you'll get my granddaughter back in about a thousand pieces. See this device in my hand? I push the button and she dies."

Jill turned her head and glared at the son of a bitch who kept boasting he was her grandfather. "You'll go with me, genius. How many times do I have to say it?"

He glared back. "Shut up!"

Boon gave her a hard shove but kept hold of the straps, so she just stumbled.

She didn't have to chastise him in any way. Decker beat her to it. "Don't do that!"

Boon let her go. "Sorry. She pisses me off."

She wanted to give Aveoth a hint of the story she'd made up, so she called out to him. "I'm surprised you even showed, Lord Ass-oth. Did you come to kill us all? I told these idiots you wouldn't give a damn about me after I ran off with one of your hot guys. They still believe you'll do anything to make me your blood whore. Even though I pointed out the one time you bit me, I bit back. I still smell like you. Gross for me!"

Aveoth folded his wings behind his back and crossed his arms. He was a smart guy. She hoped he'd follow her lead. He didn't let her down after a few long seconds.

"I do hate to be refused. And I'm not happy that you caused one of my men to betray me. Perhaps you've changed your mind about giving me access to your body?"

"Those guys on the left look like the one we shot," Boon whispered.

She hadn't thought they'd recognize Chaz. "Do you see the two who look alike, standing next to each other? They're twins. They *used* to be triplets. Should I tell them you're the one who killed their brother? I bet that would make them play fetch with your throat."

Decker inched closer and drew her gaze. "Stop provoking Boon. I didn't give you permission to speak."

"You're going to blow me to hell anyway, so what does it matter? I hope he loses his temper, that way I take all of you with me."

A muscle in Decker's jaw flexed. Jill wasn't sure if it was from anger or fear.

The shark stepped up. "Lord Aveoth won't risk losing the bloodline," he whispered. "He's addicted. We have the upper hand. He won't risk her life, so stick with the plan."

That's the rub. It irritated Jill, too. Aveoth would do anything to protect her. She couldn't allow Decker Filmore to win. He'd force Aveoth to let him come back to Alaska, to torment and murder VampLycans. Her mate would have to abide not only because of his honor, but to avoid losing her.

319

Decker cleared his throat and faced the boulder. "I'm here to make a deal with you. I'll trade you my granddaughter in return for—"

"Hell no!" Jill yelled. "I'll just run away again with the next guy who's willing to fly me out of here!" She couldn't allow Aveoth to make promises he'd have to keep, promises that would end up costing lives he'd never forgive himself over. "Don't bother making that trade, bat boy. I'm *never* going to let you fuck me or drink my blood!"

She inwardly winced at her words, but she needed to convince the men holding her that she and Aveoth didn't like each other. She'd never forget the night she'd met him. He couldn't kill Boon and Cole. He'd hated them, but he'd had too much honor to break his word. Decker Filmore wasn't going to use a good man's character against him to win. *Not today...not if I have anything to do with it.*

Decker grabbed her by the throat with his free hand, his fingers closing tight. "Do you think I won't push this button?" He waved the detonator in her face. "You'll be the *first* to die if Lord Aveoth and his men attack because of you."

She couldn't talk or breathe until he eased his hold and let her go. Air filled her lungs again as she gulped huge breaths, glaring at Decker. The crazy was written all over his face—but she also saw desperation. She mentally ticked off what she'd learned about the man. He was greedy, stupid, selfish, and had no qualms at all about fucking anyone and everyone over. He'd even admitted to killing his own mate...

Ah ha. Bingo.

Jill cleared her throat before whispering, "I want something out of this deal, or I'll remind him why he doesn't want me. You think he won't

320

do anything to make you push that button?" She arched her eyebrows, staring down her so-called grandfather. "You want me to cooperate? I'm looking at having to climb into bed with," she jerked her head toward Aveoth, standing on the massive boulder, "scary dude. You think that sounds fun for me? No would be the answer. He turns into rock, does this freaky thing with his eyes like some walking lightning ball, and he called me a fucking *concubine*. That means one day he's going to find a wife and toss my ass aside. I'll be broke, and probably really old, judging from his shitty personality. *No* woman would be eager to hook up with him. I'd rather die right now than face that kind of future. I piss him off enough and your leverage is gone. He'll want to push that button himself."

Decker would understand greed, and she was good at dealing with assholes after the life she'd led in her bid to survive.

"He keeps a treasure room. I saw it. There's this huge diamond about the size of my fist. It has to be worth a fortune. I'll be set for life."

Decker's eyes narrowed, a calculating look in his gaze. "You want me to obtain it and hold it for you?"

Yeah, he thinks I'm that stupid. "No! I wouldn't trust you as far as I could throw you. Bat boy up there will never agree to give it up unless I trick him. It's some kind of artifact that means something to Gargoyles. He wouldn't even let me touch the damn thing, yelling about some sacred oath to protect and guard it. I want to be rich when I get free, and that chunk of sparkle has to be worth millions. I'm willing to nail *anyone* if enough money is involved. You want to rule the clans and get the big guy off your back. I get what I want, and I'll promise to be bat boy's fuck-and-suck doll until he tires of me. He'll make whatever deal you want if I say the word."

Decker leaned closer, smirking. "We *are* blood."

That sickened her. She was nothing like him, but she forced a matching smile. "I was raised dirt poor. I'm not going back to that shit when I get out of here. So, do we understand each other?"

"Perfectly."

"Good. Let me talk to him then." She was the one to back away and looked upward, meeting Aveoth's gaze. "I'll tell you what, big guy. I'll agree to whatever you want on one condition. And you'll want to agree if you want me in your bed or hope to get a drop of my blood, so listen close."

Aveoth cocked his head, studying her. "What is it?"

"You have to give me a gift for agreeing to let you bite and bed me. Your word that it's mine, and that I can walk away alive and unharmed when you're done with me. Otherwise I swear I'll blow *myself* up."

He frowned. "What do you want as a present?"

She hesitated. "You have to give me the object I desire most, and you have to swear above all other oaths that it's mine, regardless of any you make hereafter."

"Why that condition?" Decker hissed at her.

She glanced at him. "Do you think his wife will want me to have it? She'll probably demand my death. That term will keep me breathing."

Decker nodded. "Smart."

It took effort to not roll her eyes but looking at Aveoth again helped. "That's the condition." She glanced at Decker. "Tell him you'll kill me if he doesn't agree to my terms."

Decker moved next to her, touching her shoulder as if they were pals or something. Jill struggled with the need to jerk away.

"Make her the promise of a gift and the oath, Lord Aveoth. You want and need her blood. I'll kill her if we can't reach an agreement on this day. She's the last of Marvilella's line. There are no more granddaughters to offer you. If she dies, you'll be forever bereft of the pleasure you seek."

"Do it, bat boy," Jill urged. "Trust me. I'll be so worth your while. I'll rock your world, and I promise to never run away again."

Aveoth said nothing, watching her.

"Come on," Jill urged. "You heard him. I swear on my life to submit to you from now on. Everyone wins. Say yes."

Aveoth glanced at Kelzeb, both of them grim-faced. Kelzeb shrugged. Aveoth shifted his stance and dropped his arms to his side. "I agree."

"Now you must agree to *my* terms." Decker stepped forward. "Your promise that I get to return to my clan—and you must end the lives of my enemies first."

Aveoth's rage was clear as he snarled, his hand gripping his sword. "You want me to slaughter the other VampLycan clans for you?"

"I deserve to lead them all!" Decker yelled.

"Just say yes!" Jill urged him. "Naked. Blood. You and me, tonight. Doesn't that sound fun, big guy?"

Aveoth stared at Jill. She nodded slightly at him.

"I agree...against my better judgment."

"I want Lorn first," Decker demanded. "Bring me proof of his death."

"Um, excuse me, but there's still a bomb strapped to my chest," Jill reminded Decker. "We'll all friends now, right? I get what I want and you get what you want. Take this thing off me."

Decker hesitated.

"You either believe him or we stand here forever. He gave his word. It's what you wanted. I'm still right here in blast radius if they attack. We'll wait together while one of them goes after this Lorn person you want killed. Get me out of this getup!"

Decker nodded to Boon. The jerk began to unfasten the straps at her back and cut the bonds off her wrists. She carefully removed the vest and handed it to the scarred thug. "Here, Fido."

He snarled as he took it.

"Don't antagonize him, Grandchild."

She wanted to tell Decker what he could do with his orders. The weight of the explosives being gone made her breathe easier. She held out her hand. "I want the detonator."

"No."

"Fine. Keep the damn thing, but if you push it, we all die. Remember that." Jill looked back at the GarLycans. "I guess we'll all stand around here while Aveoth has his number-one man go snatch the prey." She met and held Kelzeb's gaze. "You should do that right now, Stone Garden. Snatch the prey."

He hesitated but nodded. "I will."

324

"Lorn is to die first, then I want ever other clan leader dead," Decker yelled.

Kelzeb cut a sharp look to him. "I heard your demand." He spread his wings and ran off the edge of the large boulder, going airborne. His strong wings flapped, taking him into the air, gained altitude as he soared over the VampLycans.

Jill inched away from Decker and his men. They all turned to watch the GarLycan in the sky, making sure he was going in the right direction, not paying attention to her.

She heard gasps, and knew what was coming—Kelzeb must have already circled around.

Jill spun, sprinting for her life. This was going to probably hurt like a son of a bitch, but she raised her arms high. She prayed that they wouldn't throw the vest at her.

"What is she doing?" That baffled shout came from Shark. "Get her!"

Flapping sounds drowned out her ragged breathing as she ran as fast as she could, and then fingers locked around her wrists. She was violently torn off her feet, pain wrenching up both shoulders. If it hadn't been dislocated before, she was certain her shoulder was now. Tears blinded her and she blinked them back fast, watching the trees rush at them, but Kelzeb gained altitude as she dangled in his hold. He flew higher. The fall would kill her if he let go.

"What the hell are you playing at, Jill?"

"Just take me to Aveoth and get ready to dive if that stupid vest blows up. A moron probably put it together, so I wouldn't be surprised if *anything* sets it off. Will an explosion kill one of you if you shell first?"

"Doubtful. Decker wanted us high where he could see us but those boulders provide cover if we need it."

"Hopefully we won't find out."

"Aveoth will want me to take you to the cliffs where you'll be safe."

"I'm not leaving yet! Those bastards kidnapped me for a second time. I'll stand behind one of you guys but I have to speak with Aveoth."

"I'm going to release you. Stiffen your body and I'll catch you. I'm afraid I'll break your feet if I land with you this way."

"Don't you dare!"

He let her go and Jill screamed, watching the ground rush up at her. Going rigid wasn't difficult to do while falling like a stone in the sky. Kelzeb slammed into her from behind and wrapped his arms around her ribs and hips. Her stomach heaved at the way he braked their sudden fall by jerking her upward as he flew.

"Not cool," she hissed, as soon as she was certain she wouldn't puke.

He had the audacity to laugh. "Are you injured?"

"Maybe a little, but most of it happened earlier. Good grab-and-fly, though."

He slowed, twisting them in the air, and lowered until they landed on the boulder a few feet away from Aveoth and the GarLycan twins. She stared down at Decker and his goons. They appeared pissed off and confused.

"He gave me his word!" Decker bellowed. "You can't kill me."

"Calm down." Jill wiggled in Kelzeb's arms, and he gently allowed her to slide down his body until her feet touched the boulder before letting her go. She didn't look at Aveoth, afraid she'd lose it and just throw herself at him, she was so happy to be near him. She'd had serious doubts of surviving long enough to be able to do that again. "I just wanted to be far from that vest. I like my body in one piece."

"Jill," Aveoth softly rasped.

She finally met his gaze. "You promised me a present." She made certain the jerks below could hear her. "You swore to give me what I want, regardless of any other promises you made. Remember?"

"I do."

"Great. I want Decker Filmore's head as a gift."

She glared down at Decker to witness his shocked reaction. His mouth had fallen open.

"I figured you'd fall for pulling a fast one on someone else. You really are as dumb as I thought. Try telling Aveoth who to kill without a voice box." She ran her finger across her throat and then flipped him off. Her gaze went to Aveoth next.

"Do you really want me to bring you his head?" Aveoth arched one eyebrow.

"No. I just want him dead."

He broke their gazes, glancing at his men.

"They are fleeing," Kelzeb warned. "Running for their lives. I'd like to take down the one called Boon. I didn't like the way he touched our lady. I also didn't miss that shove he gave her. He needs lessons on how to treat women."

"Be careful of the bomb. He's got it," Aveoth warned.

"Not anymore. He just dropped it." Chaz snorted. "He's probably worried Decker will panic and hit the button and accidentally blow him up instead of us."

"I hate suits," Fray muttered. "They look so uncomfortable. What kind of VampLycan wears them, anyway? He *must* be crazy. He needs to be put down for the good of all kind."

"I want the dopey-looking one who never said a word." Chaz chuckled. "Just for the fun of it."

Aveoth grinned. "I shall bring you Decker's head. Stay here."

"I won't be upset if you drop it somewhere from high up on your way back. Just saying." She grimaced. "Really."

"A promise must be kept."

She understood. "You have to actually bring me the head, huh? I can live with that as long as he's dead. Be careful."

"Don't move. This won't take long." He released her and backed away, turning to his clansmen. "Let's hunt. They don't leave alive."

"It's about time," Fray grinned. "Shithead season is on!"

Aveoth jumped, his wings sharply expanding and flapping. His men followed him into the sky and Jill watched them go. She caught a glimpse of Decker and his enforcers running through the woods. Boon shifted, dropping as he ran, parts of his clothing falling off his changing body.

"Go get them and come back to me safe," she whispered to the wind.

Chapter Eighteen

Aveoth trailed his target. Decker hadn't shifted yet, he was too busy running. The thickness of the trees impeded him slightly, but Decker avoided smashing into them, despite the high rate of speed at which he dashed through the woods. The trees also kept Aveoth from swooping down to grab him.

From the height he flew, Aveoth viewed a clearing coming up. He got there first, landed, and turned as he shelled his body. He kept his wings out. They were excellent weapons, and he planned to use them. Fray came down next to him, shelling his body as well, a look of delight on the enforcer's hardening features.

"Mine is sticking close to yours. This is going to be fun. Should we play or just take them out, my lord?"

"Kill the bastards. They stole my mate," Aveoth hissed. "No mercy."

"No problem."

Decker burst through the tree line and spotted them. He skidded to a halt and tried to spin around to flee the way he'd come, but the one in the suit slammed into him from behind. Both went down.

"Ouch," Fray murmured. "That looked uncomfortable, didn't it? Think they'll shift now?"

"Only if they find their backbones and are actually willing to fight," Aveoth rumbled loudly, making certain his words carried. "They did shoot Chaz."

Decker snarled, untangling his body from one of the few men who'd stayed loyal to him. "I'll kill you, Aveoth!"

"I quiver in my boots."

Fray snorted. "Good one, my lord."

Aveoth inclined his head. "You may kneel and die a quick death, or you shall bleed first. Your choice, Decker Filmore. Make it now. Your time on this Earth has come to an end. You are sentenced to death for the crimes you've committed against the VampLycans, and for stealing my mate."

Decker appeared shocked. "Your what?"

"Jill became my mate." Aveoth had to leash his rage. "She went home to pack, and you attacked her guard while I was buying her a human wedding ring. The only reason I offer you a quick death is because you are her blood relation. Kneel, and I shall take your head off with one slice of my blade."

"That fucking bitch!" Cole hissed.

"Did you just call my lady a bitch?" Fray shook his head in disgust. "You truly *are* mad, One Who Wears Suits."

"You know my name!" Cole tore off his jacket, then began to undo the buttons on his shirt. "And I bow to *no one*. I'll fight you."

Decker growled. "No! You swore you wouldn't kill me, Lord Aveoth!"

"Are you that stupid? You threatened the life of my mate!" Aveoth glared at Decker. "Kneel or fight. You die today."

"They're really going to kill us," Cole rasped.

Decker reached back and withdrew a gun from his waistband.

"Wow," Fray sighed. "Just wow. I heard he was a pussy but this is downright sad."

"It makes sense now why he didn't try to shift as he ran. He'd have lost the weapon with his clothing." Aveoth moved suddenly, going left, allowing Decker to witness his speed. He paused about ten feet away from where he'd been. "You can try to shoot me but it's a useless endeavor." He shelled his body further.

Decker aimed and fired. Aveoth lunged right then left, avoiding the bullets. He tucked his wings in as he moved, advancing on Decker.

He leapt up, expanded his wings in a heartbeat, and spun.

The edge of his wing struck the VampLycan. The bullets stopped an instant later.

Aveoth dropped to the ground, staring down at Decker Filmore.

Cole stumbled back, crying out in anguish. The strike Aveoth had made wasn't a killing blow, but Decker's arm and part of his shoulder had been severed. Aveoth gripped the handle of his sword and unsheathed it, standing over him.

Decker stared up at him, his eyes wide. Agony and shock mixed as his features twisted. Blood rapidly stained the ground.

"I give you mercy, since you are half of the bloodline that gave me my Jill. You were just the bad side."

Aveoth beheaded him in the blink of an eye.

"No!" Cole screamed and began to shift.

Fray was suddenly beside Aveoth, but he stilled, waiting for the VampLycan to complete his transformation.

Aveoth sheathed his sword before gripping Decker's head by his hair, keeping it at arm's length to avoid getting blood on his boots.

He glanced at his enforcer. "Do you have this?"

"Yes, my lord. I'll kill him swiftly and dispose of the bodies."

"Pick up my Jill and take her to my quarters when you're done. Don't take long. You're her protection duty. I'll see you at the cliffs soon. I have a stop to make first." Aveoth took flight.

He glanced at what was left of Decker Filmore. He wanted to return to Jill, but it was important that the VampLycans know Decker wouldn't be a problem anymore. Fray would swiftly reach his mate and keep her safe. The idea of another man carrying her during flight wasn't welcome, but he trusted the twin brothers without question. They were loyal. So was Kelzeb. He knew his best friend would see to her safety as well, as soon as he'd killed the VampLycan he'd gone after.

He landed in front of the neat cabin with the wide porch. It didn't take long for the front door to fly open, and then the clan leader strode outside.

Velder came to an abrupt halt at the top of the stairs, his gaze going from Aveoth to what he held in his hand. He slowed his pace as he came down the steps and approached.

"Lord Aveoth."

"Velder."

Aveoth hated the formality of their conversations. It made his chest ache just a tiny bit. He noticed the reaction every time he faced the man.

"You caught him." Velder glanced at what remained of the former clan leader. "We owe you a debt."

Aveoth bent and set the head down, then straightened. He wiped his hands on his pants, despite the lack of blood on his fingers. They just felt dirty for having touched someone so vile. "Think nothing of it, and there is no repayment needed. It was best for all of us if Decker wasn't alive. I'm just grateful you were home. I must return to the cliffs." He paused. "I have a mate."

Surprise flashed across Velder's face. "Congratulations. I hadn't heard."

"You're the first to know outside of my clan." He looked down at the head. "At least, the first who's still alive."

He glanced around the area. None of the clan approached and few were within sight. They had privacy. He met Velder's gaze again. "I'd appreciate if you kept that news between us for a little longer. It's very new, and some of Lorn's clan might have issues with me over killing Decker. I don't even want them thinking about doing her harm. Not that they could touch her, but I've dealt with enough shitheads lately."

"I'd never betray a trust."

"Not even to your mate or sons?"

Velder shook his head. "My word is solid, and you have good reason to keep the news of your mate within your clan. I love my family, but I'm a leader as well. I can draw the line and hold it. They understand. I made sure of it, so their feelings were never hurt if I had to keep any secrets. I'm happy you found a mate, Lord Aveoth."

333

That ache expanded. "Your sons are lucky to have a father who cares for them so much."

The blue of Velder's eyes softened. "I'm sure your father loved you as well, even if he didn't show it." Then he glanced away, clearing his throat. "I apologize. That was out of line. I shouldn't have said that. It was an unforgivable assumption on my part."

"You're incorrect. Abotorus was as harsh a father as he was a leader," Aveoth divulged. "I don't believe he knew how to love anyone."

Velder's mouth opened, then closed.

"Say what you planned to. There's no need to hold back. I won't take offense."

"It's nothing. Thank you for dealing with Decker, Lord Aveoth. It is deeply appreciated."

"You may call me Aveoth. We're alone. Set aside the fact that we're from two different clans. We shall just be two men right now having a conversation."

Velder's body relaxed. "Aveoth..." He hesitated. "I would like to speak to you about something concerning our clans. Would that be too bold?"

"What is it?"

"It gets tiresome, worrying about the future. Will we continue to be allies? I'll speak freely and just spit it out. We no longer have full-blooded Lycans to offer as mates for your men. It's our concern that you will want us out of this territory." He glanced down at the head. "Decker kept the fear of war in our hearts for a long time." He gazed into Aveoth's eyes.

"We wish for peace to remain. This is our home, and we like having you as neighbors. I wish our clans were bonded better. Is there any way to make that possible?"

"I will never allow my clan to attack VampLycans. This is your home, as well as ours. We will live in peace for as long as I live and rule. That's a promise."

Velder didn't try to hide his surprised grin. "This is the best news I've heard since my mate informed she was pregnant with my sons. Perhaps we could hold a few social functions together? I could hug you right now!"

He imagined Velder actually embracing him, and tensed slightly.

Velder noticed. "I'd never dare insult you that way. It's just a saying. VampLycans sometimes hug."

"You felt joy when your mate was pregnant with both of your sons?"

"Of course. You'll know that same exhilaration when your mate becomes pregnant, once you decide to have children. They are a blessing. I feel thankful every day for Drantos and Kraven."

Aveoth glanced around again, and felt certain they were out of hearing of anyone else. "I hope to become a father one day."

"You'll be a great one. It's terrifying. I won't lie." Velder chuckled. "Babies are so small. They get stronger and bigger too fast, but the bond grows as well. I'm very close to my sons."

"I killed Lord Abotorus." He regretted mentioning that the second the words were out.

Velder lifted his hand as if he planned to touch Aveoth, hesitated, then let it drop. "He was a harsh man, as you said. I'll be honest. I was kind of glad when we got the news that you'd taken over your clan. Your father had threatened to make us leave with the full-blooded Lycans once they'd decided to start over somewhere else. We held no more use as far as he was concerned, since Gargoyles refuse to mate with anyone tainted with Vampire blood. That's how he put it. I feared for a few years that you'd feel the same, but you let it be and you've kept the peace. Thank you. My sons believed you didn't hold the same opinion of us. They grieved when you stopped meeting with them."

"You knew we spent time together?"

"I encouraged it."

"To strengthen our clan bonds?"

Velder shook his head. "There was no motive on my part. I was aware your father could never find out. He probably would have punished you. At least that's what my sons believed. You were their friend, and that's why I was happy to let them spend time with you."

Aveoth stared deeply into Velder's eyes, seeing only sincerity. A sharp pain jabbed in the middle of his chest. The VampLycan was a good man. He'd always suspected it, but now he knew with certainty.

"They would welcome your friendship again. We all would."

Aveoth wished he could spend time with Drantos and Kraven once more. Those days had been some of happiest in his youth. "I can't allow myself to become too close to your family."

"I don't understand?"

A war waged inside Aveoth, a longing so deep that had always remained, no matter how hard he'd try to keep it buried. Jill had changed him. He took a deep breath and blew it out. "Would you do anything to protect the lives of your sons, Velder?"

"Yes."

"That's why."

"Your clan would want to kill Drantos and Kraven?"

Now was the moment, if ever there was one. Aveoth stepped closer, invading the other man's personal space. Velder held his ground and didn't back off. His body even remained relaxed. It was a sign of trust between them.

"The clan will see me dead if they ever discover Lord Abotorus wasn't truly my father. He hosted my mother while she carried me inside her womb, unaware that she was already pregnant when they mated. It magnified her Gargoyle traits, so I was born with strong GarLycan blood. She never wished to mate with that cold bastard, but her family forced her to. However...she took a VampLycan lover just days before she was sent to Abotorus. And no one must ever know, or I die. They would never allow me to lead my clan."

Velder's eyes widened, and he paled.

"I stopped spending time with my half-brothers once I learned the truth, to keep us all safe. My clan will never attack yours...Father."

Tears welled in Velder's blue eyes, and he clasped Aveoth's arm. "I didn't know."

"You were never meant to. This truth remains between us."

The tears spilled down Velder's cheeks as he studied every inch of Aveoth's face. "You're my son? Your mother...she was the one who spent

337

time with me in my hunting cabin, then disappeared." Emotion choked his voice.

Aveoth gripped him back. "It would have been a death sentence for my mother and I, had she told Abotorus I wasn't his after she realized the truth shortly after my birth. It will forever be, since the clan would see us dead for the lie we've lived all this time. No one must ever know. Do you understand? I can't promise a new lord would wish to protect our alliance. The older generations look down on VampLycans."

"You have to tell Drantos and Kraven."

"I can't. *You* can't. Don't make me regret this day, Father. It's too dangerous a secret. It was selfish of me to share it but I've held it deep inside since I learned the truth. Abotorus never learned that I wasn't his, but he planned to kill everyone with Lycan blood in the clan. That included all mates and younglings. Even his own. We were all flawed to him because we had emotions."

"You're perfect," Velder rasped. "You're my son."

Aveoth had to look away, and he backed up, releasing Velder and making sure he let go too. He cleared his throat, and then held his gaze again. "Is this secret safe?"

"Yes. I wouldn't do anything to put you in jeopardy." Velder blinked back more tears and smiled. "I have another son." That happiness quickly faded. "I wish I'd known. I would have…" His voice trailed off.

"Don't go there. You found your true mate and had two sons you love. Lord Abotorus would have had my mother and you hunted down and executed if she'd fled from the promise her parents made for her betrothal. It kept both of you alive. And now I have two brothers. They are

338

"good men who I like, and as lord of my clan, I can keep them safe. This worked out the way it was meant to, and I'm grateful for it."

"That's why you let them have Dusti and Bat without a fight."

"Yes. I'd never kill my brothers."

"Now you found your own mate. Is she a Gargoyle? I have a hundred questions. I want to know everything about you."

"She's the daughter of one of Decker's sons. It's a long story, but I'll talk to you again soon. We'll meet in secret, if you wish. I'd like to get to know you better as well."

"I would love that. Anytime. Anywhere." Velder suddenly paled. "Shit! She's a VampLycan?"

"Half. Her mother was human."

Velder's mouth firmed into a tight line. "Your clan refuses to mate our women. Will they challenge you for leadership?"

"It's already been dealt with, and my clan is aware of what she is. It will be fine. I need to go now. My mate has been traumatized." He jerked his thumb at Decker's head. "The bastard kidnapped her when she went to pick up her things from her apartment, and I haven't checked her over yet to see if he harmed her in any way. She seemed okay, but I need to get to her."

"Of course."

"We should hold a gathering so our clans can mingle. My Jill might like to meet her cousins your sons mated."

"I'd like that. If you ever have any problems with your clan accepting your mate, or anything else, you have my full support, and that of every

339

other VampLycan clan. Your disposal of Decker would be reason enough for them to stand at your side. We're here for you, whatever you need."

"I appreciate that offer, though I have trusted friends and enforcers in my clan. We can hold my reign. I chose them well."

"Do they know the truth about you?"

"That you are my father? Only one. Kelzeb. We've been friends since the beginning of our lives. I must go. Jill is waiting for me at the cliffs. I'll arrange for us to meet soon."

"I look forward to it." Velder stepped forward and clasped his hand with both of his. "I'm glad you're my son, even if I can't tell anyone."

A lump formed in Aveoth's throat, and he had to swallow hard. "I'm glad to *be* your son."

Velder let him go. "Come back soon. I want to get to know you better."

"I will. Please share the news of Decker's death with the other clans. Let them know he won't ever bother them again."

"With pleasure."

Aveoth expanded his wings, getting ready to take flight. Then he paused. "Do you happen to have a box inside your home that I may have? I need it for my mate. She likes to tease me, and it's time I returned her humor."

The request seemed to surprise Velder. "Um, I'm sure there's something. Come inside."

Chapter Nineteen

Jill paced in the living room. She was aware that Fray watched her with amusement.

"Lord Aveoth is safe. You're fretting for no reason."

"Where did he go?"

"He didn't exactly tell me. He just grabbed the head and flew off, but he said he'd return soon. Lord Aveoth won't be gone from you long."

"He should have come right back."

"My guess? He needed to fly the head to all four VampLycan clans to show them proof of death. It would be best to do that before decomposition sets in."

She stopped moving, gawking at him. "Ewww."

"To view a fresh head is much better than one days old. It otherwise might have started to fall apart while it was being flown around."

"Okay, I don't want to hear any more. That's gross. I'm so glad you talked me into eating a sandwich when we first got here or I'd have just lost my appetite."

Fray winked. "I don't want you mad at Lord Aveoth."

"You're a weird man."

"I'll take that as a compliment, my lady."

She liked Fray. "Are you hungry? I could fix you something while we wait, since you're stuck with me."

"I'm fine but thank you. May I speak freely?"

"Of course."

"You shouldn't offer to fix your guards meals. It's not done."

"I'm already screwing up, huh?"

He shrugged. "It's okay with Aveoth's trusted circle. You do need to learn more about what will be expected of you as Lord Aveoth's lady."

"I'm going to be so bad at this."

"I disagree. May I sit?"

"Take a load off."

"I really do like you." He laughed as he sat on the couch. "Everyone here is pretty formal and stuffy."

Jill dropped into a seat across from him. "I noticed. The bad news is that I break into a sweat when I go to semi-nice restaurants. See my problem?"

"Why?"

"I grew up poor. I feel so out of place. I remember going on a date with this guy a few years ago, who took me to one of those really fancy restaurants. They asked what kind of *water* I wanted. I panicked."

"Water is water."

"I know!" She nodded. "But I guess you can get it carbonated or whatnot. I'm still confused about that. I just remember feeling like I wanted to run out the door. My date laughed when I got that deer-in-the-headlights look and ordered for me. I don't do well in situations like that. Now, here I am."

"You'll have to learn for Lord Aveoth's sake. His mother will help you, and so will we."

342

"Great. I hated school."

He chuckled. "So did I." Fray stood suddenly and his gaze went to the open balcony doors. "Here he comes."

Jill stood as well, and clasped her hands in front of her. "Don't bring me a head," she chanted. "Please have dropped it."

Fray softly snorted. "He's got something in his hands. I have excellent vision."

"Shit!" She bit her lip. "Okay. Don't puke. That's so not sexy."

Fray glanced back at her and arched one eyebrow.

"Pep talk to myself."

A grin flashed before he faced forward. Aveoth landed on the balcony, and Jill couldn't help but notice the blue box he held. It looked like something that should store a hat, but she knew it was something much worse. He'd brought the head home to her after all. Maybe she wouldn't have to open it.

He tore his gaze off her to nod at Fray. "Thank you."

"I'm leaving," Fray announced without hesitation. Then he quickly walked out onto the balcony, extended his wings, and leapt into the air.

Jill darted nervous glances between the box and Aveoth.

"Are you hurt at all?" He put the box down on a nearby table and closed the distance between them, reaching her face.

She jerked back. "Head-hands!"

He smiled. "I washed up at Velder's home while I was there to inform him of Decker's death." He cupped her cheeks and leaned down so their faces were almost level. "Are you hurt at all? Tell me the truth."

"I've got some bruises, my shoulder is tweaked, and I have a slight headache from being hit in the face. I'm probably not looking my best. Fray suggested I go take a bath but I wanted to wait for you."

He released her and slid his hand down his thigh, withdrawing a dagger. "My blood will heal you. Just a few swallows should do it."

"I don't want you to have to do that for me."

"You're my mate, and there's no way I'll allow you to be in pain." He offered her the dagger. "Hold this."

She took it carefully. "I'm not cutting you, Aveoth."

He tore off his shirt, baring his chest. "You're too tenderhearted." He took the dagger from her.

"I wouldn't go that far, but you haven't pissed me off lately." She felt tears prick her eyes. "I thought I'd never see you again."

"You're stuck with me forever. Of course, I won't ever allow you to leave the cliffs again."

"I should argue with you about that but after what I've been through, I don't really *want* to leave."

He lifted the dagger and pointed it at his chest near his nipple. "No goblet this time. I want to feel your lips on me. Are you ready to be healed, Jill?"

His eyes were changing colors, flashing a lot of silver and bright blue. "Yes. And I'm turned on too. We are *so* going to have sex."

He grinned. "We are." He sliced into his skin, making a small cut, and tossed the dagger toward the couch.

She stepped toward him, putting her hands on his warm chest, and went up on her tiptoes. He was really tall. She glanced at the blood, licked her lips, and opened her mouth. The taste of his blood probably wouldn't ever be something she craved, but she found she didn't mind it. He wrapped his arms around her, holding her tight as she drank from him. The wound sealed pretty fast, and she pressed a kiss to his skin where it had been.

He lifted her off her feet, walking and carrying her toward the bedroom. Her gaze went to the opening in the living room they'd used to leave the previous night. "You aren't going to close that?"

"Later."

"Good plan." She wanted him so much. "Are you mad at me for the bullshit I said when those goons had me?"

He growled low and took her into the bathroom, then gently put her on her feet. "Strip." He backed away and released her.

"Are you?" she pressed.

"I was too worried they'd set that bomb off. Killing that bastard felt good."

"Fray said they're all dead. He was telling the truth, right? Nobody got away?"

"All dead." He bent and tore off his boots. "Get naked or I'll rip those clothes off."

She took off her shirt and shoved her pants down her legs. "The sad part is that we went to all that trouble and I still don't have my things."

"We have the stuff you wanted."

345

She stilled. "My backpack?"

"Your mother's ashes are intact. The urn wasn't even chipped. I checked."

She fought tears again. "Thank you."

"You never have to thank me for anything."

He turned on the water, and she couldn't help but stare at every bare inch of him. "You are my superhero, Wings. Do you know that?"

The corners of his mouth curved upward. "You are my super-sexy mate." His gaze ran down her, then he growled, hooked her waist, and spun her, bending to inspect her skin. "You said you weren't really hurt. Your entire hip is red."

"It was probably black and blue before the blood you gave me. I'm feeling fine. It doesn't even ache anymore."

He straightened. "You're never leaving my side again."

"That could get awkward."

He frowned.

"I mean, what about when you need to take a book and sit on your bathroom throne? I *so* don't want to be near you then, or have you with *me* when it's my sitting time. There's love and then there's T.M.I in a relationship. We do have to have some boundaries, Wings. I do drink blood for you, after all. Compromise is important."

He chuckled. "Are you always going to tease me and give me hell?"

"Probably. I bet your life was boring before I came into it. I've been told on good authority that everyone at the cliffs is a bit stuffy and formal. You're being saved from that—and you're welcome." She beamed.

He wrapped his arms around her, scooped her off her feet, and stepped into the warm spray of water. His mouth took possession of hers, and Jill moaned, opening up to him as she wrapped around his big body. Wings was super strong, and she had a feeling she was about to have sex up against the tiled wall at her back. She would have told him how she'd always wanted to do that, but heat flooded her body and her clit began to throb. Every inch of skin tingled.

Oh boy. Here we go again. The mating drug is back. I'm so lucky! This is one thing I will never complain about.

Aveoth realized what was happening when Jill clawed at his back and bucked her hips against him. The scent of her arousal almost brought him to his knees. For whatever reason, his body seemed to keep releasing ravage hormones. He broke the kiss.

"I'm sorry, baby."

"Only say that if you plan on stopping." She reached up and fisted his hair. "Fuck me."

He adjusted his hold on her, braced his thighs, and aligned his hips until his very stiff cock slid against her wet folds. She was ready for him, and he needed her. He slowly pushed inside her, loving the way her pussy sheathed his shaft.

"Yes!" She threw her head forward and bit him on the shoulder.

The feel of her smooth teeth clamping down on his skin hard enough to almost hurt broke his restraint. He drove into her deep and hard, stilled there a moment, and then began to frantically thrust.

347

"My mate. My Jill," he rumbled.

"Faster," she urged. "Harder, Wings. I love this drug. The feel of your chest rubbing against my nipples is going make me come... Shell a little."

He did, and her moans grew louder. He nuzzled into her neck and bit. The taste of her blood as she climaxed, her pussy squeezing him tight, and those muscles fluttering around his dick did him in. He groaned, holding her pinned as he pumped into her until the last of his seed stopped flowing.

Aveoth carefully retracted his fangs, bit his tongue, and licked the puncture marks. "I love you."

"I love you too. No wings this time?"

"You said shell. It's easier to get them out before I do that." He played with her earlobe with his mouth. "And to think I worried that I might frighten you when we mated."

"I'm all in, Aveoth. The wings, the shelling, and the biting." She lifted her head and peered into his eyes. "I accept you. I was afraid at first, but no more."

He brushed a kiss on her lips. "Sorry about the hormones."

"I'm not. Sex is always going to be so hot between us. That's like apologizing over stupid shit. No need. I'd call this a bonus."

"You're amazing."

"I'm also super horny. I tingle and ache."

He set her down. "Let's get clean first. You have scents on you that make me want to go re-kill corpses."

She grabbed the shampoo. "You have better things to do. Me."

He loved her. It reminded him of her gift waiting in the living room. He helped her clean her hair and they washed each other. He took her against the wall again until they were both breathless and sated.

"Go get in bed."

"Okay. Aren't you coming with me?"

"In a moment." He watched her go, then grinned. "Payback is alive and well, baby." He hustled out of the bathroom and went into the living room to get the box he'd taken from Velder's home.

Jill sat naked in the middle of the bed with a smile on her face as he walked into the bedroom—until she spotted the blue box.

"Oh no. I was totally kidding about bringing me the head. I said it had to fit inside my purse, and I don't have one. Such a shame, right?"

He sat down and scooted closer, placing in between them. "I always keep my word. Honor is important to me."

She kept her hands clutched in her lap. "I respect that. So, I've been given head." She laughed and looked up. "I think I should give it to you instead." She reached out and gently pushed the box closer to him.

His dick hardened. "I would love your mouth wrapped around that part of me, but you have to actually open this and look inside."

She licked her lips, making a show of her pink tongue. "Sweetie, I'll do just about anything to not do that. Be a man and take a hint. Blow job or traumatizing your mate. Easy decision, right? Let's toss the head off a ledge."

He had to dig deep to keep the grin off his face. "I killed for you. The least you could do is peek inside."

"That was a low blow." She grimaced. "Okay. Do you have a good shrink at the cliffs? I might need a session or two after this but I don't back away from a challenge. I might have to change my motto, though, of meeting things head-on." She lifted her hands and gently used her index fingers and thumbs to pinch the lid. "I can do this. One quick flash and it's done."

Aveoth grinned.

She glanced up. "Find this amusing, do you, Wings? I wasn't raised in a cave, barbarian. I know. Adjust to my new forever-caveman lifestyle. Here goes."

Aveoth watched her face as she jerked up the lid and then slammed it back down fast. She frowned, looking up at him. "I didn't see a head. Or smell one. Not that I know what *that* would be like, but I imagined yucky."

"Take another peek."

She narrowed her eyes at him suspiciously. "You're so messing with me, aren't you?" She sucked in a sharp breath. "You're busted, Wings!" She lifted the lid, and this time kept it off.

The small black box inside had her dropping the lid on the bed. She jerked her head up, holding his gaze. "Is that what I think it is?"

He reached in and opened the smaller box. "You're my mate, but you're also mostly human. I know that a wedding ring is an important tradition when you make commitments." He showed her what was inside.

Her lips parted and tears filled her eyes. "Blue sapphires set in white gold. It reminds me of your eyes..." She held out her left hand and smiled at him. "I love it! Put it on."

He gently eased the ring out of the case and pushed it on her finger. It fit perfectly. She shoved the box out of the way and threw herself at him. He caught her, adjusting her so she was on his lap.

"I love you. This was so sweet. Thank you."

"We could hold a wedding if you want. It won't be in a church or official, but the ceremony has meaning to some humans."

"I'm touched but it's not necessary. Thank you for offering, though."

"Our relationship needs compromise. You said it, and I agree. I don't ever want you to feel that you have to leave everything you once where to mold yourself to life here."

"I'm so glad you said that. The corsets women wear should be outlawed and let's take off at least four yards of material from their dresses."

She amused him. "That's going to take some time."

"Like a hundred years or two, and then we'll be dressing like people are now?"

He kissed her lips. "You're such a smartass. Never change."

She admired her ring. "We should celebrate."

"Do you want me to arrange a party for the clan to rejoice our mating?"

"I was thinking of something more private. We *are* naked and in your bed." She winked. "And you're still giving off the sexy hormones."

He cupped her face. "*Our* bed. I was so lonely before you came. Thank you for coming to me."

"Well, it wasn't as if I was asked. I never thought I'd say this, but I'm so glad I got kidnapped."

"We'll have quite a story to tell our younglings one day."

"Yes, we will. Our bat babies will be cute too. I just know it."

"You don't really plan to keep calling them that, do you?"

"Sure. It's like Batman but cuter. They'll love it. I mean, right after you get me a television so they know who that superhero is."

He cuddled her closer. "I will get you a TV."

"And cable. The internet might be nice in this century, too."

He twisted and pinned her under him. "Do you want to know what I want to give you right now?"

"Is it big and hard?" Her hand trailed down his stomach. "Am I getting closer?"

"Yes."

"Bring it, Wings."

"Always, Jill."